The Meatball Mistress

Tiffany N. York

CRIMSON ROMANCE

F+W Media, Inc.

Published by
Crimson Romance
an imprint of F+W Media, Inc.
10151 Carver Road, Suite 200
Blue Ash, OH 45242. U.S.A.
www.crimsonromance.com

ISBN 10: 1-4405-8088-X
ISBN 13: 978-1-4405-8088-8
eISBN 10: 1-4405-8089-8
eISBN 13: 978-1-4405-8089-5

Cover art © wakebreakmediamicro/123RF

For my #2 fan, BG.

Acknowledgments

Many thanks to Julie Sturgeon, and everyone at Crimson Romance. And as always, I'm grateful for the much needed support of my mom, and my fellow pitizens.

CHAPTER 1

Cara Manzoni had two questions as she stepped through the doorway of the Bensonhurst apartment she rented with her fiancé: *Where have I seen that tacky, black purse with the pink skulls before?* Remembering it belonged to Annemarie—her hairdresser for the last twelve years—triggered her second question: *Since when does my hairdresser make house calls?*

When she reached the living room, she froze. Annemarie wasn't doing her fiancé's hair. She was *doing* her fiancé. Robbie sat on their sofa still clothed, except for his jeans, which were gathered around his ankles. Annemarie was sitting on him, naked, her tramp stamp and skinny ass in plain view.

"Are you friggin' kidding me?" Cara shrieked, causing them to spring up like burnt toaster Pop-Tarts. "We're supposed to be married in two months and you're screwing my skanky hairdresser?"

Annemarie made no effort to cover her nudity. She put her hands on her bony hips and thrust her over-inflated chest out at her. "Who you callin' a skank? Maybe if you satisfied your man a little more, he wouldn't have to get a little something from me. Or a lot of something."

Cara lunged at her as Robbie jumped between them. "Jesus!" he said.

Cara glared at him. "Jesus isn't going to help you, you cheating son-of-a-bitch! I expected this from you. You're a man, after all. But you … " She pointed her finger in Annemarie's face. "Do you know how hard it is to find a good hairdresser?"

Annemarie smiled and her voice softened. "I'll still do your hair, Cara. In fact, your roots are showing, so it's time to make an appointment for a touch-up."

Cara stared at her for a long moment. Tears welled behind her eyes. It was time to get out of there before either of them saw her break down. She headed for the front door.

"Cara, wait!" Robbie called after her.

He waddled down the hallway, his pants still around his ankles. For the first time in the four years they had been together, she found the sight of him ridiculous.

"I'm sorry, Cara, it won't happen again. Please don't leave."

"Exactly how many times did it happen, Robbie?"

He hesitated a little too long. "Twice."

"Yeah, right," Annemarie muttered from the living room.

"How many times, Robbie?"

Robbie shrugged. "You expect this from men. You've said it yourself. You know we're biologically programmed to want to spread our seed everywhere."

"That's your story?"

"Remember that show we watched about the differences between men and women, and how … hey, is that my travel mug?"

Cara looked down at his beloved cup in her hand. He hated when she used it for her coffee, because Robbie only drank tea and he claimed her coffee tainted its taste. Her eyes zoomed in on Mr. Happy, the pet name he had given his penis. She should have known anyone who referred to his penis in the third person was going to have issues. She aimed his travel mug at Mr. Happy and gave it her best shot. When Robbie yelped in pain she turned and strode out, satisfied in knowing that Mr. Happy was, at that moment, miserable.

• • •

Cara sat motionless in her 1972 Cadillac Sedan de Ville. She called it the Pimpmobile, due to its offensive size and leopard-print velour seat covers. Her grandfather had willed it to her, minus the covers.

She leaned her head on the steering wheel and started to cry. Robbie had asked her to spend the rest of his life with him; he had claimed he loved her with all his heart and soul. Being one half of a couple had given her an identity, a purpose, and she had desperately needed that after her parents' accident. How much of what he had told her was just empty words and promises?

Talk about a blow to the ego. He had always said her body was voluptuous, womanly—that her ass defied gravity. The fact that he had chosen to cheat with a woman who was her complete physical opposite both confused and pissed her off. Since when did he prefer stick-thin, fake-breasted, Botox-lipped females?

What did Annemarie have that she didn't? Besides lower BMI and silicone? What did she do for him that Cara didn't? She wasn't a prude in bed. It's not like she refused to venture south on him or insisted the lights always be off during sex.

The visual image of Annemarie sitting on Robbie came back to her and she felt the bile rise. She heard their moans in her head, imagined Robbie being inside Annemarie—*another woman*—and her head began to spin. Cara opened the car door and threw up everything she had eaten for dinner.

What was she supposed to do now? She couldn't go back to the place she shared with that lying snake. She didn't want to burden her older brother, Anthony. He had a wife and three-year-old twin girls to care for, which he wouldn't be able to do if he were put in prison for murdering Robbie.

What a prize she had turned out to be. Here she was, almost thirty, newly single and childless, and working as a cocktail waitress with no health insurance. Anthony continuously harped on her, wanting to know when she was going to get it together. Well, she thought she had been heading in the right direction until tonight.

Cara recounted the money she had made in tips that night. Eighty-seven bucks and some change. Maybe she would have made more if she hadn't left an hour early. Then again, she wouldn't have caught her cheating rat bastard of a fiancé either. There was a silver lining to everything. She put her head down on the steering wheel and began to sob again.

Come on, suck it up. I'm stronger than this. It's just another crappy experience in the toilet of life.

She wiped her eyes and started the car, taking one last look at the place she had called home for the last three years. She gave it the finger before driving off.

· · ·

The numbers whizzed by on the gas pump until finally, the Pimpmobile was sated. It had taken sixty bucks to fill up the gas-guzzler. That left Cara with approximately twenty seven dollars. She certainly wasn't going to be able to go far. Daylight was beginning to lighten the sky. She hadn't slept, her throat was sore, and a dull ache had taken up residence inside her head.

Cara needed peace. She needed calmness, so she could figure out what her next step was going to be. The ocean always gave her a sense of stability. She could count on the steady rhythm of the tide to soothe her frazzled nerves.

Her fondest memories growing up were of her parents taking her and Anthony to the Jersey Shore every August. They'd rent a house on Crabclaw Island for two weeks, where they'd spend entire days at the beach and have barbeques in the evening. Each year, her brother would catch and release sand crabs into Cara's bed in the middle of the night, and Cara would retaliate by hiding slimy seaweed under his pillow.

"I'm going to make you both do laundry next time," their mother would holler, stripping the sheets off the bed, while Cara and Anthony chased each other around the cottage.

Cara managed a slight smile. Life was so much simpler back then.

The man working inside the convenience store rang Cara up for her extra large coffee and package of eight mini chocolate doughnuts. He reminded Cara of an ostrich—all body, small head.

"Take the Jersey Turnpike all the way until you hit the shore, doll face," he told her, taking in her short skirt outfit and heels, and throwing her a look that clearly said, "I bet I can afford what you're selling."

She would change out of her work clothes when she got to wherever she was going. She knew she had some extra clothes in her trunk, a few personal items, but nothing compared to what she had left behind. She willed herself to turn the car around and go back to Bensonhurst, but then Annemarie's ugly purse flashed before her eyes and all she cared about was getting as far away as she could from Robbie, Brooklyn, and her disastrous life.

• • •

Ryan Garridy knew that look in a woman's eyes when she wanted to have a serious talk. It was a combination of apprehension and irritation. He let out a sigh. It's not like he hadn't been expecting it.

Shelly stood at the foot of his bed in nothing but a pale pink, silk chemise. Ryan considered dragging her back to bed with him in an attempt to avoid the conversation they were about to have, but then he figured why postpone the inevitable?

"Do you realize how long we've been seeing each other, Ryan?"

He leaned back onto his overstuffed pillows and said nothing. He had enough experience with women to know they'd answer their own questions.

"Three months. And while I respect the fact that you were upfront in the beginning about not wanting a serious relationship, I feel like it's time for a status update."

"A status update?" Ryan almost chuckled at her choice of words; they sounded so businesslike.

She came over and sat beside him on the bed. "I told myself I'd never be one of those women who pressured a man to define their relationship."

Ryan admired the curve of her breasts under the thin fabric while she was speaking. He found himself becoming hard.

"I'm going to be thirty-two, Ryan, which means my eggs are going to be thirty-two."

He was about to pull her on top of him and to hell with conversation, until she mentioned the word *eggs*. Ryan immediately went soft.

"I'd love for us to go to the next level, but you don't give me anything to go on. I have no idea how you feel about me. We never discuss the future. You don't even let me make plans a week in advance."

Ryan shifted uncomfortably, letting out a long exhale. "Look, Shelly, I enjoy spending time with you, but … " His voice trailed off. But, *what*? What was he supposed to tell her? That he never saw himself getting married again due to his first nightmare experience? That every time he reached a certain point with a woman it was like a noose had been placed around his neck and it slowly grew tighter and tighter until he was forced to end things with her?

She searched his eyes, waiting for him to finish.

"You deserve someone better. You'd only be wasting your time with me."

"Don't give me that 'you deserve better' line," Shelly said, jumping up from the bed. "It's so condescending." She found her clothes and started dressing quickly. "You know, I thought we might have had a chance at something more."

"When I said I didn't want a relationship, I meant it."

She stopped buttoning her shirt and looked up at him, her eyes narrowing. "Three months together and it was never more than just sex for you?"

This was the part he hated, but if life had taught him anything, it was never to lie to a woman for the sake of peace. It always came back to bite you in the ass. "I'm sorry if I ever gave you the impression it was something else."

Shelly's petite features twisted in anger. "I hate to break it to you, but you won't be winning any awards for Coveted Bachelor of the Year. You're nothing but an emotionally stunted little boy who's sadly going to wind up alone."

He scoffed at the notion of such a ridiculous idea. "What makes you think I'll ever be alone?"

She buttoned her last two buttons and slipped into her pumps. "Ryan, you can be surrounded by twenty women and you'd still be alone." Shelly grabbed her purse, throwing him one last pointed look. "A life without a special connection with one meaningful person is a life wasted."

The sound of her heels echoed down his hallway. Ryan experienced a slight twinge of regret. He'd miss her; she was a good customer at his restaurant. She'd probably be back in a few weeks, flaunting a new date in front of him as if to say, *look what you gave up.*

What part of "I don't want a relationship" was so hard to understand? He adored women. He worshipped the ground they walked on. But they always wanted *more* from him. More time, more expressions of devotion, more commitment.

Wasn't there a woman out there who could enjoy being with him without trying to change him? A woman whose primary purpose in life was not to get a man to take a trip down the aisle?

• • •

After following Route 9 for almost two hours, it turned into N. Main Street. Cara still remembered which streets to take even though it had been almost twelve years since she'd last visited Crabclaw. Left on Cedar. Last house at the end of the cul-de-sac.

She couldn't wait to see the salmon-colored cottage with the hideous sea-foam green trim and matching picket fence. Maybe the current tenants would be nice enough to let her inside the place to take a peek around.

When she reached the end of the cul-de-sac all she found was an empty lot. No quaint cottage, just a barren space with nothing but dirt and dying shrubbery. She must have gotten the street wrong. Except Cara recognized the six ceramic ducks in descending order from largest to smallest on the neighbor's lawn. The ducks belonged to Mrs. Clancy, who used to bake them oatmeal cookies with too many raisins.

Cara's vacation cottage was gone, just like her parents were gone, and now her fiancé. Her head began to throb from sadness and sleep deprivation.

She parked in front of the lot, cracked the windows, and made sure all four doors were locked. She crawled into the backseat and curled up in the fetal position. Once she got some sleep her head would be clearer. Then she could think of a plan.

By the time Cara awoke a few hours later, she was a sweaty mess. It was June after all, and sleeping in the upholstered backseat of a car without any cross-breeze was no beauty queen's dream. She would kill for a shower and a plate of meatballs. Her shower. Her meatballs. There were a dozen freshly made ones swimming in marinara sauce in the fridge. She'd kill Robbie if he'd let that bitch have any of her meatballs.

Cara shook the thought from her head. What did it matter? She wasn't going back to him. They could have the meatballs. In fact, she hoped they both choked on her meatballs. Leaning across the seat, she pulled down the mirror on the visor, letting out a weak groan at the sight of her reflection.

It was worse than any mug shot she'd ever seen. Half-moons of mascara under her eyes, deconstructed hair, and a red, splotchy complexion. At least her nails still looked good. All ten, two-inch turquoise wonders studded with rhinestones. She held them out in front of her as they glistened in the sun. At the moment, they were the only bright spot in her life.

Time to use the restroom and get more coffee. She drove to the nearest gas station and checked her trunk to see what she had inside. A few changes of clothes for work, appropriate only for the bar scene. A pair of four-inch leopard pumps. Hair spray, a toothbrush and tube of toothpaste, face wash, age-defying moisturizer, and a box of tampons in assorted sizes.

She breathed a sigh of relief when she saw the hair spray, but when she realized she had no flat iron she wanted to cry. There was no need for hair spray if there was no friggin' flat iron. The second her hair hit water it would frizz up like some demonic Shirley Temple doll. Cara grabbed everything she needed and slammed down her trunk. One of her acrylic nails went flying off into the distance. She wondered if her day could get any worse.

Apparently it could.

"Your credit card is coming up as stolen," said the apologetic kid behind the counter.

Cara couldn't believe Robbie had reported their joint credit card as stolen and this quickly. Motels and food were now completely ruled out for her. She had to hand it to him. It was a smart way to try to bring her home. Although if he wanted an exhausted, starving, betrayed female crawling back to him, he wasn't very smart at all.

• • •

"Which one of your girlfriends is coming in tonight, Ryan? The one who looks like Audrey Hepburn, Shelly, or Barbara the ballbuster?"

Ryan finished writing the specials on the board. He turned to his bartender. "Shelly is history and Barbara's been blocking my calls. Maya could be a possibility."

"Is the great Ryan Garridy losing his charm with women?"

Ryan checked his watch and debated whether four thirty was too early to start drinking. "Oz, my friend, women are like martinis. One isn't enough and three are too many."

"Not for the great Oz."

"I don't see any women beating down your bar."

Oz shrugged. "I'm picky." He went back to slicing lemons and limes.

"*Picky* is a fancy word for 'not getting any,'" Ryan said. Oz was a confusing contradiction—part walking hard-on and part choirboy. Despite constant boasting of his sexual prowess, Ryan had never seen him leave with a woman, even though the offers were many. Ryan took out a bottle of Campari from behind the bar, poured it in a glass, and added a splash of soda water. He took a long sip.

"Call it what you will. I can't help it if I have standards."

"Gimme a break, Oz. Your standards are that they walk upright and have their anatomy in all the correct places."

Ginny, Ryan's head-server, came over, weighted down with a pile of menus. "I hate to interrupt what I'm sure is a philosophical talk about the nature of the universe, but you're needed in the kitchen, Ryan."

Oz's eyes glazed over, along with a goofy smile that spread over his face. "Hi, Ginny."

Ginny grunted in Oz's direction.

Ryan sighed. "What's the problem with Brady today?" he asked, dreading the answer. It was always something with his head-chef. "Does it have to do with the kitchen or his kid?"

"He's holding a picture of Elmo and crying."

"You might as well sleep with me, Ginny," Oz interjected, "because I'm going to tell everybody we did it, anyway."

Ginny ignored Oz and walked away.

"Your delivery leaves a little to be desired," Ryan said.

"Can I help it if I'm direct?"

Ryan drained the rest of his drink. "How's that working for you, champ?" He handed Oz his empty glass and went to see about his chef's latest crisis.

CHAPTER 2

Ryan peered at his head-chef through the small window of the kitchen door. Brady was holding a butcher knife in one hand, which to some might be an imposing sight given the fact that he was easily six-foot-six and covered with tattoos. He'd look pretty intimidating in a dark alley if he weren't holding a piece of green construction paper in his other hand and bawling like a baby.

Little did Ryan know when he took over Bella Vita eight months before that in addition to restaurant owner, he'd have to play therapist. He slowly entered the kitchen and approached Brady.

"What are we looking at, bud?" Ryan stared down at the paper Brady was clutching tightly in his hand.

"My little girl drew me this picture of Elmo with her crayons."

"Yup, that's Elmo all right."

They both stood there, nodding.

"So, what's the problem?" Ryan said, breaking the silence.

Brady turned over the picture to show Ryan the words "I miss you Dad" scrawled in a child's handwriting. "She drew it in preschool." He began to cry even harder.

Ryan tried to rub out the tension from the back of his neck. His kitchen staff buzzed around him, going about their business, prepping for the dinner crowd. They were used to Brady's emotional meltdowns. Ryan, however, was still rattled by them. Wasn't there some pill Brady could take to temper his feelings like everyone else did?

What did his chef expect him to say about Elmo? Ryan had no kids. He barely knew who the red, ratty-looking creature was. He finally decided on "Shows lots of artistic potential."

Brady shook his head. "You don't get it, man. *She misses me.* And I'm not there for her."

"You live with her, don't you?"

"But I'm not there to tuck her in at night."

"Absence makes the heart grow fonder?"

"Not when you're four, man. Not when you're four," he said, rubbing his bandana-covered scalp.

"You want a drink?" Which is what Ryan always offered when he was at a loss for words.

"Maybe later. I'm trying to limit myself to five drinks a night. I'll be okay in a sec."

"You sure?" Ryan said, which was code for *you'd better get it together soon, because we open in less than half an hour.*

Brady wiped his stubble-filled, tear-stained cheeks with the hem of his apron. "Do you mind if I hang up my daughter's artwork so I can see it when I'm working?"

"Whatever gets you through the day." Ryan smacked Brady's back. "You okay now? Ready to work?"

A slow grin spread across Brady's face as he put down the knife and picked up a spatula. "I'm ready!" he said, in a voice resembling a ninety-year-old SpongeBob.

Ryan was familiar with SpongeBob, because he often watched the cartoon to zone out after a long day at the restaurant. He gave Brady an exaggerated thumbs-up and went to fix himself and her drink.

• • •

Cara went through her "does my life suck?" checklist in her mind while driving aimlessly around. No money? *Check.* No credit card? *Check.* No place to live? *Check.* No fiancé, dwindling gas, dead cell phone? *Check, check, check.*

She should just head back to Brooklyn to lick her wounds. She knew her brother would welcome her into his home with open arms, but he'd also expect her to have a five-year plan mapped out by next Tuesday. "Plan A failed. So what's your Plan B?" he'd ask. Plan A had been to become a wife and have some kids. Dammit, she didn't have a Plan B.

Swallowing made her aware of the sore glands in her throat. Her head throbbed with pain. She needed to eat something, but how many choices did she have when she was down to her last five bucks? She hated fast food and the packaged junk that came from a convenience store, so that left her without any options.

She turned down a small side street, heading away from the beach. Three blocks up, she spied a small restaurant with outdoor seating. Bella Vita. Cara smiled. The name meant *beautiful life* in Italian. The words of her grandfather echoed in her mind: "No matter what happens, always remember that life is good; life is beautiful; life is to be cherished." She considered the restaurant a good omen.

Miraculously, there was a parking space large enough for the Pimpmobile a block away. Cara had no immediate plan in mind, but she knew if she didn't eat some decent food soon, her fingernails were going to start to look really good covered with ketchup.

Pulling up alongside another car, she put the Pimp in reverse and backed up right into the curb. She let out a curse, pulled out, and tried again. This time her car slid perfectly into the space.

It was warm outside, but Cara began to shiver. *Please God; don't let me get sick right now. I don't think I can handle one more thing.*

She walked the block to the restaurant. The entire façade of the building was yellowy-orange and painted to look like peeling plaster. It reminded her of something you might see in Tuscany. A heavy planter filled with a rosemary bush stood at each side of the entrance, and a black wrought iron fence surrounded the open-seating dining area.

Cara studied the glass-framed menu outside. The meals were a little too fancy and Americanized for her taste, which probably meant the chef or the owner wasn't Italian. *Shrimp Parmigiana?* A true Italian knew never to mix cheese with seafood. There were way too many items on the menu to choose from and all the pricey dishes only made her head spin more.

"Do you see anything you like?" a deep, teasing voice next to her asked.

Cara's head jerked up. She found herself looking into a pair of smiling, hazel eyes. "I … I'm not sure," she stammered.

"Come, sit. I have a lovely table outside for you with your name on it." He placed his hand lightly on her shoulder and Cara felt a small charge shoot through her. She allowed him to lead her to a small table. When he asked her whether she was expecting anyone else, she absently shook her head. "It's a crime to have such a beautiful woman dine alone."

Oh brother, was that ever a line. Cara snapped out of her fog. "It's even more of a crime to dine with an unwanted guest," she said, giving him her best smile.

He laughed, revealing a set of immaculately straight teeth. "Very true. I'll have your server bring you a menu. In the meantime, can I bring you a cocktail to start?"

Anything alcoholic was probably not the way to go if she was getting sick. Then again, she needed something to calm her nerves, considering she had no way to pay for the dinner she was obviously about to have.

"Campari and soda."

His brow wrinkled for a moment. He seemed surprised by her choice. "I'll be right back."

Cara watched him go, admiring what she could see of his slim physique in the navy dress slacks and white linen shirt he wore. She gave herself a mental forehead flick. What the heck was she doing? She couldn't stand the male species right now. Especially one that had "player" written all over his strong jawline covered with three days' growth.

...

Impressive. Not many people knew what Campari was, especially women. The bitter liquor was rarely ordered by anyone except Italians. Ryan kept a steady supply on hand because he drank it himself. It brought him back to the months he had spent traveling Italy, where a Campari and soda was often enjoyed before dinner.

"I need two Camparis and soda."

Oz raised his eyebrows. "Are you a double-fisted drinker now?"

"Only one of them is for me. The other is for the lady outside dining solo."

The bartender squinted, looking through the front window. "Long, dark hair, dark eyes, dressed in all black?"

Ryan nodded.

Oz let out a low whistle. "Wow, she could make jogging a spectator sport," he said, referring to her more-than-ample chest. "Looks a little slutty, if you ask me."

"I didn't." Ryan took the two drinks Oz handed him and headed outside. "Table three needs a menu," he told Leah, the waitress handling the outdoor tables.

Leah saluted him. "Yes, sir."

Ginny intercepted him. "What do you want to do about the days off Brady is asking for?"

"What days off?"

"Fourth of July weekend. I told you about it last week," she said, giving him a mildly exasperated look.

Thank God Ginny had a working head on her shoulders, because half the time his was inoperable.

"Chris and Manny will be working, won't they?" Chris was his sous chef and Manny was one of his two line cooks.

"Yes, but ... "

"We're good."

Ginny appeared doubtful. "What if we get slammed? It *is* a holiday weekend."

Wishful thinking. They hadn't been anywhere close to slammed since he bought the place. "If only you ate as much as you worried," Ryan said. The poor girl looked as thin as a piece of dental floss. "We'll be fine."

Ryan shrugged off the disapproval on her face and went to join his Campari-drinking partner. He could use an escape at the moment from all his restaurant problems, and what better escape than a feminine one?

• • •

"I need something with a lot of garlic in it." Garlic was the only thing Cara could think of to help her get rid of whatever bug might have infected her.

"A lot of garlic," the waitress repeated, sounding like she had never heard the word before.

Cara's Campari and soda was set down in front of her. "Is this your restaurant?" she asked the man who had originally seated her.

He smiled proudly. "It is."

"This is an Italian restaurant. Garlic is one of the main ingredients in Italian cooking. At least it is if it's authentic."

"Something tells me you're Italian," he said, amused.

"With a wicked head cold, so I'd like something with lots of garlic in it."

He turned to the waitress. "Bring her the escarole soup and tell the kitchen to add extra garlic. And," he turned back to Cara, "how about a nice pasta?"

She shook her head. "Too heavy."

"What about chicken?"

"How about something a bit more original? I didn't come all the way to the shore for chicken."

"Fish it is, then. Leah, bring her the grilled swordfish—"

"Anything except swordfish."

"What's wrong with swordfish?"

"They're overfished," she explained to Leah, who was standing there looking helpless.

"How about the tilapia?" Leah suggested. "It's one of our specials tonight."

Cara leaned back in her chair, finally satisfied. "Sounds wonderful."

After Leah had gone, Mr. Restaurant Owner asked, "May I join you for a moment?"

Cara hadn't the faintest idea why he'd want to, unless he mistakenly assumed that since she had come in alone, she wasn't looking to leave alone. He probably thought she was a hard-up single woman alone on vacation, looking for some summer fun. The hard-up single woman part was right, anyway.

"For a moment, I suppose," Cara said. She wished he would leave her alone so she wouldn't feel guilty about having to stiff him for the meal she was about to eat. She took a sip of her Campari, noticing he was more than halfway through his already.

"So, Miss Authentic Italian, may I ask where you've come all the way from? Wait. Let me guess. Brooklyn. Am I right?"

"Gee, what gave it away? My nationality?"

"Actually, the nails."

She couldn't tell whether he was hitting on her or insulting her. Leah returned, placing a bowl of steaming hot soup in front of Cara. She bent her head down over the steam in an attempt to clear her sinuses.

"Whew!" Cara exclaimed. "Can you smell that garlic?"

"I think the entire place can smell the garlic."

Cara tried a spoonful, added a dash more salt and pepper, and tasted it again. She reached for the Parmesan cheese and sprinkled some in. Trying not to slurp, she kept her head down and ate quickly. She reached for a piece of bread and dunked it in her soup.

"I'm Ryan Garridy, by the way. I'd shake your hand, except I'm worried I might not get it back."

It took a moment for her to realize he was referring to the fact she might eat it. "You're a funny guy, Mr. Garridy. I bet it's your humor that wins over the ladies."

Her sarcasm was obviously lost on him, because he leaned in closer and in full seduction mode asked, "Is it working?"

If Cara hadn't felt so bitter and vengeful against the entire male race, she would have definitely found this man charming. Being a cocktail waitress had exposed her to more than her share of cheesy pick-up lines and men with less-than-noble intentions. Ryan was definitely classier than most, not to mention better looking than the majority of the vultures out there. The hair on his head was lighter than the darker stubble on his jaw, and his changeable hazel eyes seemed a different color each time she stared into them. And then there was that disarming smile.

She popped the last of the bread in her mouth and wiped her lips with her napkin before answering. She didn't have it in her to insult him like she would some random customer who made a pass at her. "Ordinarily, it would, but I'm heading back home tomorrow."

Leah returned and removed Cara's soup bowl. She served fish in its place. "Would you like any fresh pepper?"

She nodded. "And a glass of Riesling, please." Since she was going to Hell, Cara figured she might as well be tipsy so she didn't feel the heat from the flames as much.

She dug into her meal with gusto. Last meal before her execution. The thought made her dizzy. Her throat tightened as the hopelessness of her situation returned to the forefront of her mind. She put her fork down and rubbed her forehead.

"Are you alright, Miss, Mrs.? I don't even know your name."

"It's Tess." Why Melanie Griffith's character in the film *Working Girl* popped into her head, she'd never know. "It's *Miss*, and I'm fine."

She picked up her fork and started eating again. If she were a different kind of woman, she could have easily seduced this man so he would take her home. She'd be able to sleep in a bed for the night instead of the backseat of her car, or at the very least, be able to take a shower.

Three glasses of wine and an order of tiramisu later, the thought of going home with this admittedly sexy and personable man didn't seem quite so revolting. He had chatted about how great it was to live and work so near to the beach. He teased her about being from Brooklyn. She bragged about the pastries they made in Bensonhurst—the cannoli, especially—and told him there needed to be more espresso in his tiramisu. For a short time, Cara felt like a normal human being without a care in the world.

Leah approached the table and let Ryan know he had a phone call. She placed the bill next to Cara's empty wineglass. "I'll take this whenever you're ready."

"Will you excuse me for a moment?" he said, standing.

"Of course," Cara said. "Take your time."

Take all the time you need, sweetheart, because I am about to break one of my commandments: You shall not skip out on a bill without paying.

• • •

Ryan awoke the next morning with a pounding headache. He had vague memories of having consumed Campari, whiskey, and tequila. His body was sore. Metaphorically, he felt like he'd had some crazy, rough sex with a Harley-riding Italian/Mexican woman. What was he thinking mixing those types of alcohol?

He hadn't been thinking. He'd been pissed off. He couldn't believe the woman he had talked to for half the night ran out on the check. He still wasn't sure what pissed him off the most—that she left without paying or that he thought she might have come home with him.

He splashed some ice-cold water on his face and threw back three aspirin. A restaurant was a bitch to run. When he'd returned from Europe several months before, Ryan had thought it'd be a great venue for meeting women. He'd had no other options career-wise, so when the chance to buy Bella came up, he'd decided, why not? Women, free food, and drink. What more could a man want? He knew next to nothing about running a restaurant, except that it would piss off his father, but he figured it couldn't be that hard to learn. He couldn't have been more wrong.

Ryan brewed a pot of coffee and watched it drip. His cell phone rang from the bedroom. He knew the call had something to do with Bella Vita. It always did.

"What's up, Brady?" he said when he answered.

"I've been up all night with a sick kid, man, and my wife just got called in to the hospital to work."

"Please don't tell me you're calling off today. Can't your wife take your kid to work with her?"

"Trish works in a *hospital*," Brady said.

What better place for a sick child than the hospital?

Ryan shook his head to clear the fog. "So what's the problem?"

"Trish's mom can watch my daughter during the lunch shift, but I won't be able to get to the farmer's market in time to get the produce we need."

He sighed. "Give me your list."

After chugging down a cup of coffee, Ryan threw on a pair of jeans and a T-shirt and headed out. Luckily, everything was in close proximity. He lived one block away from the ocean, Bella Vita was two blocks from his condo, and a block from the restaurant was the farmer's market spread out over three parking lots.

Ryan managed to get all the items on Brady's list. It seemed like everybody in town was at the market that morning, including the woman Ryan had slept with in February, who was working behind a small table selling cheese. For the life of him, he couldn't remember her name. He hadn't called her again after their one night together, and because he didn't need a cheese ball to the head, he decided it was best to go the opposite way.

He headed toward the side street that would take him straight to the restaurant, but not before catching sight of the little thief who had ripped him off last night. *Tess.*

Tess was as pale as a ten-day-old corpse, slumped against the side of a building. She looked so completely out of it Ryan was convinced she had to be on some kind of drug. He hadn't pegged her for an addict, but he certainly wasn't an expert. Well, no better place for her to sober up than in jail.

Ryan immediately made a beeline for her. When she saw him coming toward her she tried to run, but he caught her by the arm, yanking her to him. Her eyelids fluttered before she collapsed in a heap onto the pavement.

"What the hell?" he said, shaking off the bags of produce hanging from his wrists. Ryan bent down and felt her pulse. Still beating, but she was burning up. Her eyes opened, and when she realized who was leaning over her, he saw the look of distress.

"What are you on?" he said, grabbing her wrist.

"What are you talking about?" she said, her voice so hoarse he was barely able to understand her.

"Tell me what drugs you're on!"

She shook her head slowly, clearly confused. "None. I've never done drugs ... " A fit of coughing overtook her. "I'm sick," she wheezed, as soon as the fit subsided.

"Do you need some help over here?" A police officer approached them, looking down at Tess, who was still sprawled on the ground.

"Yes, as a matter of fact … " Ryan began.

Tess's other hand shot out to cover his hand still tightly holding her wrist. "Please don't," she begged.

Ryan wasn't sure whether he was dealing with a drug addict, a con artist, or both, but something in her pleading look made him reconsider having her arrested. *For the moment.*

"You can help me get her up, officer," he said.

As soon as she was standing, the officer asked, "Are you alright, Miss? Do you need to go to a hospital?"

"No, I just have a bad flu. My husband … he was helping me home when I fainted."

Ryan stiffened at the word *husband*, but nodded to the officer. "We'll be fine. She just caught me by surprise. Thank you." He picked up the bags, put his arm around Tess to steady her and said, "The restaurant is a block away. Can you walk it?" She nodded. Ryan eyed her stilettos doubtfully. Who wore stilettos in a beach town during the light of day?

Please don't be a drug-addicted hooker, because the last thing I need is an angry pimp beating down my door.

CHAPTER 3

Before passing out at the farmer's market, Cara had been terrified of the murderous expression on Ryan's face as he was coming toward her. His beautifully chiseled features had been twisted in rage, and when he grabbed her she was convinced he was going to shake her senseless, or turn her in to the police. She was surprised when he hadn't.

Now she was back at the scene of the crime, being led through Bella Vita's kitchen. Maybe Ryan was planning on taking matters into his own hands, instead. Maybe he planned to kill her and use her bones for stock.

Ryan opened a door along the far wall and ushered her inside. "Go slowly up the stairs."

Her eyes traveled all the way up to the top of the narrow staircase. She hesitated, doubting whether she could make it with what little strength she had left. "I don't usually go places with men I don't know very well."

"And I don't usually take in women who steal from me."

Cara winced. Now she had felon to add to her already impressive résumé of waitress and telemarketer. She made her way up the stairs, with Ryan following.

At the top of the landing he told her to open the door. She stepped into what appeared to be a studio apartment. There was an open living room with a chestnut-colored leather couch, two easy chairs, and a large flat-screen TV on the wall. To the left was a king-sized bed, and to the right, an oak desk flanked by two metal filing cabinets. Another door led to a small bathroom. The only thing missing was a kitchen.

"Let me guess. This is where you have your afternoon trysts."

"It's where I go to get away if I need to, and it's also where I do most of my paperwork."

Another wave of dizziness hit her and she hoped she wasn't going to faint again. Cara reached out to steady herself against the wall.

"Why don't you lie down?" Ryan said.

"In your bed?"

Ryan gave her an odd look. "Uh, okay."

For once a bed sounded better to Cara than a homemade cannoli. She had never experienced exhaustion like this before. In fact, she could be dying, which might not be terrible, all things considered. Dying would certainly end her problems.

She sat on the edge of the massive bed. She and Robbie had shared a full-size, forcing them to snuggle up against one another. This bed would make you feel like you and your lover were vacationing on different continents.

Thinking of Robbie only made Cara feel sicker. She lay down and curled up in a fetal position. It felt so good to be on a soft bed. She'd rest for ten minutes, and then be on her way. Her muscles began to relax. She was vaguely aware of her pumps being pulled off and a blanket covering her.

"Thank you," she mumbled before drifting off to sleep.

The next time Cara opened her eyes the room was cast in shadow. "Hello?" she called out weakly.

Ryan brought over a bottle of water and a glass of orange juice, setting them down on the side table. Cara sat up slowly, reaching for the water. She took a long sip and shivered.

"How long have I been sleeping?"

"All day," Ryan said.

"Have you been here the whole time?"

"I was downstairs for a few hours." He studied her closely. "Do you feel any better?"

"No. I think I'm dying."

"You're not dying." Ryan chuckled. "You have a bad flu. Here, take these." He handed Cara two aspirin.

She swallowed them with water and laid back down, closing her eyes. "Well, if I'm not dying, feel free to kill me, because I wouldn't wish this misery on anyone."

"Don't be such a baby."

Cara opened one eye. Ryan had changed into nice slacks and a hunter-green shirt that brought out the green in his eyes. "Are you leaving?"

"I need to go downstairs for the dinner shift, but then I'll be back." He hesitated. "If I leave you here alone, will you promise not to steal anything?"

"I'll try to restrain myself," she said, before rolling over and knocking out again.

• • •

Cara needed to use the bathroom. She had no idea what time it was or how long she had been sleeping. Her clothes were damp, which meant her fever had broken. That was good. She hadn't showered in four days. That was bad.

She tiptoed to the bathroom and shut the door. She almost screamed at what she saw in the mirror. She looked like the crack whore who hung out on 20th Avenue: runny mascara, bags under the eyes, pale skin visible through her fake tan. No wonder Ryan thought she was on drugs. Cara's purse was in the car, so she had no way to fix herself up. She desperately needed a shower; actually she needed to take a jog through a car wash, but the thought of getting back into the clothes she was wearing after she was clean was just too icky.

Cara crept out of the bathroom, hoping the creaky floorboards weren't making too much noise. Ryan was sleeping on the couch in nothing but a pair of gym shorts. He was lying on his back, not leaving a whole lot to the imagination. She was able to appreciate that he was a breathtaking specimen, but that's all he was. A specimen walking upright on two legs with the ability to massacre an entire army of unsuspecting females.

"See anything you like?"

His voice startled her. "Hardly." She snorted.

Ryan pushed himself up into a sitting position. "How do you feel?"

"I think my fever broke."

An awkward silence followed, filled only by a ticking clock somewhere in the apartment.

Cara cleared her throat. "Thanks for not calling the cops on me."

Ryan stared at her without saying a word, which made her extremely nervous. She shifted from one foot to the other. "I'll find a way to pay … "

He held up his hand. "Look, Tess, why don't we cut through the bullshit and you start by telling me who you are."

She gave him a sheepish look. "Well, for starters, my name's not Tess."

•••

A thief *and* a liar? Boy, he sure knew how to pick 'em.

"What *is* your name?"

"It's Cara. Cara Manzoni. I'm from Bensonhurst."

"You want to tell me what you're doing on Crabclaw Island, Cara Manzoni from Bensonhurst?"

"I'll tell you everything you want to know, I swear. But can I please take a shower first? Look at me!"

Ryan had to agree she looked a wreck. Her shoulder-length, greasy hair hung down around her mascara-streaked face. Her upper eyelids were smeared with neon-blue eye shadow. He was sure there had to be orange spray tan smeared all over his pillow, and to top it all off, her fingernails were frightful.

Cara rubbed her eye with one of her fingers, accidently pulling off a false eyelash. She groaned. "I'd like to at least attempt to salvage what little dignity I have left."

"Fine." He didn't know what he had been thinking the other night; she definitely wasn't the type of woman he was usually attracted to. He preferred women more put-together and less artificial. He really needed to cut back on his drinking. It was clouding his vision.

Relief filled Cara's face as she gave Ryan a big smile.

She does have a nice smile, though.

"I just need to get my purse from my car."

"You have a car?"

"How do you think I got here from Brooklyn?"

"Bus?"

"Oh, please. You'd never catch me on one of those filthy things," Cara said, wrinkling her nose. "Do you know how many germs are inside one of them?"

"This coming from a woman who hasn't taken a shower in, how long?"

"Very funny." She headed for the door. "I'll be back in a sec."

"If I believed that, then I'd look like an idiot for the second time in two days. Why don't I come with you?"

"Suit yourself," she said, giving Ryan a one-shouldered shrug.

He followed Cara down the stairs, noticing she was barefoot. "Let's go out the side door in the kitchen," he told her. "Where's your car parked?"

She mumbled something about it being one block up and they walked the distance in silence. What was he was doing with this girl? He was going to let her take a shower. And then what? He knew he wasn't ever going to see any money from her, so why should he bother helping her? He had to admit he was interested in hearing whatever story she was going to come up with to explain her thievery.

Cara stopped in front of a mammoth powder-blue car that reminded him of an oversized Crayola crayon. A bumper sticker on the back read "Kiss me, I'm Italian."

"*This* is your car?" he asked, in complete shock. He rubbed the stubble along his jaw. "Damn, you really *are* a hooker."

•••

Cara spun around so fast she almost fainted again from dizziness. "What did you just say?"

Ryan opened his mouth to say something, but then closed it again.

"Did you just call me … " Her eyes became dark angry slits as her pulse raced. "A hooker?"

"Aren't you?"

She had to bite her fist to keep from clocking him one. Jesus, her car was called the Pimpmobile for a reason, but not for that one.

"First of all, I am *not* a hooker, despite my appearance. And this happens to be my dead grandfather's car. Second, I have never done any drugs in my life, so I am *not* a drug addict.

"Okay," Ryan said warily.

Cara went to her trunk and unlocked it. "I happened to have run into some bad luck, is all."

Ryan glanced inside her trunk. "This is not the trunk of a woman on vacation."

She grabbed what few clothes and toiletries she had and shoved them inside her purse. "I'm not on vacation," she said, slamming down the trunk.

They headed back to the restaurant. "Are you on the run?"

Cara stopped in her tracks. "Let's see, you think I am a hooker, a drug addict, and now, a fugitive," she said, ticking them off her fingers. "What about puppy torturer and child-slave broker?"

Ryan cracked a smile. "I was getting to those." He placed his hand on her back, urging her to start walking again.

"If you think I'm such a horrible person, why didn't you turn me in when you had the chance?"

"I still might, unless you have a really good story for why you stiffed me."

She whirled around to face him. "A really good story? How about I walked in on my fiancé banging my hairdresser? I was supposed to be married in two months. How about I took off with only the clothes on my back and less than a hundred bucks in my wallet, only to find out he canceled our joint credit card? How about … " Her voice trailed off. She was suddenly very tired again.

"How about a shower?" Ryan said.

His voice was soft and soothing, like a hot toddy on a freezing night. Cara wanted to curl up in bed with that soothing voice and have it lull her to sleep.

She still wasn't sure why Ryan was helping her out at all. She hoped he didn't expect a sexual payback. He was a man after all, although she was certain he had no shortage of women wanting to sleep with him. Besides, he would have to be deranged to want to sleep with her after what she'd seen in the mirror earlier.

Because she had no one else to turn to, Cara was going to have to rely on the kindness of strangers, even if they were male.

• • •

Another love affair bites the dust. It made more sense to Ryan than the whole hooker/addict/fugitive thing. They'd had great conversation together that first night; she had seemed witty, intelligent, and feisty, even if she had been sick.

He would have taken her to bed, despite not being his type. He usually dated women with ballerina bodies, ones who shopped at Nordstrom and decorated their homes in colors like ice blue and white truffle.

Cara was Fiestaware. Judging by her short skirt, stiletto shoes, and excessive cleavage, it was obvious she wasn't conservative. She wore makeup like a drag queen and her fingernails could be classified as weapons.

It wasn't like Ryan hadn't seen her type before; they were all over the Jersey Shore. But they didn't come into his restaurant to eat, and he definitely didn't approach them in bars.

"There's a robe hanging on the back of the door," he told Cara before she slipped into the bathroom.

He should probably make her something to eat. She had to be starving. That's what he'd do. Get some food in her, fill up that monstrosity of an automobile with enough gas to get her home, and send her on her way. That'd be his Good Samaritan Deed of the Month. Maybe it would cancel out one of his Deeds with Questionable Intentions.

Ryan went downstairs to the kitchen to get Cara some toast and a glass of orange juice. She probably wasn't feeling one hundred percent better yet, so best to go light. Plus, she'd been so picky the other night, who knew what she'd want to eat?

He was just putting the plate and glass down on the coffee table when he heard the bathroom door open.

"I brought you some toast and … " Ryan froze. He was completely dumbfounded by the woman who stood before him, because she sure as hell didn't look anything like Cara Manzoni from Bensonhurst.

CHAPTER 4

Why was Ryan staring at her like she was a bearded lady at the carnival? She already felt self-conscious enough without her "face." Gone were the false eyelashes, the tanner, and the makeup. She had even ripped off her six remaining acrylic nails. And now that she had washed her hair, her frizz would come back with a vengeance. Cara looked nothing like herself.

"Why are you staring at me like that? Stop it."

"I've never seen anything like it. Such a complete transformation," Ryan said almost reverently. "You're like a completely different person."

She tried to hide her face while padding over to the couch. "Yeah, well, don't rub it in. I know I look terrible."

"If you think you look terrible right now, what did you think you looked like before?"

"That was different." She sat, tucking her feet underneath her. "There were circumstances beyond my control. Usually, I'm much more put-together."

"You don't usually look like you've been tied to a car bumper and dragged a mile?"

She threw him a look that said, "Did you really just say that?"

He held up both hands. "I'm kidding. You're stunning now. Natural and beautiful, without all that war paint on your face."

Cara's cheeks grew warm. "Oh."

After a long silence he said, "You should eat a little something."

She picked up a piece of toast and broke it in half. Ryan sat down in one of the chairs opposite her.

"Thanks for letting me use your robe."

"Looks better on you than it does on me," he told her, letting his eyes drop below her neck.

Cara glanced down to make sure she wasn't spilling out of his terrycloth robe. She wasn't, but she pulled it tightly closed, anyway. She nibbled on her toast, knowing Ryan was waiting for her to explain how she wound up at his restaurant.

He cleared his throat and leaned forward in his seat. "I figured once you got cleaned up and had a little to eat, I would take you to fill up your car, and you could head home."

A wave of panic shot through her. Home? She couldn't go home. She was willing to bet fifty bucks Robbie had already changed the locks on their apartment so she'd have to beg him to be let in. That macho bastard always needed to have the upper hand in their relationship.

At the moment, home and everything familiar resembled a noose around her neck, choking the life out of her. What did she have to go back to? A dead relationship, her dead-end job? She didn't want to couch-surf with friends for the next three months until she found a place to live, and even then she wouldn't be able to afford to live on her own. She'd have to live with two roommates, vie for bathroom time, and fight about whose turn it was to buy toilet paper. Plus, she'd forever feel guilty for stiffing Ryan. A Manzoni never ran out on their debts. What she had done was cowardly and desperate, and made her feel like a crummy person.

"How about I do something to work off that meal from the other night?" she blurted out. Anything to keep her from having to return to Brooklyn and her cheating fake of a fiancé.

Ryan slowly smiled and leaned back, crossing his arms. "What did you have in mind?"

Cara mirrored Ryan, slowly smiling while she leaned back and crossed her arms. "Waitressing. What did *you* have in mind?"

• • •

He had a lot of ideas, but none he should probably share with her unless he wanted to get slapped. He couldn't help it. Cara looked so different. Fresh-faced, like the girl next door. And she wasn't wearing anything underneath his robe.

"Hello! My eyes are up here," Cara said, directing Ryan's attention away from her breasts.

He sat up straighter. "I don't need a waitress. Besides, you need to go home and work things out with your boyfriend."

He didn't want some *goombah*, or whatever a testosterone-filled Italian jerk was called, banging on his door looking for his girl.

"I don't have a home to go back to."

What Ryan was about to say he didn't actually believe, but he said it, anyway. "Look, Cara, every man does some crazy things before he gets married. Your fiancé was probably getting one last woman out of his system … " He wanted to say, "before being sentenced to sleep with one woman for the rest of his life." Instead, he said, "before settling down."

"That's just the kind of comment I'd expect from a man. You're justifying the act of cheating."

"I'm not justifying it. I'm explaining it from a man's point of view."

"So when a man realizes he's only going to be allowed to have sex with, God forbid, *one* woman till death do us part, he panics? Is it too scary a concept for him to wrap his weak, small mind around?"

Ryan put his feet up on the coffee table. "Pretty much, yeah."

She stood and started pacing. "Even if he's had sex with more than five hundred women already?"

"If he's had sex with more than five hundred women already in his lifetime, a shrine should be erected in his honor." He let out a laugh. "Pun intended."

Cara stopped pacing and glared at him. "Infidelity is a joke to you?"

"Absolutely not," Ryan said with a somber expression.

She resumed her pacing. "Why is it so friggin' hard—*no* pun intended—for a man to have sex with one woman only?"

All this talk about sex while watching a voluptuous woman walk around in his robe was getting Ryan aroused. Cara's fieriness turned him on.

"Why even bother getting married then?" she asked.

He imagined silencing her with his mouth while he tore open the robe—

"Hello! I asked you a question."

He sighed. Just silencing her would be okay for him right now.

"Why get married?" she repeated.

"I'm the wrong person to ask."

"Don't you ever want to get married?"

Now she was irritating him. How had the conversation turned to him when they had started out discussing Cara and her need to go home? He took his feet down from the coffee table and pointed a finger at her.

"You need to sit down and eat. You're making me nervous," Ryan said, in a more stern voice than he had intended.

She sat back down on the couch. "I just asked a simple question is all," she said.

"There's nothing simple about the subject, so let's leave it at that."

. . .

Cara was hungrier than she thought. She polished off the rest of her toast and juice. Raking her fingers through her now almost-dry hair, she could feel it starting to frizz. She couldn't remember the last time she let her hair go curly. How was she supposed to be able to control her life when she couldn't control her hair?

She could have her flat iron if she went back. Along with her makeup, clothes, and pillow. If she were able to forgive Robbie and pretend this whole nightmare had never happened, she could go on with her life as planned. His family had welcomed her with open arms. Being a part of it had been important to her, especially since the only family she had left was her brother.

If only she could forget him being inside another woman. But she couldn't. The most intimate act between two people had become an act between three.

The toast came up in her throat. Cara ran to the bathroom and threw up. When she returned, Ryan handed her a bottle of mineral water. She nodded her thanks and curled up on the couch.

"I can't go back to my … " To her *what*? Robbie wasn't her fiancé anymore. "I can't go back home."

"Don't you have any family you can stay with until you get back on your feet?"

She shook her head.

Ryan stared at her without blinking. He touched his index finger to his temple, which Cara thought made him look very studious. All he needed was a pair of round glasses and he'd look like a sexy teacher.

She gave him a warm smile.

"No," he said simply.

"No, what?"

"I've seen that look from women when they want something. I know what you're thinking, and the answer is no."

Cara's lip jutted out.

Ryan looked away. "And that pouty lip thing isn't going to work, either."

What was she expecting to have happen? A man she hardly knew was supposed to offer her a job? Even if he did, she was out of money and had nowhere to stay. The desperate, panicky sensation in the pit of her stomach returned, causing the tears to flow.

"Please don't cry again. I can't stand it when a woman cries." Ryan ran both hands through his hair. "Didn't you have a plan when you left Bensonhurst?"

Ugh, he made her sound like such an idiot, just like her brother always did. She pushed herself up into a sitting position. "I had a plan for the rest of my life, but my plan didn't go according to plan."

"Life never does," he said more to himself than to her.

She tried to stop the tears, but the tighter she held her mouth closed the more choked her sobs sounded.

"All right, calm down," Ryan told her. "We'll think of something."

• • •

Ryan knew what it was like to think your life was going to go one way and then—bam! You were blindsided by a curveball. Just like his aborted baseball career. And marriage. He and Cara had that in common. Except Ryan had run off to Europe to hide for almost two years, and Cara had run to the Jersey Shore.

Now that she was here, what was he supposed to do with her? He knew what he'd *like* to do with her, but that would only take one night. Then what? This woman was trouble with a capital T, the kind prone to public outbursts and grand displays of emotion.

"What about friends? You must have a friend you can shack up with."

"They're all married with young kids running around," Cara said.

"Let me guess. They're about thirty years old. Am I right?"

Cara's face lit up as she laughed. "How did you know?"

"Think about it. Most people get married around twenty-six or twenty-seven. Babies tend to come about two years after that."

"How old are you?"

"I'm coming up on thirty." Ryan winced just saying it.

"Me too. Unfortunately, it means something very different for a woman than it does a man."

"So I've been told," he said dryly. "More than once."

Cara gave him a knowing look and nodded. Then she looked down at her hands in her lap. "All I'd need is some work as a cocktail waitress and a place to stay for a short time. I promise I won't be any trouble."

Trouble. There was that word again.

She chose that moment to glance up at him with doe-like eyes, and against his better judgment, Ryan found himself in an almost trance-like state saying the words, "Fine, you can stay here."

Was he trying to atone for being an uncommitted jerk to all the women he'd dated since his divorce? He wasn't a jerk intentionally, and he was genuinely sorry when they walked away with that opinion of him. He always tried to be honest in the beginning so they wouldn't expect more from the relationship, but it never seemed to make any difference. Whenever women didn't get what they wanted, they weren't happy. End of story.

Ryan was no stranger to commitment. Marriage had been sacred to him. He had chosen one woman above all others to spend the rest of his life with until death. But that dream had died when his wife had betrayed him. In an instant, all hopes and plans for the future fell apart, and with it, any desire to love and fully commit. He couldn't handle that kind of upheaval to his life again.

So, yes, he knew exactly what Cara was going through, and he was genuinely sorry for her. Hopefully, she'd learn to trust again. Just because he was a lost cause when it came to love didn't mean everyone else should be, too. He heard her let out a deep exhale.

"I'm a fabulous cocktail waitress," she bragged. "You won't be sorry. I know every drink in existence. Honestly, it's like I have a photographic memory when it comes to ingredients."

Ryan didn't answer her. He sat there shell-shocked.

"Say something."

"I can't. I've lost all power of speech."

"You're not regretting your decision to let me stay, are you?"

"It's just … " His voice trailed off. He leaned his head back and stared up at the ceiling. "I'm trying to remember whether I've ever helped out a woman I wasn't sleeping with."

"If you think I'm going to sleep with you … "

"No! Jesus, that'd be a disaster waiting to happen."

"Are you saying sleeping with me would be a disaster?"

"Absolutely!" He caught the deadly look she shot him and quickly said, "I mean, absolutely not!"

Cara shrugged. "It doesn't matter either way, because I've sworn off all men. As far as I'm concerned, they're all mangy dogs. Except you, of course," she amended.

Ryan stood up and headed for the door. "No, I'm one, as well. If I weren't, I would have told you five minutes ago your robe was open," he tossed back.

CHAPTER 5

Was he completely out of his mind? Did he really just agree to let Cara stay in the apartment? Now he wouldn't be able to use it as an office. Instead, he would have to make do with the closet-sized office off the kitchen, with the tiny desk and single filing cabinet.

As for needing his bed upstairs, well, every woman he'd been involved with recently was now mad at him, so he had no prospects, anyway. Ryan leaned both hands on the cool stainless steel counter and took a deep breath. He closed his eyes and envisioned the part of Cara's breast he had seen. He wished he'd seen more.

Okay, he had to get over this fascination with her breasts. He was beginning to feel like some horny high school kid. He couldn't help it though. They were large and round and real. Usually he was a leg man, but Cara's cleavage was rendering him stupid.

She was going to work for him now. Which meant she'd be an employee of his. Which meant no messing around unless he wanted to be slapped with a sexual harassment suit.

He didn't need a cocktail waitress. He certainly couldn't afford another employee on his payroll. But Ryan knew what Cara was going through firsthand, which was why he agreed to help her. Maybe if he'd had someone lend him a helping hand after his wife had emotionally slaughtered him, he wouldn't be such an aimless screw-up now.

He knew he was a coward for running away to Europe after filing for divorce. Left behind all his responsibilities and commitments without saying a word. But the disappointment over his life had been strangling him little by little every day. He needed to bolt or he surely would have lost his mind. Or killed someone.

Ryan shoved the memories down into his gut like he did every time they entered his mind and went to find a white button-down shirt that would fit Cara. What was he going to tell his staff? Why was he bringing in another person when the restaurant was already struggling? It was summer, the busiest season on Crabclaw, but not busy enough to make up for the last six financially disastrous months.

"You up to starting tonight?" he asked Cara. She was still in the same spot on the couch as when he'd left. She was staring down at her chipped nails with disgust.

"Sure. What does it matter if I look like hell? Not like I'm trying to attract anyone."

"You don't want to scare the customers away, either."

"Are you saying I look scary?"

"Actually, you look much better than you did before, without all that … " He motioned up and down her body.

"I feel naked," Cara said shyly.

I'll show you how naked feels, Ryan wanted to say, and then quickly replaced that comeback with *Employee*. He threw her the shirt.

She held it up and grimaced. "When I get my first paycheck, I'll be able to buy some … necessities."

"Here's the deal, Cara." He hesitated, still not quite believing he was going to let a woman inhabit his personal space. "You can stay here in this apartment. There's only a mini fridge, so if you want to cook something you have to go downstairs to use the kitchen. The only time I'll be up here is when I need some papers or want to use the treadmill." Cara's eyes followed his thumb as he pointed to the monstrous beast of a machine in the corner.

"I said I didn't need a cocktail waitress because the restaurant isn't busy enough. I'm not sure how much money you'll make, so we'll have to see how it all works out."

"Okay," she said.

"I'm also not sure what to tell my staff about you."

"What do you mean?"

"Who are you, and why did I hire you?"

Cara gave it some thought for a moment. "Tell them I'm a friend of yours who needed a job."

"I'm not friends with any women." Ryan laughed as he noticed Cara's upper lip curl in disgust.

"Say I'm your cousin."

"That reeks of nepotism."

"Well then, tell them I'm some chick you want to nail," she said, exasperated. "From what you tell me, that seems to be the most believable explanation."

"You're probably right."

Cara gave him the biggest eye-roll he had ever seen.

"Come down at four-fifteen to eat, and then I'll show you around before the shift starts." He made his way toward the door. "You need anything else before I go?"

"Nope, I'm good."

Ryan stepped out, but popped his head back in again. "I have only one rule: no men are allowed up here, unless they're paramedics trying to revive you." He waited, expecting to hear a snide remark.

"Yes, Daddy."

He cracked a smile and went downstairs.

• • •

Had she made the right decision by staying in Crabclaw? The question gnawed at her for the rest of the afternoon. She knew her brother, Anthony was probably worried sick over her. He would take her in; of course he would. *Sempre Famiglia* had always been his motto. Family Forever. The fact that she hadn't gone to him for help would be a knife in his heart.

Cara couldn't go home. Not when she felt so humiliated and broken and worthless. Her entire identity had been stripped away.

She wasn't a fiancée or a girlfriend, or a student, or a career woman. No longer a daughter or a granddaughter.

Who was she now?

An almost thirty-year-old nobody.

Not to mention makeup-less, acrylic-less, and flat iron-less.

At four-ten, Cara stepped slowly down the stairs in her stilettos. She had on the white button-down top Ryan had given her to wear, tucked into the waistband of her short, black skirt. Even though her hair was pulled back in a rubber band, runaway curls kept escaping from it.

The kitchen was a whirl of activity. A prep cook was peeling, slicing, and chopping vegetables. One line cook was preparing the grill, another one the sauté station. The dishwasher was in the middle of washing enormous, steel pots. She tried to stay out of their way as she headed toward the double doors leading to the dining room.

A very large man in a perfectly pressed white double-breasted jacket and chef hat jumped in front of Cara, startling her half to death. His shoulder-length hair was tied back in a ponytail and his neat goatee was flecked with gray. He stood there squinting at her, hands on hips. He reminded Cara of a gunslinger deciding whether or not he should shoot.

"Hi, I'm Cara, the new cocktail waitress," she said, feeling awkward and out of place.

"Since when do we need a cocktail waitress?"

"Since the boss realized he didn't have one?"

He tipped back his head and laughed so hard, she was able to see all the silver fillings in his teeth. "Brady," he said, as soon as he caught his breath. "Executive chef. Of course, my number one position is 'Pop-Pop'"

"Pop-Pop?"

"That's what my precious girl calls me. I'm the proud father of a four-year-old daughter. Want to see a picture of her?"

"Uh, sure." She braced herself for a wallet full of photos.

Brady yanked up his chef's jacket to expose his entire torso. "Here she is." He pointed to a portrait of a little girl tattooed above his left breast.

"Wow," she said. She pointed to the massive image of a duck tattooed on his belly. "What's up with the duck?"

"Drunken night when I was in the military. My buddies thought it'd be funny if I woke up the next day with it on me."

"You didn't know what was happening?"

"Nah. I was passed out cold."

Ryan came bursting through the double doors, concern plastered all over his face. "I see you've met our chef."

Cara smiled. "And his daughter, as well as his duck."

Ryan stared at Brady's pudgy, hairy gut. "How about you pull your jacket back down, Brady? We're trying to make Cara feel welcome, not send her running for the hills."

"Will do. Let's get smurfin'!"

"Come on," Ryan said, leading Cara out of the kitchen.

She gave Brady a wave over her shoulder. "He's not as scary as he looks," she told Ryan.

"Not when he's quoting cartoon characters, which, I must warn you, he does a lot. And he's got a thing for knock-knock jokes. Usually ones told by his daughter that day."

"I think that's cute."

Ryan shrugged. "In a crackpot sort of way, I guess."

They traveled through the dining room, past tables set with white linens atop red tablecloths. An unlit fireplace with a row of ten votive candles on its mantle stood off to one side. Oil paintings of the Tuscan countryside in hues of olive green and blood orange hung on the golden-colored walls.

A red-brick archway separated the dining room from the bar area. The bar itself was a majestic looking, solid oak structure filled with bottle after bottle of every liquor imaginable. A guy was behind the bar, preening in a mirror. He saw Cara and his mouth fell open.

"Oz, this is Cara. She's our new cocktail waitress. Oz is my bartender."

Oz turned around, still open-mouthed.

"You catch many flies with your mouth hanging open like that?" she said.

Ryan snickered as the bartender immediately closed his mouth. He started to say something, but Ryan's cell rang. "Show her around, while I take this call."

"Why are you called Oz?" she asked.

His head was shaved, which made his moss-green eyes and thick, dark lashes stand out. He had a nice muscular build and smooth, clear skin. He was definitely in the *hot* category.

Then he spoke.

"Because I'm here to grant any and all of your wishes, preferably of the carnal nature."

"You're kidding me, right?" Cara immediately downgraded him to *warm*.

He winked at her. "Remember my name, baby, 'cause you'll be screaming it later."

"I guess that makes you a legend in your own mirror."

The waitress who had served Cara the other night came rushing in. "How late am I? I had a goddamn flat tire. Jeff said, 'Call AAA.' I said, 'I don't have time to wait for AAA. Change it for me.' 'I don't know how to change a flat,' he told me. What man doesn't know how to change a fucking flat?"

Oz raised his hand.

"I expect it from you, Oz, but not my own husband."

"So what did you do?" Cara asked her.

"I changed the fucker myself. Who are you?"

"I'm Cara." She prayed the waitress wouldn't recognize her.

"She's our new cocktail server," Oz said.

"We don't need a cocktail server. We're not busy enough." She looked Cara up and down. "You must be screwing Ryan. Since when does he hire one of his girlfriends?" she asked Oz.

"What? No, I'm not sleeping with him!"

"Not yet, anyway," Oz muttered under his breath.

"I'm Leah." She stared at Cara for a long moment. "Why do you seem familiar?"

"I have no idea," Cara said quickly. "I'm not from around here."

"Where are you from?"

She considered saying Long Island, but with her luck, Leah would know someone who lived in whatever town she chose. "Bensonhurst."

"Get out! I have an uncle who lives in Bensonhurst. Except he's in prison, so technically he's not living there at the moment."

Cara admired Leah's hair—*straight*, above the collarbone, dyed Marilyn Monroe blonde and held back with a rhinestone barrette—and wondered if it was too weird to ask someone she had just met whether she owned a flat iron, and if so, could she borrow it?

Ryan came over to them, his face tight with tension, even though the restaurant wasn't open for business yet. "Where's—?"

"I'm right here," said a woman no wider than one of Cara's thighs. Her dark hair was pulled into a tight, severe bun, which accentuated the hard angles of her face.

"This is Ginny," Ryan told Cara. "Any problems, you go to her."

"Hi, Jenny," Cara said.

"It's Ginny."

"That's what I said."

"No, you said Penny with a J. It's Gin, like the liquor, and also short for Giovana. Ginny."

Cara's head started to pound. "Got it."

Ryan's cell rang again, so he stepped away from their chatter to answer it. Brady came up to the bar and without having to ask, Oz poured him a shot of Jack Daniels. After Brady slammed it, he turned to Cara, eyes glistening and said, "Knock, knock!"

She glanced at the others for guidance. They had knowing smiles on their faces. "Who's there?"

Brady looked like he might explode from excitement. "Gorilla."

"Gorilla who?"

"Gorilla me a cheese sandwich! Ha ha ha ha …" and back to the kitchen he went.

This entire staff is a few peas short of a casserole.

Leah must have read her mind, because she nudged Cara with her elbow and said, "Don't worry, you don't have to be crazy to work here. We'll train you."

•••

Still unsure as to what he should tell his staff about Cara, Ryan tried to avoid their questioning stares. He knew they were all dying to know where she had come from, what she was doing here, and why she was staying in Ryan's upstairs apartment.

He had Oz pour him a Scotch and soda an hour before closing.

"How's Cara working out?" Ryan asked.

"Seems chatty and friendly enough with the customers."

He nodded.

Oz leaned in closer to him. "Are you going to tell me the real story about her?"

"I don't know what you're talking about."

"She's the chick from the other night. I almost didn't recognize her, but Ozzie here can never forget Ben and Jerry, or as Brady would say, Bert and Ernie."

"What?"

"You know, Thelma and Louise. Bonnie and Clyde."

It wasn't until Oz made a motion to his chest that Ryan realized what he was referring to. "They're called breasts, Oz. The sooner you learn that, the more chances you'll have of getting a date with someone who has them."

"So, what's the story with Cara?"

He sighed. He may as well set the record straight before gossip started to spread around the restaurant. "She's someone I just met who happens to be a little down on her luck right now. I'm helping her out until she can get back on her feet."

"You mean, get back on her stilettos," Oz said, ogling Cara's legs from across the room. "You're not doing her?"

"No, I'm not *doing* her. And you won't be, either. She's an employee."

"You're helping out a gorgeous woman without expecting anything in return?"

"That's right."

"Where's she staying?"

"Upstairs."

Oz tried to keep a straight face. "Let me get this straight. You've given her a job. You're letting her sleep in your apartment. No doubt you'll have to feed her. It will essentially be like you're living and working together, yet you won't be sleeping together?"

"That's correct." Why did it sound more absurd when Oz said it than it did in his own mind?

Oz laughed. "Good luck with that. You must be a saint."

Since Ryan knew he couldn't be farther from a saint when it came to women, he had to wonder whether to question his sanity or his libido.

CHAPTER 6

The next morning, Ryan was about to blast into his apartment to retrieve a file before he remembered he needed to knock first. Cara answered the door in bare legs and one of his college T-shirts.

"You look better in my clothes than I do," he told her.

She looked down at herself and blushed. "I hope you don't mind. I have hardly any clothes with me."

He imagined a sexy Cara in her black mini skirt and heels. Then the image of her going to the beach and having her heels sink into the sand ruined it for him. "Here's some money," Ryan said, opening his wallet and pulling out four twenties. "Buy yourself some things to wear and get a pair of flip-flops. This is the beach, for God's sake."

"I know, right?" she said. "Thanks. I promise to pay you back."

Ryan got the file he needed, stared longingly at his large desk, and trudged downstairs. He made himself an espresso behind the bar, finished it quickly, and made another one. Cara wearing his T-shirt brought up a range of surprising emotions. It was uncomfortably intimate on the one hand, yet an incredible turn-on to see her in a piece of his clothing.

The bell rang. It was Pisarro and Sons' fish delivery.

"The boss said not to unload until I had a check from you," Mario, the fish guy, said.

"Come on, Mario. How long have you been delivering fish to Bella Vita? You know I'm good for it."

Mario didn't budge. "I gotta follow orders. What my boss said, stands."

So, Pisarro finally had enough of extending his unpaid credit. What was Ryan supposed to do now?

"No problem. I'll write you a check," he told Mario. *Just don't cash it until sometime next year.*

Mario handed him the purchase order and started to unload the delivery. When he was ready to leave, Ryan handed him a check. Mario folded it in half and stuck it in his shirt pocket.

"See you Friday," Mario said, climbing into his truck.

Not after you find out that check has been returned for insufficient funds.

Ryan's next order of business for the day? Find a new fish purveyor.

• • •

Without having to do her makeup and hair in the morning, Cara was able to shower and be out the door in fifteen minutes. It was somewhat freeing, in a Bohemian kind of way. She could use the money Ryan gave her to buy some cosmetics, except she only wore MAC and eighty bucks wouldn't go far there. She could buy a flat iron, but then she wouldn't have much left over for clothes.

But her hair would be straight, instead of a mess of curls a pair of hamsters could burrow in.

But then she wouldn't have any money for clothes.

And Cara wasn't going anywhere unless she put some gas in her monster of a car, so practicality won out. Gas, a couple pairs of shorts, tanks, flip-flops, curl relaxer, and lip gloss. The money was gone already and she hadn't even bought anything yet.

She left Ryan's T-shirt on, slipped into her skirt, and traipsed barefoot down the stairs. Ryan was in his tiny office with his forehead down on the desk.

"Are you sick?" she asked, worried he had caught whatever it was she had.

"No, I'm banging my head against the desk," he said, without looking up.

"Well, stop. You'll give yourself a headache."

He lifted his head up. "That would be the least of my problems today," he said as his cell rang. "Ryan Garridy," he answered in a tired voice.

Cara slipped out the side door. *Poor guy*, she thought. He looked worn-out. How had Ryan became involved with Bella Vita and did he enjoy running a restaurant? She had never worked in a restaurant, only bars and clubs, but she knew it was a lot of labor. She went to high school with a guy who'd had a big crush on her. Used to ask Cara out three times a week. It became a running joke between the two of them. After they graduated, he took over his family's pizza place in the neighborhood and lived, breathed, and ate the place. He never had the time to ask her out again.

When she reached the Pimpmobile, the words "Wash Me" had been written on her back window.

She snorted. "Like that'll happen any time soon."

Robbie was the one who used to take care of washing her car. *Robbie*. He would be at work right now, no doubt goofing off with the other guys at Eddy's Auto Body Shop.

Was the jerk even worried about her? She was dying to know how many times he'd called her brother looking for her. Then again, maybe he hadn't called at all. Maybe her ex-hairdresser had moved in right away with her ex-fiancé, and they had packed up all of Cara's stuff.

Insane and irrational feelings of jealousy slammed her. For the millionth time, she asked herself what Annemarie had that she didn't. What more she could have done to make Robbie not want to cheat on her. Maybe if she had been sexier or cleaned the house better, or been sexier while cleaning the house.

She needed to stop this nonsense. She had never felt insecure before and she hated Robbie for making her feel now like there was something lacking in her. Every girlfriend Cara had ever known had gone through this low self-esteem period with their cheating boyfriend. "It's them, not you" Cara would tell them. "They're the rats. You're too good for them." They'd nod absently with that doubtful look in their eyes—the look that said these guys could call the next day and be welcomed back with open arms and legs.

Well, she'd never be that gullible or stupid. She wasn't unattractive to men. She saw the way Ryan had looked at her wearing his T-shirt this morning, like he had wanted to lift it up with his teeth. That counted for something.

She started the car, feeling slightly better about herself. After getting gas, she headed for the strip of stores near the beach. She bought a few things, threw the bags inside the Pimp, and took a walk on the beach. The feeling of warm, grainy sand between her toes and the smell of coconut suntan lotion soothed her. The familiar beach sounds surrounded her and took her back to her childhood. The waves pounded against the shore as children shrieked, running to avoid the incoming water. Argumentative seagulls swooped down, in an attempt to snatch unattended cheese doodles or potato chips. Music blared from radios and small planes overhead bearing advertised messages rumbled by.

She strolled over to a man sitting on a multicolored beach chair that looked as though it might collapse under his weight. He was maybe early sixties, with dyed black hair arranged in a pompadour. In front of him was an easel set up with a large pad of thick paper. At the moment, the man was chewing on the wooden end of the paintbrush. He glanced up at Cara.

"Whaddya think?" He had a thick Brooklyn accent that made her instantly homesick.

She studied his half-finished painting of the shoreline. A shoreline that looked like it had been terrorized by a chainsaw-wielding killer. "It's strangely unique."

"Watercolor is a bitch to do. Pardon my French."

She smiled. "You're from Brooklyn."

"You are correct in that assumption. However, I now inhabit the island of Crabclaw with the wife. Not for nuttin', but I would kill for a decent slice from the old neighborhood. Here, you gotta order an entire friggin' pizza pie."

"What neighborhood you from?" she asked, lapsing into her Brooklynese.

"Carroll Gardens, home to the yupsters now."

"I think you mean yuppies."

"Whatever," he said with a wave of his paintbrush.

"I grew up on 64th Street in Bensonhurst."

"Ah, yes. I had many business acquaintances from Bensonhurst. They got good cannoli there. I notice you don't have much of an accent."

"My mother told me if I ever wanted to sound like a lady I needed to get rid of it."

He nodded slightly and added another violent brushstroke to his picture. "Dino," he said finally, putting down his brush and extending his hand.

She shook it. "Cara Manzoni. What brought you to Crabclaw?"

"Three heart attacks." He laughed when her mouth fell open in surprise. "Too much fried calamari. The wife decided I needed to slow down and get healthy." Dino picked up his brush again. "So I took up painting, even though I am aware my interpretations leave much to be desired. I'm going to college now, too. My classes are filled with young Wisenheimers I'd like to smack into tomorrow." He dipped his brush in water, dabbed in some color. "I grow vegetables in my backyard, zucchini mostly. I wish I could make furniture out of zucchini, that's how much zucchini I have." He leaned forward and added more color to his picture. "And I try to perfect my red sauce, which is a friggin' never-ending process."

He shifted his body weight, causing the lightweight chair to sink further into the sand. "You remind me of my granddaughter,"

Dino said. "Especially the hair—wild and unruly curls, like fusilli pasta."

The more Dino kept bringing up food, the more her stomach cried out for something meat-filled and rich in carbohydrates.

"You wouldn't happen to know any place that makes a decent meatball sub, would you?"

"Yeah. Nino's Pizzeria on Henry Street in Brooklyn," Dino said wistfully. "You could try Avenue C Grocery, four blocks south of Broadway."

"Thanks. I'll see you around."

"I'm here every other day during the week. Any less and my blood pressure shoots up."

Cara drove to Avenue C Grocery, an old shack of a place with red screen doors and a rusty 7-Up sign over the entrance. The store looked like it had been there since before the invention of the automobile. She gave her order and began salivating as soon as she saw her meatballs being placed on an Italian roll.

She sprinted back to her car, unwrapped the tin foil, and bit into the saucy sandwich.

Eh. It was alright, but not as good as what she could make. The meatballs were dry, which usually meant they'd over-mixed ingredients or the balls had been packed too tightly. Not enough people understood that making meatballs was an art, as was lasagna, and a red sauce.

If only there were a kitchen in the apartment. The thought of using the commercial kitchen was too scary. She'd probably accidently set the place on fire by turning a wrong knob. Or put something back in the wrong place, sending crazy Chef Brady running for his cleaver. Cara laughed at the cartoonish image of Brady chasing after her, swinging his meat cleaver left and right.

The visit to the beach did her good. She drove back to Bella Vita with a surprising feeling of contentment, instead of that too familiar feeling of waiting for the other shoe to give her a swift kick in the ass. She planned to go up to Ryan and give him a great big hug for all he was doing for her. He was a good person, a lifesaver, and she couldn't wait to tell him so.

She parked and grabbed her purchases. The front door to the restaurant was wide open. Ryan was probably airing the place out before opening for business. She walked in and stopped in mid-step. Sitting at the bar was a pretty redhead in short shorts and a peasant top, laughing at something Ryan had just said. He was leaning into her with a posture that clearly said, "I want to take you right here, right now."

Ryan looked up, giving her a relaxed smile. "Hey, Cara."

He hadn't moved away from the woman, not even a millimeter, and for some illogical reason that pissed Cara off.

A phone rang somewhere in the restaurant. "Excuse me, ladies," he said and went to answer it.

The woman gave Cara a friendly smile. "I'm Charisse," she said in a Southern drawl.

"Cara," she said. "I work here."

Charisse seemed relieved. "Oh good, because I only came in here for directions, but Ryan charmed me into staying longer." She ran her fingers through her long, straight hair. "He's precious, but I sure wouldn't want to tread on your territory."

"Oh no, Ryan is definitely not my territory. You have free reign over that precious one."

"That's great to hear. I'm on vacation and it's been a little dull so far." Her face brightened as Ryan made his way back. "Ryan said he'd show me a good time, didn't you, sugar bear?"

"Huh?" he said, looking preoccupied.

Cara chimed in. "Charisse said you were going to show her a good time."

"Oh, right. Starting with the best Italian restaurant in town."

Charisse checked her watch. "Well, goodness gracious, it's almost dinner time!" She hopped off the barstool. "I need to hurry back to my hotel and put my face on. I'll see you again before you start to miss me."

All eyes were on her tight junior-sized body as she fluttered out. "Don't women eat anymore?" Cara grumbled under her breath.

"Don't women *what*?"

"Oh, never mind," she answered in a snippy tone.

"What's the matter with you? Bad day?"

What *was* the matter with her? She was having a perfectly fine day until she saw those two together.

"Well, goodness gracious, it's almost dinner time!" she exclaimed with an exaggerated Southern accent. "I need to scoot myself on upstairs, so I can work out for an hour-and-a-half and get my butt nice and tight. Then I need to make myself look *beauti-ful*, so you'll show poor lil' ole me a good time here in Crabclaw. I am just sooo bored out of my lil' ole mind, I don't know what to do."

Ryan stroked his jaw, a far-away look in his eyes. "I always fantasized about being with a helpless, ditsy Southern Belle."

Cara made a growling sound in the back of her throat and stomped away.

• • •

It was a slow night at the restaurant. Cara knew she wouldn't be able to count on much in the way of tips. The tables outside were all filled, as well as half the bar area, but there were only a few occupied dining room tables.

A waiter known as Johnny-boy was handling the tables inside. About mid-twenties, he was the spitting image of James Dean. Every time Cara caught a glimpse of him, she felt like she was in a wax museum.

"How's your night going?" she asked Leah.

Leah's face twisted. "I had a huge woman who ordered chicken with the sauce on the side. Then she complained the chicken was dry. Well, no shit. Everyone knows chicken breast tastes like you're eating a mattress. That's why chefs put sauce on top!"

Cara liked Leah. She was thirty-two and had been married for five years, no kids yet. She had gone to school for clothing design, and was in the process of creating a line of lingerie.

"Sluts & Goddesses," she told Cara. "How's that for a name? Every woman has a little of both in them, so I have designs to fit either mood." Leah's eyes travelled slowly up Cara's body, then down, and then up again. "I would love for you to test out some of my stuff," she said. "I want my pieces to work for every body type, but without knowing how they work on different bodies, I won't know what details need to be tweaked."

"Have you had anyone else try them on?"

"Ginny has tried on a few pieces. And obviously I have, but we're … "

"Way skinnier than me?"

Leah smiled. "A different body type than you."

"What's up with Ginny? Is she anorexic or something?"

"Ginny doesn't eat wheat, dairy, or anything with sugar in it."

"That means no pasta, no cheese, no cannoli, no … "

"That means no to *a lot* of things."

"What does she eat?" Cara tried to think of foods that didn't have wheat, dairy, or sugar in them. She came up with meat, vegetables, fruit, and tofu. *I'd be that skinny, too, if that was all I ate.*

"I don't ask," Leah said. "It's too fucking depressing to talk about."

Leah went to check on her station, so Cara wandered over to the bar. Oz was busy flirting with the bevy of females who sat in front of him. She had worked with many bartenders like him— good-looking, aggressively charming guys who took a different girl home every night. They had never bothered Cara, but that was before she became bitter and cynical over the opposite sex. Now she believed if all promiscuous men could be space-launched onto their own planet, the world would be a much better place.

The night was dragging. Cara knew she wasn't going to clear much in tips. "Hey, Oz, do you have the time?"

He sauntered over. "The better question is, do you have the energy?"

Luckily, she was a seasoned pro at smart comebacks. "Please, save your breath. You'll need it later to blow up your date."

"Oooh, you're a sassy calzone, aren't you? Have I told you how much I love to eat Italian?"

Now that one was funny. "You're too much, Oz." She spotted Ryan and Charisse huddled together at a table. "It's a wonder he has any time to run a restaurant."

Oz followed her eyes. "Ryan? Are you kidding? It's the only reason he bought Bella Vita in the first place."

"To meet women?"

"It wasn't because of his restaurant expertise, that's for sure."

"There are less expensive options for meeting women. How about joining a dating site like everyone else?"

"I don't think Ryan is looking for Mrs. Right. He's only looking for Miss Right Now."

That statement had always incensed Cara. "What is wrong with men nowadays?"

"I don't think every … " Oz started to say.

"Are you all unable to make a commitment and remain faithful?" she asked, cutting him off.

"Not all men … "

"Is there some gene that prevents you from doing so?" Oz opened his mouth, but no words came out. "Well?" she said.

"To lump us … "

"Just forget it," she said, throwing up her hands. "I don't want to talk about it anymore."

Leah handed Oz her customer's credit card. "Are you pissing off our new addition already, Oz?"

"We were having a conversation about the inadequacies of men," Cara said.

"Oh crap," Leah said.

"Tell me about it," Oz said. "I feel like I'm taking one for the whole team."

Leah shook her head. "No, I mean, oh crap, look who just walked in."

A statuesque blonde with a super short, razor-cut hairstyle and skin that looked like it had been airbrushed smiled at Oz.

Oz greeted her with a nervous laugh. "Allison, long time, no see."

"Don't be silly. I was in here last week." She looked around. "Where's my man?"

"Why don't you have a seat at the bar and I'll find him for you," Leah said.

"All right," Allison said in a singsong voice.

Oz handed Leah the credit card and receipt with his right eyebrow raised. Leah raised her left eyebrow back at him. Cara raised both her eyebrows at them, wanting to know why they were acting so weird.

Leah headed back to the dining room. Johnny-boy came in the front door and handed his ticket over to Oz.

"Hey, Jimmy D," Allison said, waving. "Seen my Ryan?"

Johnny-boy shook his head no.

Ryan was Allison's man?

"What can I get you to drink, Allie?" Oz asked.

"White wine spritzer."

Cara scoffed at her choice of drink. She could only begin to guess what would happen when Allison realized *her man* was dining with another woman.

Before Allison was able to take a sip of her wine, Ryan was beside her. "What are you doing here? I thought you were mad at me."

"You know I can't stay mad at you for long." She put her arms around his neck and gave him a kiss full on the lips.

If Ryan felt nervous about having two girlfriends in the restaurant at the same time, he sure wasn't showing it.

"So *this* is your man," Cara said to Allison, staring directly at Ryan. "How long have you two been … whatever it is you're doing together?"

Ryan gave her a look that clearly told her she was venturing into dangerous territory. "On second thought, it's really none of my business," she said quickly, backing away. "Forget I asked." Helping along the inevitable train wreck was not a smart thing to do. She didn't want to be fired this soon.

Cara returned just in time to see Allison throw her drink in Ryan's face, followed by Charisse calling him a "two-timing non-gentleman." Both women stormed out of the restaurant as everyone sitting in the bar area applauded, including Oz.

Ryan wiped spritzer out of his eyes, took a slight bow, and headed toward the restroom.

"This kind of thing happen often?" she asked Oz.

"Only to the best, baby," Oz said, laughing. "Only to the best."

CHAPTER 7

Ryan ran the credit card tips and printed the register tapes. "Thanks, guys. Good job tonight," he told his staff as they were leaving, just like he did every night.

He shut everything down and poured himself a Scotch. Ah, his favorite time of the day. The restaurant was quiet. Phones were quiet. All lights were off, except for the small one over the bar that illuminated the liquor bottles. He was finally able to relax even though he still felt sticky, despite efforts to wash off the wine.

Couldn't say he didn't deserve that drink in the face, although he would have wished for a more discreet plan of attack. Why did women always have to be so emotional? He had been humiliated in front of his staff and his customers. Even worse, he was going home alone to eat ramen noodles while watching the news. Lately, that seemed to be Ryan's nightly ritual: Scotch and ramen for dinner, news for entertainment, solitary sleeping arrangement.

He belted back the Scotch and poured a second one. He needed to stay away from women altogether until he was ready for a serious relationship. Focus his energies on the restaurant, instead. Bella Vita had turned out to be way more than he had bargained for, and if he didn't do something soon to turn sales around, he would no longer have a restaurant to worry about.

If Ryan had been a betting man he would have wagered all his money on Bella being a huge moneymaker. Boy, had he been wrong. The overhead was enormous, from payroll to utilities, to credit card processing fees, to repair and maintenance. It wouldn't be such a problem if the place was packed every night, but the reality learned too late was that he had bought a restaurant already in trouble.

Cara padded barefoot into the bar area. She hopped up onto a barstool. "You servin'?"

"You buyin'?"

"How about some Frangelico?"

"As you wish, milady." He reached for a snifter.

"Trying to forget tonight?"

He placed the liqueur in front of Cara, watching her lips as she took a sip. When her tongue traced her bottom lip, he looked away and poured himself another drink. "I don't think there's enough Scotch here to make me forget tonight."

"Is this what you do every night once the place closes? Drink in the dark, alone?"

"Seems that way lately."

She tipped her head to one side. "What's the matter, Ryan? Have you run out of girls to play with in Crabclaw?"

"Why do women always have to take everything so seriously?" he said, frowning.

"There's a sweeping generalization if I've ever heard one."

He came around the bar and stopped behind Cara. He lightly touched her bare left shoulder. "Is that a tattoo?" He squinted, trying to make it out. "Three testicles?" he guessed, still tracing the design with his finger.

She smacked his hand away. "They're meatballs! Geez, why would you say something like that?"

"Testicles, meatballs. They're both about the same size."

"You wish. The meatballs are in memory of my mom and dad, and my grandfather."

He instantly sobered. "They're … ? They've all passed away?"

She nodded. "My grandfather, who I was very close to, did all the cooking for the family. He was known around our neighborhood as Meatball Manzoni, because he made the greatest Sicilian meat-a-balls." She took another sip of her drink. "As a kid, everyone would come over to our house on New Year's Day.

There would be two huge pots of sauce. One with meatballs and one with sausage. Everyone would watch football all day, and you would just go and make yourself a sausage or meatball sandwich on an Italian hard roll whenever you felt like it."

"Was it a secret family recipe going back for generations?"

She nodded proudly. "You're looking at the first female in the family to learn it. Apparently, none of the women ever cooked. It was always done by men. Go figure."

Ryan sat on the stool next to her, waiting for her to mention her parents. She stared down at her hands in her lap. In the dim light, Cara looked about sixteen, but when she finally looked up, her eyes were those of a woman much older than twenty-nine.

"Both my parents were killed in a car accident eight years ago."

"I'm sorry. That must have been horrible for you."

"Yes."

She said nothing more, and he didn't push it, but her situation began to make a little more sense to him. "That's why you can't go home. You don't have anyone to go back to, do you?"

"I have an older brother who has a family of his own to take care of. He's felt responsible for me for years." She reached up and wiped underneath one eye. "It's time for me to learn how to stand on my own two feet. You know what I mean?"

Not only did Ryan know what she meant, he admired her obvious fortitude and wanted to tell her so, without it coming out sounding like he felt sorry for her. Maybe it was the whisky, but instead of telling Cara he admired her, Ryan found himself leaning into her and asking, "What would you do if I kissed you right now?"

If she was surprised she didn't show it. "I think I'd throw the rest of my drink in your face."

He leaned back in his seat. "Since it's already been done once tonight, I'll rescind the question."

"Oh, Ryan." She sighed. "I'll see you tomorrow."

She walked away, fading into the darkness. Hadn't he said less than an hour ago that he was going to stay away from women? *It's time to call it a night, Garro,* he told himself, using the high school nickname from his baseball team. Three strikes in one night was a record for him. He hadn't struck out this badly since junior high, when he wore braces and had a consistently bad haircut.

•••

After being out all morning scouring the town for an authentic Italian bakery, Cara concluded there weren't any. Unless you counted the one in the local supermarket, which she didn't. They sold a sorry excuse for an éclair. Doughy and too sweet.

She would kill for a *sfogliatella* to dunk in her cappuccino. Nonna's, the bakery around the corner from her apartment in Brooklyn, made the best ones: crispy, clam-shaped, paper-thin flaky pastry on the outside, with a subtle orange-flavored ricotta on the inside.

She had to settle for an apple fritter instead—a poor substitute and definitely not worth the calories. Armed with peaches, plums, cherries, and ears of corn bought from a roadside stand, Cara trudged up the stairs to the apartment. She heard the sound of a running motor coming from inside.

What in the world was that? Did she leave something on?

She pushed open the door. Ryan was running on the treadmill, with an iPod blasting in his ears. His back was to the door, so he didn't see her come in. She stood frozen, mesmerized by the sight of him in only a pair of thin nylon gym shorts. A sweaty, toned, glistening, hard Ryan. He was like a work of art, sculpted out of stone, every muscle in his back defined.

Cara had never been one for hard bodies before. She used to tease Robbie by poking his soft tummy and calling him "dough boy." But she was experiencing such an intensely primal, physical reaction watching Ryan, it made her wonder if this was what it felt like to be a man. Was she experiencing the female equivalent of an erection?

If he asked her now whether he could kiss her, she wouldn't bother answering. She'd wrap her arms around his sweat-drenched torso and lay a deep, hot kiss on him—

"Christ, you scared me!" Ryan exclaimed, which in turn startled the hell out of Cara, snapping her out of her delusional fantasy. He ripped the headphones from his ears. "How long have you been standing there?"

"I just came in," she lied.

Ryan slowed down his pace, mopping his face with a hand towel. He pressed a button and came to a full stop. Opened a bottle of water and took a long sip.

"I can come back," Cara said, unable to tear her eyes away from him.

"I'm done."

Cara was now able to gape at Ryan full frontal. His shorts were drenched with sweat and molded to every bump, line, and curve. He took another sip, some of the water spilling down his chest. It dripped down his stomach, which, she noted, was way flatter than hers.

"You're in pretty good shape, considering." She tried to appear as nonchalant as possible.

"Considering *what*?"

"Considering the fact that you drink like a sailor."

He grimaced. "About last night ... "

"No explanations necessary. You're a man."

"So?"

"So, since I was the only girl there last night, I was the logical choice for your advances." Cara made her way over to the couch and plopped down. She took out a ripe, plump peach from her bag and polished it with the hem of her shirt.

"You make it sound like I would have made a pass at any woman, regardless," he said, stretching his hamstrings.

She didn't want to tell him that as far as womanizing went, he gave Italian men a run for their money. "Look, you can kiss, screw, screw *over* as many women as you'd like. It's none of my business."

Ryan stopped stretching. "I don't screw over women."

Cara took a bite of the peach and savored its sweet juice.

"I'm upfront and honest with women. Always."

She continued to eat her peach.

"I can't help it if you women always want more."

She stopped in mid-bite. "You mean, more than a one-night stand? More than just a roll in the hay? Excuse us for having some morals and values."

"Why can't women be content with just dating? Why does it always have to go somewhere? And then when it doesn't, *I'm* the asshole."

"Try dating one woman at a time, instead of treating us like rides at a fair. You're on one and then as soon as you get off, you want to immediately ride another."

"As long as I'm not married, why can't I date more than one woman at a time as long as I'm upfront about it?" He reached behind to stretch his broad shoulders.

Cara's teeth clenched in anger. "You're exactly the kind of man I despise!"

"You mean the kind who's putting you up for free?"

"You're going to throw that in my face because you feel guilty for treating women like cattle?"

"Cattle? I don't treat women like cattle. All of them know the rules from the beginning. I tell them I don't want anything serious, and they agree. 'Oh no, me neither,' they always say, and then inevitably down the line, they change the rules. Why?"

She felt sorry for every single one of this callous jerk's past and future girlfriends. "God forbid they start liking you too much, Ryan. What a character flaw on their part."

He shrugged. "Nothing wrong with liking a person. Love's a whole different story. That's what screws everything up."

She stared at him for a long moment, considering the truth in his statement. How had he become so bitter about relationships? He even had her beat in that department. "Not everyone has such a tight rein on their emotions as you do. I'm sorry you think women are weak and pathetic creatures."

"I didn't say women were weak and pathetic; you just complicate everything." He crossed in front of Cara and headed to the bathroom. "I'm jumping in the shower."

She had finished her peach and was now sucking on the pit. "It's a wonder we've managed to evolve as a species. The differences between men and women are mind-boggling."

"Life was much simpler back in the Stone Age," he said before shutting the bathroom door.

"You mean when you clubbed a woman and dragged her back to your cave?" Cara shouted at the closed door.

Ryan opened the door and peeked out. "I meant before women learned how to speak," he said, slamming the door before she could throw something at him.

• • •

Cara, along with the rest of the Bella wait staff sat around a table, ready to sample the specials of the evening. Brady presided over them like a power-hungry dictator. She lost count as to how many tattoos covered his arms—enormous shaved arms, filled with various fruits and vegetables battling one another with kitchen utensils, tumbling into pots and pans.

Oz leaned into her, whispering, "If I said you had a great body, would you hold it against me?"

"Can I ignore you some other time?" she whispered back.

"For an appetizer, the special is Polenta Bianca made with chicken livers, dried dates, and wild mushrooms." Brady passed the dish around and everyone took a bite.

Cara declined. She didn't like chicken livers, or anything liver. Brady raised an eyebrow at her but said nothing.

"For the main, we have a spinach ravioli stuffed with goat cheese, kale and wild mushrooms, and *coniglio*, a rabbit *confit* with eggplant, squash blossoms, tomato, and red bell pepper."

Cara scrunched up her nose at the choices. Way too fancy for her taste. She took a bite of the ravioli, which was creamy and somewhat bland, but passed on the rabbit. She'd had one as a pet.

"Hey, new girl with the hair," Brady said. "What's the problem?"

Chatter ground to a halt, and all eyes were suddenly on her. "I don't eat liver or rabbit."

"When a customer asks about them, what are you going to say?"

"Ask your server?"

Oz snickered, Ginny clucked her tongue, Ryan shook his head, and Leah muttered, "Oh, crap."

"I can't help it if I prefer simpler cuisine," Cara said.

Brady put both palms on the table and loomed over them like a vulture. "If you have an uncivilized palate, then you shouldn't be working in a restaurant."

"I'm a cocktail waitress. Alcohol is my specialty, not food."

"Listen here, you little barnacle."

"Barnacle?"

"It's from SpongeBob," Leah said.

Brady had his hands on his hips, looking as if fire were about to shoot from his nostrils. "You think you're such an expert on liquor, do you?"

Cara stared him down. "Your drink is Jack Daniel's, right?"

"Yeah," he said gruffly.

"Jack Daniel's distinct taste is a result of a process called charcoal mellowing. In case you don't know, that means every drop of the whiskey gets filtered through ten feet of containers packed with sugar maple charcoal, which makes J.D. a Tennessee whiskey and not bourbon."

"Can we all get to work now?" Ryan said, trying to hide his smile.

Cara went up to Brady and patted his back. "Just don't expect me to eat organs or cute, fluffy animals and we'll get along fine."

"Humph," was all he said.

Leah put an arm around Cara's shoulders. "I don't know you very well, but I love you already."

Cara decided that was as good an opening as she could get to ask Leah if she could borrow her phone. She was dreading the call, but she needed to let her brother know she was all right.

"I promise I'll only talk for a few minutes."

"Don't worry about it," Leah said. "Talk for an entire goddamn hour if you need to. I have unlimited minutes."

Cara headed to the quiet of the dining room and dialed Anthony's number. Anthony thrived on routine. He taught high-school math, and pulled into his driveway at four-thirty every day. He expected dinner at five-thirty on the nose, after which he spent an allotted time with the twins—one hour and fifteen minutes—and then proceeded to prepare lesson plans and grade papers for the rest of the night. Any deviation sent him spiraling toward a panic attack.

It was almost five.

"Hello?" he answered hesitantly.

"It's me, Anthony."

"Jesus H. Christ, Cara! Where the hell are you? I've been trying to find you. Robbie came by and dropped all your stuff off. Said you flipped out on him and took off."

"He did *what?*" She focused on one of the serene Tuscan landscapes to calm herself. "Anthony, I walked in on him with another woman."

"I'll kill him! Tell me where you are, so I can get you."

She felt comforted by the fact that her brother always wanted to protect her. "Leave him alone. The jerk's not worth it."

"Tell me where you are, so I can get you," he repeated.

Anthony could easily come and bring her back to his place. She might even be able to get her old job back. She'd have money again, makeup, nails, a flat iron, a kitchen. But she couldn't go back. Not yet. "I'm down the shore staying with a friend. As soon as I figure out what I'm going to do, I'll come home."

Anthony gave a frustrated grunt. "Can't you think up a plan over here in Bensonhurst?"

Sure. She could get to that during her 30 to 40 for the double murder she'd commit if she returned to Bensonhurst. "The salt air is doing me good. Listen, I gotta run. Give the twins a hug from their Auntie Caca." *An unfortunate nickname, yet the only one the twins seemed to be able to pronounce.*

"At least give me a number where you can be reached. This one came up *Private*."

"We're gonna get cut off. I'll call you soon." She disconnected.

Hearing that Robbie had moved all her stuff out of their apartment was a blow she hadn't expected. How was he going to swing the rent all by himself? And what if she had planned on returning to him? Cara thought it was awfully presumptuous of him to assume she wasn't going to marry him. Plenty of women overlooked infidelity and went on to live head-in-the-sand lives.

She found Leah and handed the phone to her. "Can you be my voice of reason?"

"Sure. What's up?"

"What do you think about a man who cheats on his fiancée?"

Without hesitating, Leah said, "I think he should be strung up by his scrotum and hung naked in the town square for a public flogging."

Cara grabbed Oz by the back of the shirt as he passed by. She asked him the same question.

"Uh, he's not ready to get married?"

"Have you ever cheated on a girlfriend?" Cara asked.

"No."

"Liar," Leah said.

"It's true!" Oz said, his cheeks reddening.

"Are you blushing?" Oz might have some redeeming qualities after all.

He nervously cleared his throat. "Oz doesn't have to cheat. He informs all the ladies from the get-go that if they want a piece of the Oz pie, they're going to have to share."

Cara and Leah stared at him, their lips curled in disgust. Luckily, Ryan called for Oz, because the idea of doing him bodily harm seemed mighty attractive.

"Don't worry, there's more than enough of the Oz to go around," he said, wiggling his eyebrows suggestively before scurrying off.

Cara rolled her eyes. "When Oz dies, they'll have to bury him face down, so he can see where he's going."

Leah laughed. "I'm sure it'll be mighty crowded down there with the rest of the men."

• • •

The double espresso slowly dripped into a demitasse cup. Ryan stared at his reflection in the polished brass of the machine, wondering how he was going to get out of the financial mess he was in. Nights at the restaurant were easy to get through, with the hustle of the customers and staff. The bright light of day was a different story. It was then he was forced to face certain realities, like the fact he'd written three checks that wouldn't clear the bank until the deposit was credited tomorrow morning. Or that the tax payment was overdue and he had no idea how he was going to come up with the cash to pay it. He was on a COD basis now with every vendor, because they no longer trusted they would get paid. He dreaded the next payroll.

His credit was tapped, a bank loan was out of the question, and crawling to his father to ask for money … well, Ryan would rather gargle with a lye solution. It was bad enough he had to pop antacids again like they were candy. He hadn't had to do that since his divorce.

"What happened to my 'golden boy'?" his father would say. "You were so full of promise. You let your injured throwing arm and some woman get the best of you, and now everything you touch turns to shit." Which wasn't exactly true, since Ryan hadn't attempted to succeed at anything since he had returned from Europe.

Fast money. Ryan thought owning a restaurant would be an easy way to make fast money and meet women. He didn't think about having to pay labor, taxes, and repairs. His stomach twisted just thinking of the long list of expenses: food, equipment, maintenance, advertising, laundry. He was in too deep. Shutting the place down and walking away was looking better and better.

"Good morning." It was Cara. Without makeup, she looked fresh-faced and vibrant, reminding Ryan of the many natural beauties he had seen throughout Italy.

"Espresso?"

"Please." She smiled, revealing a slight gap in her two front teeth he hadn't noticed before. He found it sexier than a row of straight, unnaturally white veneers.

Ryan placed Cara's espresso on the bar in front of her and pushed the sugar toward her. "*Signorina*."

"*Grazie, signore*."

Impressed with her authentic Italian accent, he told her so.

"My grandfather's English was horrible. He preferred speaking Italian, so he taught it to my brother and me. It came in handy, because my parents spoke Italian when they didn't want us to know what they were saying." She smiled sweetly at the memory. "It took awhile for them to catch on that we understood everything they said."

"Were they mad when they finally figured it out?"

"Nah. They were impressed we had learned another language."

Cara added three spoonfuls of sugar to her espresso. She stirred it, letting out a loud sigh.

"What's up?"

"What makes you think something's up?"

"If you stir your espresso any more, you're going to wind up with butter, and also, you're not your usual spunky self."

She stopped stirring and stared at him long and hard. "Can I ask you something?"

"No, I did *not* sleep with her." He laughed at his little joke, but she didn't share in his amusement. "Sorry, it's a reflex. Go ahead."

"What does it mean when my fiancé—"

"You mean your *ex*-fiancé, don't you?"

"Of course."

"Just checking."

Cara leveled her eyes at him. "What does it mean when my *ex*-fiancé moves all my stuff out of our apartment?"

"It means the relationship is over." He was surprised when she let out a muffled cry. "It *is* over, isn't it?" She gave a weak nod, but he still wasn't convinced. "Listen, the guy's a bum."

"I know that, but it should be *my* decision to move my stuff out, not his."

"I thought the decision was clear when you walked out the door."

"That has nothing to do with it."

Ryan wished he knew of a series of online classes he could take to better understand women, because he sure as hell needed them.

Cara threw up her hands, exasperated. "Why isn't he begging me to come back?"

"Does he know where you are or how to get in touch with you?"

"No!"

For once, Ryan wasn't sorry to hear his cell ring. "I don't need another credit card," he said into the phone. "I don't have time to shop." He clicked off. "Look, I would love to finish this conversation, but I have vendors I'm trying to avoid today." He finished off the last of his espresso.

"Fine. All you men stick together anyway. I don't know why I expected anything different from you." With pursed lips and her head held high, she left him to the mess that was his life, which, in Ryan's opinion, was undoubtedly easier for him to deal with than the female species.

CHAPTER 8

Dino sat in the same spot on the beach as before. This time he was painting demonic-looking seagulls—bloody orange and purple birds attacking a fish.

"I'm exercising artistic license today. It makes me feel more edgy," he explained.

Cara plopped herself down on the sand next to his chair. She stared at her chipped, blue toenails. There wasn't a time when her toes weren't nicely painted. *Oh, how the well-manicured have fallen.* Embarrassed, she buried her feet into the warm sand.

"I went over to Avenue C like you suggested."

"What did you think?"

"The meatballs were a little bland. I'm used to mine."

"The secret to meatballs is to simmer them in the sauce."

"Yeah, that's what my grandfather used to do. He'd make them fat and round, like the size of a billiard ball, and then he'd let them cook in a heavy garlic tomato sauce. Sicilian-style balls."

"Get outta here. You're Sicilian? I'm Sicilian. My family's from Palermo." Dino shook his head in amazement. "Small world, I tell ya. The wife is from the north, near Milan, so I don't get a lot of spicy Sicilian meals like my mother used to make. The wife bakes her meatballs. She says there's less fat that way."

"My grandpa Manzoni taught me to make the balls with a mixture of freshly ground veal, lean pork, and beef chuck. You wanna know what his secret ingredients were?"

"I'm listening."

"A handful of raisins and toasted pine nuts. I haven't found anyone who makes them like that."

"I'd bet they'd taste like my *mama*'s meatballs," he said wistfully. "A hint of sweet, with a whisper of crunch."

She started to laugh. "How come every time I see you we talk food?"

He reached inside his lunch pail for a bag of sliced carrots and celery. "Maybe because this is all the wife ever packs me for a snack. I'm so hungry for some real food I'm ready to eat my arm." He offered the bag to Cara and she took a carrot stick.

"She's only looking out for you. She doesn't want to be a widow and have to wear black the rest of her life."

"Yeah, I suppose." Dino munched thoughtfully on a piece of celery.

"How long have you two been married?"

"Forty-two years in September," he said automatically.

"Why do all men cheat?" she blurted out.

Dino frowned. "First, let me start off by amending that statement: all men do *not* cheat. Only the scumbags. Pardon my French. Never once did I go out on the wife, although I had many opportunities. All men will have many chances to cheat in their lifetime, but if you choose a man to marry who has some character, some integrity … " He pounded his chest with his fist. "Not a *shem*, then you won't have to worry about nuttin,' *capisce?*"

"Yeah, I *capisce*." Cara's skin was starting to burn. She stood, brushing sand off her. Robbie had been a *shem*. But it's not like he had been a jerk when they first started dating. Except for the mother thing. He always disrespected his mother. In Cara's family, if you disrespected Mom, you got a smack in the back of the head. Her father once told her, "You can always tell how a man's going to treat you by the way he treats his mother." She should have listened to those wise words.

"Thanks for the carrot."

He grunted.

She waved goodbye and started up the beach. "Hey, girlie." Dino's words stopped her. "Do you know what a *mensch* is?"

"A decent, honorable person?"

"You find a *mensch* to marry and you'll be all right."

•••

"Do you have internet on your phone?" Cara asked Leah later that evening.

"Of course. Why?"

"Do you mind if I check something on it?"

Leah reached into her pocket and handed her phone to Cara. "Knock yourself out."

Cara made her way over to the service area of the bar. As soon as she logged onto Facebook, she felt nervous jitters in the pit of her stomach. How pathetic after almost a month in Crabclaw she was still religiously checking up on Robbie. The need for some sort of closure, an understanding as to why he had cheated still gnawed at her. She was concentrating so intently on working Leah's phone that she was unaware of Oz by her side. She glanced up, startled.

"What do you say we go back to my place later on and do some math? Add the bed, subtract the clothes, divide the legs, and multiply?"

Cara looked down at the phone again. "Gee, I'd love to, Oz, but the voices in my head say no."

"I know how to please a woman," he said in a suggestive tone.

"Then *please* leave me alone." Robbie's page came up on the screen. Photos of them as a couple were still there. His status read "in a relationship." Nothing had changed, yet everything had changed.

"Is that your fiancé?" Oz asked.

"Ex." Cara could barely get the word out.

"The guy's an idiot."

Even though Cara knew Robbie was an idiot, it didn't stop her from still wanting him. Or rather, the life they'd had together and the future she had been dreaming about.

Leah stomped toward them. "If business doesn't start picking up soon, I'm going to have to become a surrogate for a rich, infertile couple."

"It's the busy tourist season. Seems like Fridays and Saturdays have been the only decent nights in a while," Oz said.

Ginny tapped Cara on the shoulder. "'The rattlers' at table six need more drinks. They're rattling their ice at me."

"That's just as bad as 'the tapper' I had the other night," Leah said. "You know, when they hold up the glass and tap on it?"

Oz said, "Personally, I prefer 'the snapper.' They snap their fingers to get your attention."

"I'll get the drinks," Cara said in a trance-like state, still staring at Leah's phone.

"What's with her?" Ginny asked.

"It's a tragic case of ex-longing," Oz said.

In a soothing voice, Leah said, "Give me the phone, Cara. Come on."

She handed over the phone and turned her attention to Ginny. "Why do men cheat?"

Ginny put her chicken wing of an arm on her hip. In a matter-of-fact voice, she said, "Infidelity is genetic. There's a cheating gene called the 'love rat gene.' Scientists say one in four is born to be unfaithful."

"Ah-hah!" Oz exclaimed. "That includes women, too." All three ladies glared at him. "Or not," he quickly said.

Ginny went on. "My father had many occupations throughout his life, but he excelled at being a womanizer. He had half a dozen children in and out of wedlock. He'd take off for months at a time, but he always came back to my mother. And my mother always took him back."

She studied Ginny's face, expressionless as she said the words. Cara didn't detect sadness or anger or even absurdity over the situation. Ginny seemed to accept it like it was an inevitable fact of life.

"How did your mother put up with that for so many years?" Leah asked.

Ginny shrugged. "She said she loved him. After thirty-six years, she finally left him."

"Good for her," Cara said.

"Yes, but bad for me. I'm genetically doomed to cheat the same as my father. Table six, Cara. More drinks." Ginny walked away.

"Genetically doomed," Cara echoed.

"Don't listen to her. Your guy wasn't genetically doomed, he was just an asshole," Leah said. "Listen, we have a night off tomorrow. Why don't you come over?"

It wasn't like Cara had any other plans.

"I'd love to have you try some designs I've been working on. It'll be fun. We can order take-out," Leah urged.

Cara had eaten so much take-out in the last few weeks she could fill an entire drawer with packets of ketchup, salt, and pepper.

"I'll come over, but only if I can cook," she said.

Leah laughed. "Not only can you cook, the hubs and I might ask you to move in. Both of us are terrible cooks."

"Shall I bring the wine?" Oz said, handing Cara the drinks for her table.

Cara gave Oz one of her sweetest smiles. "Did you hear in the news about the woman who slashed off her husband's penis, threw it in the garbage disposal, and switched it on before calling 911?"

Oz swallowed. "I just remembered I have something to do tomorrow."

Cara turned to Leah. "How's four o'clock sound?"

• • •

The anticipation of a home-cooked meal filled Cara's every waking moment. The meals she ate at Bella Vita were good, but most of the time they were too fussy for her taste. She preferred her food simple—the kind of meals she grew up on, where you didn't need to use seventy-five ingredients just to make one dish.

Leah lived in a one-bedroom apartment in a third-floor walk-up with her husband. Cara trudged up the stairs with two bags of groceries and found the door to Leah's apartment wide open. She knocked anyway.

"Come on in," Leah's muffled voice called from inside.

A haze of incense enveloped her as soon as she stepped into the place. Healthy green plants grew in each corner. Black and white prints of naked men and women hung on the walls. And books. Lots and lots of books everywhere—paperbacks, hardcovers, coffee table, and textbooks.

Leah sailed out of the bedroom, pulling a loose T-shirt over her head. "Welcome to *mi casa*."

"You have a lot of books. And plants," Cara said.

"What I lack in culinary skills, I make up for when it comes to all things green. Jeff's the smart one. Most of these books are his. I married a nerd."

"Is Jeff here?"

Leah led her to the kitchen. "He should be home from school in about an hour."

Cara dumped the grocery bags on the counter. "College?"

"Grad school. He'll be finishing up this December."

She was impressed by anyone who picked a path in life and stuck with it. "What's he studying?"

"Art history. He wants to be a professor at a university, preferably in Florence, Italy." She laughed. "But for now, Jersey will have to do."

A fluffy orange kitten sashayed over to Cara's calves and began rubbing against them. She wasn't a cat lover, but this one was kinda cute, so she crouched down to pet it behind the ears. "What's this little guy's name?" The kitten bit down hard on her finger. "Ouch!"

"How'd you guess his name? Ouch, be nice to our guest."

"Your kitten's name is Ouch?" The kitten rubbed against her again, and then stood on its hind legs reaching for her finger.

"Appropriate, don't you think? He's a jungle cat trapped in a kitten's body. Wants to play all the time, but he's so damn rough. I have scratches up and down my arms." Leah showed her the undersides of both her arms covered with red gashes.

Cara started to unpack the groceries. "Thanks for letting me come over and cook in your kitchen."

"No, thank *you*. Jeff only knows how to make scrambled eggs and tacos, and I just plain suck at anything involving a stove. Plus, you're helping me out by trying on some of my designs. I need to make sure my more well-endowed customers won't fall out of my lingerie."

She gave her a sideways glance. "Are you talking boob-wise?" Leah nodded. "It's good to know my breasts come in handy for something." Cara had lined all her ingredients up on the counter. "I need a mixing bowl, a cutting board, a large skillet, and sauce pan, and I'll be good to go."

Once Leah had given Cara all the things she needed, she said, "You work your magic and I'll get things together in the bedroom, which also doubles as my office."

Cara grabbed a sharp knife and went to work chopping garlic and onions. When they hit the heated saucepan, she inhaled deeply. Few things comforted her more than the aroma of those two ingredients being sautéed. It made her feel safe and reminded her of family.

She emptied Italian plum tomatoes into a bowl and crushed them with her hands. "Eyeballs," her grandfather used to tease when she was younger. "They feel just like eyeballs." She had never thought to ask how he would know such a thing.

Into the pan they went, along with spices, and the heat turned down to simmer. Now to make her meatballs. It had taken some time for her to get used to the consistency of raw meat through her fingers, but her grandfather had insisted the meat be mixed by hand, not spoon. The process soon became therapeutic. It allowed her to quiet her mind and focus only on the task of making meatballs.

She combined all the ingredients and began to blend the mixture, only she wasn't able to shut off her mind. She should have been standing in her own kitchen she'd shared with Robbie. Cara caught herself beginning to knead the meat a little too roughly. She eased up a little; too much kneading would make the meat tough.

By the time she was finished, she had made thirty-six meatballs. Leah came back into the kitchen to see how she was doing.

"Wow, look at them lined up like little fat soldiers."

"All I need to do is brown them lightly before dropping them into the sauce to simmer for about an hour," she said.

"You'll make a mean wife some day." Leah smacked herself in the forehead. "Oh, shit, I'm sorry. That was a dumb thing to say."

She brushed it off. "Don't worry about it."

Leah chewed her bottom lip while watching Cara gently place each meatball in sizzling olive oil. "Can I ask you something?"

"Of course."

"How do you know Ryan?"

Cara's posture stiffened slightly. How truthful should she be? She hated lying, not to mention trying to remember her lies. It was easier to just spill it all. "I was the one you waited on a few weeks ago who ran out on the check."

Leah gasped. "I knew you looked familiar, but I couldn't figure out where I had seen you before. Damn, you look different."

"I didn't want to tell anyone. I'm so embarrassed about that night. I swear, I've never done anything like that before, and I'd certainly never want to stiff a waitress out of a tip."

"It's all good. Ryan took care of me. It's him you screwed over."

Cara inwardly cringed at the memory, especially considering Ryan's generosity toward her. "I ended up getting really sick and passing out on him at the farmers market the next day. I had nowhere to go. I had no money, and Ryan was kind enough to take me in until I get on my feet."

Leah wiggled her eyebrows suggestively. "So you're sleeping with him."

"No!" she said. "I'm not." She placed the last of the balls into the sauce and turned to face Leah. "He's just helping me out."

Leah looked doubtful. "Let me get this straight. Ryan gave you a place to stay as well as a job, and you're not having sex with him? That doesn't sound like Ryan, my friend."

Cara filled the sink with dirty dishes and was about to start washing them when Leah stopped her. "Leave them for Jeff," she said.

"You don't think Ryan is going to expect me to sleep with him, do you?"

Leah fiddled with the ends of her short hair. "From what I know of him, he likes the ladies. I'm not saying he doesn't have a good heart, but I'm not used to seeing him think from the heart."

She gave her a confused look. "What do you mean?"

"I mean, I'm used to him thinking with his head."

"Meaning?"

"Thinking with the little general." Cara now understood what Leah was trying to say, but decided to have a little fun and see how inventive Leah could be. Her deliberately blank expression encouraged Leah. "His bald butler, his clam digger, his dangling participle?"

"I don't have any idea what you're talking about."

"Oh for crissakes, Cara, I'm talking about Ryan only thinking with his man-sized manicotti. His bony cannelloni!"

"Oh, you mean his penis?"

Leah threw up her hands. "Whatever you want to call it. Come on, let's get to work before Jeff gets home."

She followed Leah into her bedroom. On the way there, Leah's crazy kitten jumped out at her from behind a chair and attacked her foot. "Ouch!" she screamed as he proceeded to encircle her ankle with both paws and push on it with his hind legs.

Leah grabbed him by the scruff of his neck. "I forgot to tell you he does sneak attacks."

Cara looked down at her ankle, which now had bleeding scratch marks all over it. "He sure is a cute one," she said through gritted teeth.

"Bad kitty," Leah told Ouch while tapping his nose. She plopped him down onto the floor and he charged over to a small table piled high with rolls of multicolored ribbons. Before she could get out the words, "Ouch, no!" he had already jumped up onto the table, sending the rolls crashing down to the floor. She tossed the kitten out and shut her bedroom door. "The day he shreds any of my silk fabrics is the day we'll need to renegotiate his living arrangements."

Cara pitied Leah's husband who had to sleep in what looked to be a cross between a dressing room and a designer's showroom. Rolled bolts of fabric lay piled up against walls and sketches of designs were pinned onto a large corkboard. Three dress dummies stood in the corner in various stages of undress, alongside a sewing machine.

"How does your hubby put up with all this?"

"I model all my lingerie for him." Leah handed her a deep blue-gray satin bustier that laced up the back. "Try this one on first."

Cara squeezed into the tight garment, barely able to breathe as Leah laced her up. Leah studied her from all angles. "Take a deep breath," she told Cara. Cara breathed in, which resulted in both of her breasts unleashing themselves from the confines of the barely-there cups. "I was afraid that would happen," Leah mumbled, deep in thought. She made a few notes on a clipboard.

"Large breasts present a challenge," Leah explained, "because the regular rules don't always apply. I refuse to design anything just for looks. You have to able to wear it underneath your clothes for the entire evening without falling out of it."

Cara nodded. "I've always had the hardest time finding a bra that fits me. One that doesn't look like something my grandmother would wear. Even if I did find something halfway sexy, it was usually so uncomfortable, I couldn't wait to take it off."

"I have a few pieces I want you to test-drive for me," Leah said excitedly. "Maybe you can wear them while you're working and let me know if I need to alter anything."

"Sure." She admired Leah's passion for her work and wished she felt the same passion for something besides heartache. And meatballs. She smelled the aroma of simmering sauce and her mouth began to water.

"Take off the bustier," Leah said. "Try these on. This color will bring out your olive skin tone." Cara took a look at herself in the full-length mirror wearing a magenta lace bra and high-cut panties. "Now raise your arms over your head for me so I can see whether you—"

Cara stretched her arms toward the ceiling. Both her nipples peeked out from the bra as the bedroom door swung wide open.

"Sweet mother of Jesus! I didn't see anything, I swear!" Leah's husband exclaimed, backing out of the room.

Leah rolled her eyes. "With any luck, now Jeff won't have to watch any porn for a week."

"I hope I haven't scarred him for life."

"If anything, he's just realized what he's missing. The fact that you can also cook may very well seal my fate. Come meet my dork of a husband."

Cara peeled off the bra and panties and got dressed. It took awhile for Jeff to be able to look her in the eyes, but as soon as he tasted her meatballs, he couldn't praise her enough.

"Oh man, these are out of this world! *Magnifico* as the Italians would say."

"They're fuctastic," Leah said between mouthfuls. "You should go into the meatball business."

She was pleased with the way her meatballs had turned out. They were firm, yet moist and flavorful. She ate three of them with a bit of spaghetti and felt like she might explode. It was worth it.

Leah ate two. Jeff consumed six, plus a huge plate of pasta. He crawled to the couch and collapsed onto it. "Oooh," he groaned. "I think I overdid it."

"You think?" Leah said. "You ate like you might never eat again."

"I might never eat this *well* again," Jeff said. Leah threw her crumpled-up napkin at him.

Cara laughed. "Don't worry, you'll have leftovers."

"If Leah were able to cook like this, I'd weigh three hundred pounds in no time."

Jeff was pushing six feet and probably weighed one hundred and forty pounds tops, so that seemed unlikely.

"You're on dish patrol tonight, my love," Leah informed him.

Jeff grudgingly rose from the couch. "Anything you say, cookie."

Listening to their playful banter made Cara smile. And feel a touch of sadness for what she didn't have any more.

"Can I borrow your cell for a sec, Leah?"

Leah tossed it to her. "Don't tell me you're checking your ex-douchebag's Facebook page again."

"So what if I am?"

"You're turning into a stalker."

Robbie's page came up. "Single? He changed his relationship status to single?" She was lucky it was Leah's phone, because if it had been her own she'd have thrown it across the room. She looked up at Leah with tears beginning to form in her eyes.

Leah came over and put an arm around her shoulder. "You know the best way to get over someone, don't you?" Cara shook her head no. "Get under someone."

She snorted. "Oh yeah, that's what I need. Another man to break my heart."

"You're thinking about it all wrong, sweetie. I'm not telling you to have a serious relationship with someone. Find someone to play with to make you forget the obsession with what's-his-name."

Cara crossed her arms over her chest. "I despise men right now."

"Then I guess you'll have to find a man who turns you on like no man ever has before."

• • •

It was the times after speaking with his father over the phone that Ryan wished he had a heavy bag to punch.

So he did the next best thing to alleviate his angst: drink. He considered scrolling through the list of female contacts in his phone and calling one of them to come over for a few whiskey sours, but he wasn't up to the effort of making conversation. He didn't want to entertain and he didn't exactly feel charming at the moment, so he chose to drink alone at Bella Vita.

The conversation with his father had gone as it always did, with Ryan ending up feeling grossly inadequate as a son, and as a man. It wasn't so much what his father said, it was more what he *didn't*. So when he asked Ryan what his numbers were for the restaurant and whether he was out of the red yet, what his father really wanted to know was, *are you making a lot of money, so I can be proud of you?*

And when his father mentioned there was always a position in his company for Ryan, what he was really saying was, *when you get this silly restaurant business out of your system, come and work for me so you can be under my thumb again.* When he was fresh out of college and newly married, it was fine to work for his father's company. He was working toward a future, toward stability. But Ryan was his own man now, out to please only himself. He wanted to make it on his own, however unlikely that seemed, without his father's help.

He sipped the Scotch, his fourth of the night, appreciating its numbing effects. When he was numb from drink, the prospect of losing the restaurant didn't seem too bad. And his failed marriage and dream of being a major league pitcher didn't incapacitate him like it did when he was sober.

Surveying the inside of the restaurant from his position at the bar, he took note of the peeling paint in one corner he couldn't afford to do anything about, and the old, worn barstools that needed to be sanded down and stained. He remembered the ailing beverage case and the shorting light in the reach-in fridge.

And here I thought owning a restaurant was glamorous. Boy, did I take stupidity to a whole new level.

He laughed aloud at the irony of his life.

"Are the voices in your head amusing you?" Cara asked, entering from the dining room. Ryan laughed harder. Maybe he *was* losing it. It might actually solve some of his problems if he made a complete break with reality.

He was genuinely glad to see Cara. She walked across the room toward him and he became hypnotized by the sway of her hips and the fullness of her breasts. She had on white shorts and a T-shirt with the shape of the island, a crab's claw, on it. Her bra was visible through the sheer material, and for some nonsensical reason he felt like snapping the back of her bra strap like he used to do to the girls in junior high.

"Care for a drink?" he asked.

"No, thanks. I had wine at dinner."

An irrational twinge of jealousy shot through him. "You had a date already?"

"Hardly." She snorted. "Leah had me over for dinner." She held up a plastic container. "I made meatballs."

"Ah, your famous meatballs."

Cara peeled off the lid of the container and dug her fingers inside. "You have to taste them while they're still warm." She came closer, so close she was practically sitting in Ryan's lap. "Open wide."

Ryan opened his mouth for the piece of meatball. Her fingers brushed his bottom lip slightly. An innocent gesture on her part, yet it sent a sexual surge through him.

"Cara, this is amazing," he said, chewing. "I taste raisin and … ?"

"Pine nuts."

"Can I have another bite?" He was enjoying having her stand so close to him. She brought another piece to his mouth and some sauce dribbled down his chin.

"Sorry," she murmured, using her finger to wipe the sauce up into his mouth. He captured her finger with his lips before she could pull it away and drew it inside his mouth. He began to suck on it and her eyes widened, but she allowed him to alternately suck and run his tongue over her finger. He smelled a hint of garlic, which turned him on more than any perfume ever had.

Ryan kept his eyes on her. She cocked her head to one side, keeping her eyes on him, and boldly placed another finger in his mouth. He grabbed her wrist and pulled her fingers out of his mouth.

Not a good idea. She's an employee.

Cara laughed under her breath, her eyes shining. "Are you going to tell me what was so funny before?"

He welcomed the change in mood. "I was laughing over the fact that I knew absolutely nothing about the restaurant business when I got into it. I thought a masters in business would be enough. The owner of Bella was going through a divorce and needed to sell quickly. We met here at the restaurant about four times before the purchase and every time I asked about the sales, he'd order more drinks and a dessert."

"You didn't think that was a little strange?" she asked, sitting down next to him.

He shrugged. "The last time we met, when I asked about it again he opened his briefcase filled with cash and showed me a stack of credit card deposits from a year of restaurant sales. I mean, here was this guy who seemed to hardly work, yet walked around with a few thousand dollars in cash. His total monthly sales, cash excluded, were about fifty thousand dollars. I did the calculations in my head: rent was $3,500, my loan payment about $3,000, food cost would be based on sales. How could I possibly screw this up?" He started to laugh again.

"How much are you screwing up, Ryan?"

He took a moment before answering. "If I don't figure out something soon, we're all going to be out of a job."

Cara stared at him a long moment before sliding off her stool. "I'll help you come up with a plan." She placed the lid back on the container of meatballs and handed it to him. "Here, take it. You seemed to really enjoy them." She gave him a sexy little half-smile that had more of an effect on him than he was sure she intended—that effect being a state of arousal and confusion.

CHAPTER 9

What the hell had just happened? Cara's heart was pounding, even though she had appeared as cool as gelato with Ryan. She let her boss suck on her fingers. And she enjoyed it.

She closed her eyes, remembering the feel of his soft, warm tongue against her fingers. She imagined how it would feel in her mouth against her own tongue, or inside her—*No, no, no!* She couldn't get involved with Ryan; she worked for him. She couldn't get involved with Ryan; she had just gotten out of a serious relationship. She couldn't get involved with Ryan; he was an unapologetic, womanizing commitment-phobe.

Cara stripped off her clothes and pulled Ryan's T-shirt over her head. She had thought of all the reasons why she *couldn't* get involved with him. She *could* get involved with him, because he was more of a friend than a boss. She could get involved with him, because she needed to completely purge Robbie from her entire being, and what better way than with someone more intelligent, more successful, and way sexier?

The fact that Ryan was an unapologetic womanizing commitment-phobe still stood, but she didn't want a commitment from him, or from any man. Commitment was definitely off the menu for her.

What was wrong with "getting under someone to get over someone," as Leah had so bluntly put it?

Cara saw Ryan's eyes in her mind, eyes that changed from green to brown to gray, depending on his mood. His strong jawline covered with dark growth. His shirtless, sweaty torso that day on the treadmill. Oh yes, if she were going to have a steamy, no-strings-attached sex fest, Ryan would be at the top of her list. Only problem was she couldn't think about being intimate with another man. She wasn't ready. A part of her still felt engaged to Robbie.

She was now one day closer to thirty. Had she figured out what to do with her life? Nope. She likened herself to a piece of slightly rotted driftwood, floating on the ocean's surface, going in the direction of wherever the tide wanted to take her. She had made enough money to pay back Ryan for her meal. Maybe not enough for all his generosity toward her, but she could at least give him something. She knew she couldn't stay here forever, but the idea of going somewhere else made her stomach queasy.

She used to define her goals and write them down in a small notebook. They started out modest: Learn how to flat iron hair. Stop biting nails. Drink more water. Then they grew in importance: Go to college. Find a job. Get married.

Cara had been two semesters away from graduating with a degree in psychology. Her parents' accident had changed everything. Her motivation to finish college was gone, because really, what did it matter anymore? Both her parents were dead.

She'd found a job as a cocktail waitress, a job that didn't demand much from her, and when she'd met Robbie, he had offered her much needed distraction and companionship. Robbie required constant attention, nurturing, and encouragement, so whenever Cara thought about going back to get her degree, he would always convince her to wait. For what? She had no idea and never thought to ask.

She crawled into bed and curled up on the left side, practically all the way to the edge. Sleeping alone was the worst, and the humongous bed made her feel like she was the only person left on the planet. She missed snuggling, spooning, hugging a warm body. She hugged the pillow instead, willing herself not to cry over how lonely she felt. Memories of her parents, her grandpa, and her childhood provided solace. She dreamed of a world without loss or heartbreak. And a world with calorie-free comfort food.

•••

The Fourth of July fell one month after Cara first stepped foot on the island of Crabclaw. Everyone expected the restaurant to be bursting to capacity. Brady had taken the weekend off to go camping with his family, so the assistant chef was fully prepared to handle the onslaught of customers that never came.

Ryan paced the bar area, nervously running his fingers through his hair. Every once in a while, he'd step outside, his eyes sweeping left to right. Then he'd sigh and come back inside to pace some more. Cara wished there was something she could do to make Ryan less agitated, but short of standing outside naked holding a sign advertising the restaurant, she had no idea how to get more people in to eat.

When Ginny said, "I have an unhappy guest who's complaining about her spaghetti swimming in oil," Ryan pulled out a roll of antacids from his pocket and popped two of them before dealing with the disgruntled customer.

Ginny turned to Oz. "I need a ring-up for a cheesecake."

"Do you—" he started to say.

Ginny held up her hand to stop him. "Save it, loverboy, I got a screaming baby at table nine and one of my customers just asked me how much a soda costs, which gives me a glimpse of the tip I'll be getting. I'm not in a good mood."

Oz switched his attention to Cara. "Do you have a library card? Because I'm checking you out."

"That doesn't even make sense," she said to Ginny.

"Did you expect it to?"

Oz was summoned by a group of three giggling girls at the end of the bar.

"I think Oz might have a crush on you, Ginny," Cara told her, even though she knew Oz had about as much chance with Ginny as she and Brady had going to get a mani/pedi together.

"Lucky me, I already have a boyfriend," she said.

Ryan returned with a fake smile plastered on his face. "Give her the filet mignon and bill her the same price as the spaghetti. Oh, and she wants the steak cremated," he said through gritted teeth.

Ginny shook her head sadly and went to put the order in to the kitchen.

Oz used the moment to bring up his problem. "The girls sitting over there are asking for a drink called What the Hell." He gave Ryan an exasperated look. "Apparently, there's an Avril Lavigne song with the same title, because they keep singing it to me."

"I've never heard of that drink before," Ryan said. "Unless they can tell you what goes in it—"

"Gin, dry vermouth, apricot brandy, and a dash of lemon juice and grenadine," Cara said.

Ryan and Oz stared at her. Finally, Oz said, "You're good," and went off to make the drinks.

"Make an extra one for me," Ryan called out. "How in the world did you know that?" Ryan asked Cara.

"It's a gift."

Johnny-boy came shuffling over. "My last table just left. Mind if I take off since it's slow?"

"How's it going?" Cara asked him.

"Can't complain," Johnny-boy answered.

She waited for him to say more, but he didn't. He just stood there, rocking back and forth on his feet. Cara was starting to get a complex over the fact that he never said more than two sentences in a row to her.

Ryan checked his watch. "I suppose so. Go watch the fireworks."

Johnny-boy went up to an older woman who was sitting on one of the bar stools and kissed her on the cheek. They left the restaurant together arm in arm.

How sweet. That must be his mom.

"Johnny-boy never says much, does he?"

"One less headache for me." Oz handed Ryan the drink and he took a sip. "It's not half bad for an 'Estro' drink."

"An 'Estro' drink?" Cara said.

"There's 'Estro' drinks and 'Testo' drinks. You know, estrogen and testosterone drinks. Frou-frou drinks and manly men drinks," Oz said.

"Oh brother. Let me guess. Examples of 'Estro' drinks would be Sex on the Beach and a Screaming Orgasm, whereas 'Testo' drinks would be a Kamikaze or anything involving Jägermeister?"

Oz clutched his chest. "Brains *and* beauty. You're killing me here."

Cara bit her tongue to refrain from calling them both chauvinistic idiots. "I think I'll go check on my last table."

She returned in time to see Ryan ushering a couple into the restaurant. "It's only nine fifty-nine and we don't close until ten," he told them in an overly enthusiastic voice. "You are more than welcome to have dinner." He pulled Cara aside. "Let the kitchen know there's one more order and tell Ginny she can leave if she wants. I'll take care of this."

When she poked her head inside the kitchen and said, "Hey guys, one more damn order and then you're done for the night," they all groaned and spat out curses. One of the line cooks threw a dish towel at her. "I'm just the messenger!" she shrieked, making a hasty retreat.

And when she let Ginny know she could take off if she wanted, Ginny practically left skid marks in her wake.

Everyone has a life but me. Here it is, Independence Day and I'm finding independence to be way overrated.

Even Oz had plans for the night with friends.

"You're invited to come along," he said.

"I think I'll hang around to see what Ryan's doing."

"Knowing Ryan, I'm sure he has someone lined up for tonight."

What was Cara thinking? Ryan was a horny man like the rest of them. Of course he would have plans for later. She waited around until the last couple had finished dinner and dessert. When she was sure they were done drinking for the night, Cara slid out without saying goodbye. She went down by the pier in search of fireworks, but the show had been over for a while. Smoke lingered in the salty air. The crowds had thinned. The only people left were obnoxious drunk guys egging each other on to see who could burp the loudest, so she made her way back to the restaurant.

Cara had just reached the side alley to the kitchen when she noticed a man with a bicycle standing at the back door. He looked to be in his seventies and had a fierce resemblance to Abraham Lincoln. He rapped on the door three times. She stepped back into the darkness and waited.

Ryan stuck his head out. "Hi, Edward. How are you this Fourth of July?"

"Very good, sir. How's business treating you?"

"Could be better, my man. Give me a minute and I'll wrap some things up for you."

Cara watched Ryan disappear into the kitchen. When he returned, he handed Edward a plastic bag filled with two large take-out containers.

"We had lots of leftovers tonight."

"Thank you, sir. You're a good man, Mr. Garridy."

"Let's keep that between you and me." Ryan took out his wallet and handed Edward a twenty.

Edward bowed, and then rode off into the night with the bag of food swinging from his handlebars.

So, Mr. Ryan Garridy, you're a man who tries to pass himself off as an emotionally unavailable, womanizing jerk, yet you take damsels in distress into your life and feed the homeless.

She wasn't sure what to make of this revelation, but it certainly made her see Ryan in a kinder, softer light.

Cara spotted the half-empty bottle of Scotch on the counter right away. Ryan was sweeping the kitchen floor with a push broom in one hand, an empty glass in the other.

"Did the kitchen staff leave a mess?" she asked.

He looked up at her with eyes that were tired and bloodshot. "Brady may be a drunken nut, but at least he's a neat freak." He leaned the broom against the wall and went to pour himself another drink.

Cara took the bottle away from him. "Speaking of drunk, don't you think you've had enough?"

He leaned in so close to her, she could smell the liquor on his breath. "You sound like my mother, Cara." He grinned. "Do you think I need another mother?"

"No, but I don't think you need another drink." She held the bottle behind her back.

"What do you think I need?" His voice was low and seductive.

She inched back slowly until her tailbone hit the counter. "I think you need to stop this self-destructive path you're on."

He narrowed his gaze. His eyes had turned a fierce, dark green. "That's not the right answer." Ryan moved toward her slowly, like a jungle cat about to pounce. His arms trapped her in place. "Try again."

She gave him a small nudge. "Alcoholics Anonymous?"

Ryan pressed his body against hers. "I don't like that answer, either," he whispered, his hot mouth pressed up against her ear. "You have one more chance."

He was hard against her. Cara's mouth went dry as other parts of her became wet. "I think … "

He ran his lips down her neck, then his tongue. "Tell me."

She felt chilly and feverish at the same time. "You need … " *to kiss me just once so I can see if it makes Robbie disappear.*

He took her hand and placed it on his crotch. "Can you feel how much I want you right now?"

"Ryan?" a female voice called from the doorway.

He spun around. "Barbara? What are you doing here?"

The woman ventured further inside. She was thin and blonde, with excellent bone structure. "I hated the way we left things and … " She caught sight of Cara. "I'm sorry. I didn't realize you weren't alone."

Cara placed the bottle of Scotch back on the counter where she had found it. "I was just leaving." She rushed up the stairs to the apartment in the blink of an eye before anyone was able to get a word out.

•••

Ryan eyed Barbara warily. He had no idea why she had come to see him, considering she had been blocking his calls for more than a month now.

Barbara cleared her throat. "As I was saying, I hated the way we left things."

"You mean, you calling me every name in the book and then throwing me out of your apartment?"

"Yes, well, that was definitely not one of my finer moments," she admitted. "But I've come to make amends." She slinked toward him and put her arms around his neck. She smelled of new clothes and expensive perfume.

He unwound her arms from his neck and poured himself another drink, against his better judgment. "What do you think has changed since that time?"

She flinched slightly. "You're referring to your need to see more than one woman at a time?"

"Yes."

There was no mistaking the determination on her face. "I'm willing to accept that. For a while."

Ryan laughed. "And then what?"

"Surely that unfortunate compulsion can't last," she said, taking the glass from his hand. She sniffed it, her nose wrinkling, and set it down. Her hand slid up his thigh and cupped his balls. "I want you, Ryan. I'll take you any way I can have you."

He was flattered, but he knew he would never be able to give her what she wanted: commitment, fidelity. A month ago, he would have bent her over the counter and had his way with her, but things were different now. The only woman he wanted to bend over the counter was upstairs in his apartment. The realization hit him suddenly, with force.

Still, it turned him on knowing he could find quick release with Barbara. Ryan had to clench his fists and pull away from her. "I can't."

"Why not?"

He hesitated. What should he tell her? That he'd had too much to drink?

"Are you involved with that woman I walked in on you with?" Ryan found himself nodding yes. "So?" She smirked. "That never stopped you before."

The room began to spin. "She's different."

Barbara stared at him, disbelief and hurt rampant on her face. "Is Ryan Garridy finally going soft? Are you in love with her or does she simply turn a blind eye to your wandering ways?"

He was willing to say anything just to get her to go away. "I don't wander anymore."

"I see," she said quietly.

"You're a great—"

She brushed past him. "You are such a bastard."

He let her leave without trying to explain himself. There wasn't any point in telling her it was all a lie.

• • •

Common sense told him he was too drunk to drive home. Usually he spent the night in his apartment under these circumstances, but the present circumstances had changed. Now there was a woman upstairs in his bed. A feisty, fresh-faced woman with a body unlike any he'd seen before. He was desperate to feast his eyes on her curves without the hindrance of clothing. To touch her skin and know for sure whether it was as soft as it looked. Explore her mouth with his tongue instead of his fingers.

He weaved up the steep stairs. It was dark when he entered the apartment and he did his best not to make any noise that might wake Cara. He stripped off his pants and shirt and left them lying on the floor in the living room. Then he made his way over to the bed where Cara was curled up on the left side, sleeping peacefully. Sliding in on the right, he slowly inched his way toward her. She still hadn't stirred.

Ryan lay his head down on the pillow. The room began to spin, his stomach became queasy.

Throwing up on Cara would be a definite turn-off.

He turned onto his side, facing away from her, and prayed for his head to stop feeling like a horse on a merry-go-round. Cara moaned in her sleep. She moved closer and threw an arm across his waist, snuggling closer.

"Robbie," she mumbled, which royally pissed off Ryan. Then again, it served him right for sneaking into her bed without permission.

Usually when he spent the night with a woman, he scrambled to the other side of the bed as soon as she was asleep to get as far away as possible. Cara's nearness comforted him though. Unfortunately, he knew that comfort would be short-lived as soon as she realized she wasn't alone.

CHAPTER 10

When Cara woke in the morning, she thought she was in her old bed with Robbie. There were broad shoulders and a head of dark, wavy hair next to her. That was where the similarity to Robbie ended. What was lying next to her had chiseled biceps, well-defined stomach muscles, and wore briefs, not boxers.

She didn't remember getting ridiculously drunk and sleeping with Ryan. No, she had been stone-cold sober.

So then why was Ryan in bed with her?

Cara gave him a shove to wake him. He didn't budge. He had been drinking a lot the night before. What she did remember was that the two of them had been dangerously flirting in the kitchen, but then the blonde walked in and Cara had fled. Which was just as well, since it had reminded her of the kind of man Ryan was. A player.

Why hadn't he gone home with the woman? It was obvious what she had come for and it wasn't to sell Mary Kay Cosmetics. Cara's expression soured. For all she knew, Ryan had fooled around with the blonde in the kitchen, sent her home, and came up to finish what he had started with her.

A double header.

Cara went to the bathroom and filled a small plastic cup with water. She stood at the edge of the bed, holding it over Ryan. She tried to wake him by saying his name. Three times. When that failed, she was forced to choose the more extreme tactic.

"What the hell?" Ryan shot up as soon as the cold water hit his face. "What do you think you're doing?"

"What am *I* doing? What the hell are *you* doing in my bed?"

He ran his hands over his face, wiping away the water. "*Your* bed?"

She waved her hands in front of his face. "No, don't even try and pull the 'it's my bed' crap. Answer the question."

"I was too drunk to drive home," he said, glaring at her.

"That's what *your* couch is for, Ryan."

His glare changed to a sheepish expression. "I was on my way to the bathroom and I tripped and landed here?"

She crossed her arms and tapped her foot impatiently. "Sorry. Try again."

"I wanted to finish where we left off." He reached for her, but she jumped away.

"Didn't Blondie take care of you?"

He groaned and sunk down on the pillow. "I don't think that whole thing ended too well from what I can remember."

"So you didn't … ?" Ryan shook his head no. Cara experienced a strange mix of surprise and pride. How come every time she pegged Ryan as a typical womanizer, he did something to refute that title? "You look like the devil's ass."

"I probably smell like it, too." He closed his eyes and started to rub his temple.

"Can I get you anything?"

"A bullet straight to the brain," he answered, without opening his eyes.

She went to the bathroom, and returned with three capsules of ibuprofen and another glass filled with water. Ryan winced as he swallowed them.

"Aren't you getting too old for all this drinking and carousing?"

He lay back on the pillow. "Yes."

"Then why do you do it?"

"You're the psychology major. You tell me."

"I happen to have a few theories."

"Look, if you're going to try to analyze me, don't bother. You won't get anywhere. Therapy is for crazy people, like Brady. I'm not crazy."

Cara persisted. "Therapy isn't voodoo, you know. It's a means to help you become the best person you can be. Maybe you're sabotaging your own success. Perhaps you have an aversion to being happy."

He propped himself up on one elbow. "If you start in on how I want to subconsciously sleep with my mother, I'll throw this pillow at you."

She sat next to him on the bed. "How is your relationship with your mother?"

He frowned. "I'd rather not talk about my mother while I'm in bed. Especially with a beautiful woman so close to me."

"Hmm, obvious issues with mother regarding sexuality. How about your father?"

"Wait—what?"

"It's okay. Most men do."

"Do *what*?"

"Have sexual issues stemming from their mothers. Robbie's mother showered with him until the age of ten, and it's obvious he can't keep Mr. Happy in his pants." Cara stopped to take a breath. "Although in your case, I'd suspect your inability to commit has more to do with issues involving your father."

"I'm going to ignore the fact that the sheer act of moving my lips hurts, just so I can tell you how dead wrong you are. I don't have an inability to commit to a woman, nor do I want to sleep with a version of my mother or whatever Freud's theory is. The only problem I have with my father is that he equates money with success, and I don't." Ryan collapsed back down onto the bed. "If you really wanted to help me, you'd go down and make me some breakfast to settle my stomach, instead of psychoanalyzing me and making my headache worse."

"Okay."

"No smart-mouthed comeback? No 'You men are all the same. You all suck'?"

She smiled sweetly at him. "Nope."

He threw her a skeptical look. "Who are you, and what have you done with Cara?"

"I'll be right back with food."

Oh, this man had definite issues all right. She was sure of it. And the more issues she found with him, the easier it would be for her to ignore how sexy he looked lying in bed with nothing but a sheet loosely covering his bottom half.

• • •

Ryan had to hand it to Cara. She knew how to nurse a man's hangover. She served him a fried egg, Black Forest ham, and provolone cheese sandwich on crusty, buttered Italian bread. The egg was the perfect consistency. Just enough runny yolk to mesh in harmony with the melted cheese, yet not run down his chin. And she had topped it off with a Bloody Mary.

It couldn't get any better. Well, it could, but he had to force himself to ignore the primal urges he was feeling toward her, and focus instead on his food. She had dragged one of his director's chairs over to the side of the bed where she now sat with her legs crossed, top foot bouncing. Bouncing her foot resulted in subtle bouncing breasts, and Ryan was trying his hardest to keep his eyes above her neck.

He stopped chewing. "Why are you staring at me like that?"

"I was just wondering why it's so difficult for you to make a commitment."

He was so sorry he asked. His headache had just started to go away.

"We're back to this?"

"I want to understand men better. I want to know why it's so difficult for them to settle down."

He let out a short laugh. "I am definitely not the one to enlighten you."

"I'd still like to know why you're so screwed up when it comes to women."

Ryan put his plate on the bedside table. He took a last sip of Bloody Mary and set the glass on top of the plate. Pushing the covers off, he swung his legs around the edge of the bed to a sitting position. He didn't care that all he had on was a pair of cotton briefs. If that made her feel uncomfortable, then too bad.

"Not that my personal life is any of your business, but I'll go ahead and satisfy your insatiable curiosity anyway. I did settle down once. I was married for fifteen months. It didn't work out. End of story."

They stared at each other for a few moments without saying anything.

"And now you're out to punish all women because of one bad experience."

He wasn't sure whether he wanted to throw her down on the bed and kiss her or throttle her. "I treat the women I'm with quite well. To me, all women are goddesses until they prove themselves otherwise. When a man finds 'the One,' he has no problem committing to her. Until then, the world is his playground."

He realized he'd touched a nerve when she immediately sat up straighter, like her spine had just been starched. "With women being the toys in that playground," she said.

That wasn't what he meant, but because she'd been hurt, he knew her views on men were tainted. "Listen to me, Cara, the best thing you can do is to stop trying to figure out men. Forget about them and switch the focus onto you. Finish school, decide what you want to do with your life, and then worry about finding a nice husband to make babies with."

She surprised him by agreeing. "You're right. I was two semesters away from graduating with a BA in psychology when my parents died. I told myself I'd go back to school as soon as I was able to, but then … " Her voice trailed off.

"But then?" Ryan prompted.

"Another day turned into another year. I met Robbie, and it was more important for us to make as much money as we could to pay off his debts. Somehow *me* became *him* and *him* became *us*, although it was never really *us*, it was always still *him*."

"You need to turn the attention onto yourself for once."

She jumped up and hugged him. "Thank you for being my voice of reason."

"I wouldn't go that far," he said, enjoying the feel of her body against his. She was warm and soft, and smelled like vanilla.

"From now on, I'll keep my head on straight. I know what my priorities are, and they are definitely not men."

He didn't know what to say. He would have liked to have been her priority—at least for a few hours in bed. Since he didn't want to ruin whatever epiphany she had just had, he mumbled, "Good girl" instead.

Cara pranced over to the closet, her T-shirt barely skimming the tops of her thighs. She reached up to grab some clothes and the shirt inched up. He couldn't tell whether or not she was wearing underwear, but the idea that she might not be made him pull the covers tightly around him.

"I'm going to take a quick shower and then I'll be out of your way," she said, heading to the bathroom.

Ryan stared up at the ceiling. He was beyond sexually frustrated at the moment. Had he really just told an attractive, sexy woman to forget men? A woman who was naked in his shower and probably soaping herself up that very moment. He let out a loud groan. Cara was right. He was screwed up when it came to women.

• • •

Brady came back from his mini-vacation even more surly and unpredictable. Cara had come to dread his tastings before dinner. Brady never got mad at Ginny, who only tasted the meat or vegetables as long as they were made without wheat and dairy. He seemed to take personal offense to Cara not gushing over his food.

"I can't help it if I like my beef cooked," she said.

"You call yourself a true Italian?" Brady scoffed. "This is *carpaccio*. It's supposed to be raw."

No one else had any problems tasting it. Oz, Leah, even Ginny took a bite. But Cara just couldn't do it. "What's that?" she asked, pointing to another dish.

"Ah, my bacon and cheese-stuffed quail with parsnip puree. I added—"

"Sorry to interrupt you, but how many people do you think eat quail? And I have no idea what parsnips are, but this is exactly why we're not filling tables."

All chatter ground to a halt as everyone gaped at Cara. "Oh crap," Leah muttered under her breath.

"Tell me, Cara from Bensonhurst. Why *exactly* are we not filling tables?" Brady's voice was steely.

She faltered a moment. Going head-to-head with Brady was not her idea of a good time, but she was tired of watching this restaurant die a slow death. If she was the only one willing to speak up, then she'd take that risk, for Ryan's sake. It was the least she could do.

"I've been coming down to the shore since I was a kid and it hasn't changed much. The majority in Crabclaw are families. Simple, middle-class, hard-working families. A family of four does not want to go out and eat raw beef, quail, and parsnips."

Brady looked like a bull about to charge. "And what do they want to eat?"

She glanced over at Ryan, who was giving her a knife to the throat motion. She ignored his warning. "Heartier food like pastas, basic fish dishes, meatballs."

"Do you realize I've worked with the assistant of the assistant of Mario Batali?"

She tried not to smile. "Yeah, but this is South Jersey, not New York City."

Ryan quickly came over and put his arm around her. He steered her out of the room as Brady shouted, "You'd better shut the duck up if you know what's good for you, Miss Food Network!"

"Are you purposely trying to piss off my chef?" Ryan said. "Because if he quits, I may as well lock the doors now and officially declare us out of business."

"Can't you see I'm trying to help you stay in business?

"By insulting Brady?"

"Brady is not in touch with the clientele you need to succeed."

"And you think you know who my clientele needs to be?"

Ginny came between them. "Time for you to do damage control with Brady. He's stomping around the kitchen like a spoiled child."

Ryan's hand immediately went to his stomach. "Like I don't have enough problems already. You," he said, pointing at Cara, "lay off my chef."

He headed off to the kitchen. "You do realize Brady is a ticking time bomb, don't you?" Ginny said.

"He can't take a little constructive criticism?"

"The last time a customer complained about his food, he went back to the kitchen and punched a hole in the wall."

She swallowed. "Good to know." Cara stopped Ginny before she walked away. "Hey, I've been meaning to ask you why you don't eat any wheat, dairy, or sugar."

"Believe it or not, I once weighed over two hundred pounds. I was fatter than you."

Was that supposed to be an insult?

"By cutting those things out of my diet, I was able to lose the weight," she said.

"You never cheat once in a while?"

Ginny shook her head. "If I did, I might lose control. Then where would I be?"

"Blissfully satisfied?"

"Hardly," she said. "I'd be fat again."

Considering Ginny looked like she weighed all of ninety pounds, Cara doubted she'd balloon up from just one cheat fest.

"Here comes Oz," she warned, taking off in the opposite direction.

He came up to Cara and whispered, "I'm here to fulfill your every sexual fantasy."

"You mean you have a horse *and* a Great Dane?"

His brows knitted together, confused.

"You know, Oz, if I gave you a penny for your thoughts, I'd get change." She patted him on the back and went to punch in for her shift.

CHAPTER 11

It was Cara's wedding day. Well, Saturday, August 3 would have been her wedding day if she were still getting married. The vows were to be exchanged at the courthouse with only a few people in attendance, and then a small reception in Anthony's backyard. Not exactly every girl's dream, but it suited Cara just fine. She had her eye on the prize—to be a wife and a mother, to finally have an identity.

Who was she now? Single, homeless drifter seeking ... what was it she was seeking?

Cara thought about hauling herself out of bed, but then figured, *Eh, what's the point?* She wasn't on the schedule to work that evening. What was she supposed to do with herself? Get pampered to make the sting of rejection go away? She didn't have the money to get pampered. Should she write a cathartic letter to Robbie and burn it immediately after? She had once read that would help diffuse anger toward an ex. The only thing Cara knew would diffuse her anger was if she could smother Robbie with a pillow.

Which just went to show how much she had healed emotionally since arriving in Crabclaw.

There was a knock at the door that she didn't answer. Ryan barged in.

"Up and at 'em!" He sounded like a drill sergeant.

Cara groaned and pulled the covers over her head.

"It's laundry day. Come on, strip the bed, and give me whatever you need washed."

"How many espressos have you had?" she asked from underneath the covers.

He yanked the covers off her. "Four too many. Get your lazy butt up. It's past ten."

She wasn't about to tell him why she felt the need to sleep the rest of her life away. She didn't need a stupid pep talk that would make her feel a hundred times worse.

He stared at her, frozen.

"What?"

"Pull your … " He cleared his throat. "You need to pull your T-shirt down," he said.

Cara looked down and quickly covered herself. "Sorry, I'm out of underwear." He made a fast beeline to the bathroom. "Was that blushing I saw?" she called out.

"No. I'm grabbing the dirty towels."

She pulled on a pair of shorts and began gathering her clothes that needed to be washed. He came out of the bathroom, arms piled high with towels. Cara piled her laundry on top of the mound. Her lacy panties in an array of fluorescent colors sat at Ryan's mouth-level. "Why don't I put these in a bag?" she said, scooping them up. She filled a grocery bag and handed it to him.

His expression was a strange one. Irritation, lust, confusion— all three? Cara wasn't sure, but she wasn't in the mood to figure it out.

By ten-thirty that night, she had almost forgotten why she had bought a bottle of cheap Cabernet to drink on the beach. And another one to drink upstairs in the apartment. She was rip-roaring drunk, no doubt about it. In addition to the wine, her other consolation splurge that day had been a set of eyelashes and a bottle of bright red nail polish. Cara had misread the color of the polish as "Slut Red," which she thought was hilarious, so she started giggling uncontrollably in the drugstore aisle. Turned out the color was "Sleigh Red," which wasn't nearly as amusing.

It was a good thing she had applied both the eyelashes and polish before the second bottle of wine or else she'd be wearing her lashes on her nose and the polish on her knuckles.

"I survived this day," she announced to the empty room. "Even though I may not have survived it sober, hurray for me, anyway." She shook imaginary pom-poms and cheered for herself.

She was starving and feeling bold enough from the wine to brave the restaurant kitchen. She hoped Ryan would already be gone for the night, so she wouldn't have to pretend she was less drunk.

Cara tiptoed down the stairs, holding onto the wall as she went. All the lights were off, except for one underneath the stove that shed a soft glow over the entire kitchen. She crept through the dining room and peeked into the bar area. All was quiet until she stubbed her bare toe on a chair leg on the way back to the kitchen. She spewed a few loud curses in Italian, which echoed off the walls of the empty room.

The trouble was she didn't know where everything was kept in the kitchen; she had only cooked simple breakfasts. She wanted to make meatballs, and even though there weren't that many ingredients involved, she doubted she would be able to find them.

"If my son-of-a-bitch fiancé hadn't been screwing my hairdresser, I'd be back in my own goddamn Brooklyn kitchen able to make my friggin' meatballs!"

Maybe if she was prettier or thinner, or had been better in bed, her fiancé wouldn't have cheated on her.

Maybe if she had been a completely different person.

Tears streamed down her face as she slumped to the floor.

•••

Ryan headed home after Bella closed so he wouldn't be tempted to drink as much. He needed to keep a clear head in deciding what his next step would be regarding the restaurant. He was about to pull into his driveway when he realized he had forgotten the reports he had printed out. They were on the desk in his office.

Damn. He turned the car around and made the quick drive back. Run in, run out. That was the plan.

He wasn't expecting to see Cara on the floor of his kitchen, sobbing.

"Jesus, Cara! What's wrong? Are you okay?" He crouched down and grabbed her by both shoulders. Horrible thoughts went through his mind. She had fallen and broken her ankle. Somebody followed her home and attacked her. Or worse. "Do you need me to call an ambulance?"

She shook her head no. "I'm fine," she managed.

"You're not fine." He searched her body and face for signs of cuts or bruises. "Tell me what happened. It's okay. You're safe now."

Her sobs began to subside. She leaned back against the leg of the counter, wiping at her eyes.

"Did someone hurt you?" He was already reaching for his cell to call 911.

"Yes. No. Yes, but not in the way that you think."

Ryan waited for her to explain. "Cara?" he finally prodded, staring into her bloodshot eyes.

She bowed her head, sheepishly. "I'm not hurt. I'm … hungry." She started to laugh.

"Are you drunk?"

"Yes, extremely," she said with a hiccup.

That explained some of her erratic behavior, but not all of it. He felt his heart rate slow to where it had been before discovering her on the floor. His knees cracked as he slowly stood.

"That doesn't sound good," she said. "How old did you say you were?"

"Pushing thirty, but in knee years that's about sixty, thanks to sports." He held out his hand to help her up.

She squinted up at him. "You played football?"

"I was too small for football. Baseball was my game. I was a pitcher."

Cara took his hand and he pulled her up. "My brother played shortstop. For three years, I went to all his games."

"So you're a baseball fan?"

"After being forced to attend all my brother's games, I grew to despise the sport. Although I have to admit I think baseball players are sexy." She smiled, leaning into him. "I bet you looked really hot in your uniform."

"I did. Until I blew my shoulder out and couldn't play anymore." He led her over to the center island. "My dream of playing major league ball was shot."

"That sucks."

"And so began the series of disappointments I now call my life." He grabbed her by the waist and lifted her onto the island. "Do you think you can sit there without falling off?"

She snorted. "Of course I can." Cara leaned back, supporting herself with her hands, and stared at the ceiling.

He admired her long, slender neck and collarbone. Her skin was lightly bronzed from the sun, making her rich olive tone more pronounced. He could see a lot of skin in the sundress she was wearing. It was short and skimpy, and had tiny buttons running down the center.

She waved her hands in front of his face. "Hello! I asked if I could have some water. Ryan?"

He blinked twice. "Sure."

He went to the fridge and grabbed a large bottle of mineral water, as well as a slew of other things to tempt her. When he handed her the water she drank straight from the bottle. Her nails looked very red against the green of the glass. And her lashes seemed absurdly thick and long.

You can take the girl out of Brooklyn …

Ryan busied himself with unwrapping wax paper and cellophane, twisting off jar lids, and choosing a very sharp knife.

Why did he feel nervous all of a sudden, like he was trying to impress a date?

"Simplicity of flavors. That's what authentic Italian cuisine is all about," he said, slicing open a honeydew melon at its peak of ripeness.

"Humph! Tell that to your psycho, stubborn chef."

"Brady is a master in the kitchen."

Cara rolled her eyes. "He's a master of complication."

Ryan dangled a slice of prosciutto over her. She reached up and grabbed it with her mouth. "Mmm," she moaned, tasting it. "Pure heaven."

He popped a chunk of sweet, juicy melon in her mouth to counterbalance the meat's saltiness. Her eyes lit up, no longer dulled by alcohol and tears. That she was able to be pleased by the simple flavors of food delighted him. Maybe she wasn't so high-maintenance after all.

"More," she whispered to him with her eyes closed and her mouth semi-parted, waiting for him to surprise her with a taste of something else. In went a silky morsel of buffalo mozzarella. "So creamy."

Ryan mopped his forehead with his sleeve to remove the sweat he imagined had to be all over it. He sliced into a beefsteak tomato, its lush contents spilling out all over the cutting board. His hand shook as he neared her.

She opened her eyes and led his hand toward her mouth. Some of the tomato dripped down her lip when she took a bite and he wanted desperately to lick it off. He settled for wiping it gently with his finger.

She was smiling up at him, her dark eyes shining. "There is nothing like a ripe Jersey tomato."

Ryan took a bite of the velvety mozzarella, savoring its milky taste. "Sometimes the simplest things can give you a sense of home, or in my case, a sense of peace." He was thoughtful for a moment as he ripped off an end of a loaf of crusty bread. He handed it to Cara. "Wait," he told her, fishing out a green olive and slipping it into her mouth.

"Why do you think I always want to make meatballs? It gives me that sense of home I no longer have." She spied the piece of salami Ryan was cutting for her. "You're going to make me delirious on food."

"I can think of worse things," he said, placing the salami gently on her tongue. "Let's see how good an Italian you are. Tell me what kind of salami this is."

She answered right away. "Genoa."

He was impressed. "Wow, you're good."

"You don't know the half of it," she said, smiling devilishly.

Their eyes held for a beat. Was he supposed to take that as an invitation to find out?

"So, when were you in Italy?"

Ryan had to think back. He shaved off a sliver of salty Pecorino Romano cheese and fed it to Cara. "Almost three years ago. I traveled all over Europe, but once I arrived in Italy, she seduced me and I stayed put for awhile."

"You fell in love there."

His jaw tightened. "I fell in love with the customs, the people, and the food."

"And not with an Italian woman?" she said teasingly.

"No," he said in a clipped tone.

Cara took another sip of water, waiting for him to say more. He sighed. "The reason I left the States in the first place was to get *over* a woman. My wife."

"Did she break your heart?"

He nodded.

"I think the people with the hardest hearts are the ones who've been hurt the most." She spoke so softly he almost missed what she had said. "Today was supposed to be my wedding day." Her eyes filled with tears.

"Cara, listen to me." Ryan came up to the edge of the counter and wedged himself between her legs. He looked her straight in the eye. "He's not worth it. You're too good for him."

"I know," she said without conviction. "'It's him, not me,' and all the other things people say to make a person who's been cheated on feel better."

"You're beautiful, and smart, and sexy. You'll get over this."

"How can you possibly know I'll get over this? Maybe I'll take it to the grave."

He despised her bastard of a fiancé for putting her through this pain and self-doubt. "Because I've been where you are."

"Obviously as the cheater," she said bitterly.

"No, as the poor sap being cheated on. I caught my wife in bed with another man."

Cara cupped a hand over her mouth. "Oh no, Ryan."

"It's fine. I'm over it."

She let out a strangled laugh. "No, you're not."

"Of course I am," he said quickly.

"Okay, you are." She wiped under each eye with a red-tipped finger. Her eye makeup was smudged beyond belief and one of her lashes was crooked.

"Why do you wear those things?" he said, pointing to her fake eyelashes. "They're hideous." He pulled one off and it stuck to his finger.

She peeled the other one off and placed it in his outstretched palm. "Happy now?" Ryan was careful not to let them fall on the ground. He didn't need Brady thinking there were spiders crawling around the kitchen.

She wrapped her legs tightly around his waist and stared up at him. Something had shifted in her eyes, her body language, and that *something* was giving him permission to kiss her.

"Tell me again how beautiful I am. And smart and sexy."

"You're beautiful, Cara."

She started to unbutton his shirt from the bottom. "And?"

"And smart." He closed his eyes as he felt her cool hands on his warm, bare stomach.

"And?"

She unbuttoned the last remaining button and trailed her fingers through the hair on his chest. His eyes opened when he felt her warm breath an inch from his mouth.

"And?" she prompted, pressing against him. He became so hard, so fast. He tried to remember whether he had a condom stashed anywhere in his office.

"Sexy." He debated whether it'd be tacky if he took her right there on the stainless steel.

She kissed him lightly on one cheek, then the other. She moved to his mouth, brushing her lips against his in a feathery motion. Her tongue flicked his bottom lip. Ryan had his fingers twisted in her hair before he even knew what hit him. He pulled her toward him, kissing her with raw hunger that had been building for a while.

His tongue demanded he taste every inch of her body. He needed to suck, bite, lick her, fill her. She urged him on with her moans, reaching for his belt. The anticipation of being inside her made him ache. He hadn't wanted a woman this much since—

His wife. He pulled away suddenly.

"What is it?" Cara whispered. "Do you want to go upstairs where it's more comfortable?"

Don't screw with this one, warned a small voice inside him.

"No, I—" Ryan stopped himself. He stared at Cara. Beautiful, smart, sexy Cara. He had to be out of his mind to say no to her. *Couldn't he just—?*

No, the voice said.

He let out a harsh breath. "I have an early meeting tomorrow with a fish vendor."

She gaped at him, mouth open.

"I have to go."

Cara let her legs fall from his waist. She pushed him away with her foot.

"I completely forgot about it."

She slid off the counter and grabbed her purse. "Where are my stupid sandals?"

He found them and handed them to her. She snatched them out of his hands. "Good night, Ryan," she said, her eyes avoiding his.

"Cara, wait … "

She looked up at him, her large brown eyes filled with hurt and disappointment.

Let her go, Ryan.

"Good night," he said.

CHAPTER 12

"The strangest thing happened last night," Cara said to Leah at the end of their shifts. "I pretty much threw myself at Ryan and he turned me down."

Leah stopped counting her tip money. "Ryan, who?"

"Our boss, Ryan."

"Not possible." Leah started to count her money again. "Ryan doesn't turn women down. Maybe if they had no arms or legs he would, and even then I'm not so sure."

"Great, so that means I'm the only woman on this earth he won't sleep with."

Leah stopped counting again. "Holy crap, you're serious. You came on to Ryan and he didn't, I mean, he wouldn't … ?"

"Is there something about me that repels the opposite sex?"

"Of course not." Leah started to laugh.

"What's so funny?"

"The only reason I can come up with is maybe he was on his period."

Ryan walked by with his head down and mumbled, "Thanks for your help this evening, ladies."

"See what I mean? He can't even look at me."

Leah scratched her head. "That does not sound like Ryan. Tell me what happened last night and don't leave out any details."

After she recounted the entire story of what happened, Leah seemed as confused as Cara. "It doesn't make any sense. One minute he's got his tongue down your throat and the next, he's telling you he has to meet with some fish guy? I don't buy it."

"So then, what's the problem?"

Leah shrugged. "You got me. I don't know how men think. I'll have to ask Jeff."

"You can't tell your husband about this," Cara said, horrified.

"Why not? Maybe he'll shed some light on the issue."

"But he doesn't know me or my history, or—" She groaned. "You told him all about me, didn't you? I can tell by the look on your face."

"Of course I did. Husbands and wives tell each other everything. Besides, he wanted to know why a hot piece of ass like you was single."

She groaned again.

"Actually, I called you 'a hot piece of ass.' He called you 'my lady friend.'"

"You told him I found my fiancé with another woman?"

"Yes. Speaking of which … " Leah handed over her phone. "Do you want to check Dickwad's page?"

Cara waved the phone away. "No, I have too much on my mind."

Leah let out a big gasp and hugged her. "Cara, do you realize what this means?" she said excitedly. "The situation with Ryan has made you less interested in Dickwad. I'm so happy for you!"

"I've traded one dickwad for another."

"I don't think Ryan is a dickwad. He's, well, I'm not sure what he is yet, but it's not that."

Cara was hardly comforted.

"Cheer up. I'm bringing you my latest design to wear tomorrow. I want you to keep it on during your entire shift so you can tell me whether I need to modify anything."

"How would I know what you need to change? I'm not a designer."

"No, but you're the consumer. You're the best person to tell me what works and what doesn't. I can design the most exquisite piece of lingerie, but if it rides up the crack of your ass and you feel like Big Bird's nesting there, or your tatas fall out at dinner in front of the waiter and that causes him to spill hot soup on you, that's not sexy."

She did have a point.

"My slogan is, 'Sexy isn't only for the bedroom.' A woman has to be able to wear my lingerie in comfort even while she's scrubbing the toilet bowl."

"Feel free to use me as your human guinea pig."

"You have an amazing body, Cara. Double-Ds, full hips, firm thighs, and a round ass. If I weren't a married heterosexual, I'd want to fuck you four ways to China."

"Thanks, that makes one person in this world."

"Two if you count Oz," Leah said, winking at her.

• • •

Cara jumped out of bed in a good mood, determined not to obsess over what had happened, or *didn't* happen with Ryan. Her hair was behaving and her nails were growing longer on their own, without the aid of acrylic. When she went to get something to eat at Avenue C Grocery, she was pleasantly surprised that everyone who worked there knew her by name; it made her feel like she was part of the neighborhood. To top off her day, she hung out with Dino on the beach for a while, where they had had a friendly debate over whether it was better to bread and fry the eggplant for *parmigiana* or bake them dusted with flour only. Dino, of course, was all for the fried version.

It was when she returned to the apartment that things took a turn for the worse. The shower was running. Cara looked over at the treadmill and noticed a damp towel hanging from it. *Ryan.* He must have just finished a workout.

She needed to get out of there, and fast. She had no desire to be face to face with the man who had rejected her. The water turned off. Cara grabbed her purse from the couch just as Ryan strolled out of the bathroom, whistling, wearing nothing but a towel around his waist. He stopped short when he saw her. His torso was still wet, his hair was slicked back, and he looked more delicious than he should.

Cara tried to think of something to say, but her mind went blank. Her eyes drank him in, and she forgot for a moment she was still pissed at him. He just looked so damned hot. She wondered how he'd look without the towel. Then she remembered how close she had been to seeing him without that towel and her anger returned.

"I'll get out of your way," he said, avoiding her gaze.

"No rush," she said, planting herself on the sofa. She planned to make him as uncomfortably aware of her presence as possible.

He pulled out a pair of clean shorts from a gym bag. "Are you going to sit there and watch me change?"

"It's not like I haven't seen a penis before."

"You haven't seen mine."

She crossed her arms. "And why is that, Ryan? Seems like every other woman in Crabclaw has."

He let out an exasperated sigh, dropped his towel, and slipped on his shorts. "Happy now?"

Cara was almost rendered speechless. *Almost.* No way was she going to let her mind exhaust itself doing mental gymnastics like it had over Robbie. If another man was going to reject her, she wanted to hear why.

"What the hell was that about the other night?"

"Can you be more specific?"

"Don't play dumb with me, Ryan. First you run hot, then cold."

"I told you, I had an early meeting."

"Let me get this straight. You turned down sex with me because you had a meeting in the morning?"

He hesitated. "If I say yes, it'll make me look like an idiot, and if I say no, it'll still make me look like an idiot, so I'd prefer to plead the Fifth."

"Do you not find me attractive? Were you saying all those nice things to me just to make me feel better?" She bit her bottom lip to keep it from quivering.

"Yes—I mean, no. Arrgh!" He ran his hands through his wet hair. "I can't give you what you want, Cara."

"What is it you think I want?"

"What all women want. A relationship."

He couldn't have shocked her more than if he'd just gotten down on one knee and asked her to marry him. "That's why you wouldn't sleep with me? Because you think I want a relationship with you?" She burst out laughing.

"Why is that so funny?"

"I don't want a relationship with you."

"That's what every woman I've ever gotten involved with has said in the beginning. 'I don't want anything serious, either, Ryan. Let's take it slow, Ryan.' And then a few months later, I'm the asshole for leading them on. I'm tired of it. You women always want more."

"Don't flatter yourself," she said. "It doesn't take a rocket scientist to figure out you're not relationship material. I realized that within the first five minutes of meeting you."

He frowned. His eyes turned a rich, dark-brown color, making him appear slightly menacing. "What's that supposed to mean?"

"Oh, come on. You have man-whore written all over you. I'd have to be insane to get involved with you. All I want is a sexual Band-Aid for my gaping wound."

"A *what?*"

"Something to forget about my unfaithful ex-fiancé." Cara stood, swinging her purse around her shoulder. "I understand if you're not up to the task. I'm sure Oz can be of service." And with that, she stalked out of the apartment, leaving him standing there with a stunned expression on his face.

The last words she heard from him were, "Stay away from my bartender!"

· · ·

A sexual Band-Aid?

That had "dream come true" written all over it. So why did it bother Ryan so much? Because it was the first time a woman wanted to use *him*? Cara couldn't be serious about Oz. At least he hoped not. Oz was a damned good bartender; he hoped he wouldn't have to fire him. Which is what he'd do if he laid a finger on her.

If anyone was more of a man-whore than Ryan, it was Oz. Wait, Ryan wasn't a man-whore. He respected women. He wasn't callous with their feelings and he was always upfront with them in the beginning. He didn't pull away until they started throwing around certain words, like *relationship, commitment, future.* Besides, players looked at sex as a sport. Ryan looked at baseball as a sport, and sex as recreation.

He drummed his fingers on his desk, staring at but not seeing the computer screen in front of him. This woman was making him crazy. He wanted her, yet he knew he shouldn't have her. They'd be hot and heavy in the beginning, having sex all the time. Ryan let himself indulge in imagining sex all the time with Cara, imagined his mouth full with one of her breasts, her hand wrapped around the head of his—

It would never work. She'd inevitably want more. He'd break her heart, and she'd end up doing something irrational like spray-painting the word *man-whore* all over the front of his condo. He'd heard about Italian tempers and their lust for revenge. There was no way it could end well. He genuinely liked Cara; he'd never want to intentionally hurt her.

It was decided. No getting involved with her. Ryan needed all his focus to be on the restaurant. One by one, he began going through the stack of unopened mail. Most were past due notices or service reminders. There was a six-month reminder to clean his hood and duct system. That was important. He didn't need a grease fire in the kitchen. He saw how much it would cost and cursed under his breath. It would have to wait, just like everything else.

• • •

All Cara wanted to do was have sex with the man, not marry him. The only "M" words in her vocabulary now were *meatballs* and *masturbation*. It'd be a long time before she considered marriage again.

Ryan had definitely taken her mind off Robbie. When they kissed that night, Ryan was all she was thinking about. She wanted him and she knew in her gut he wanted her, except he had lumped her in the category of "women who had marriage on the brain." That may have been her not too long ago, but it wasn't any longer.

How could she get him to change his mind?

Subtle manipulation. She would somehow make him realize on his own that he wanted her. Desperately. But how?

There was a knock at the door. It was Leah, holding a large tote bag and a bunch of hangers covered in plastic.

"Here we go, my muse," she announced. "Tell me what mood you're in and I'll match it with one of my designs. Are you feeling slutty or goddessy?"

"How about sexually frustrated?"

Leah dumped all her stuff on the couch. "Hmm, I don't have any chastity belts."

"Let's go with slutty."

She showed Cara a hot pink corset. "How about this one?"

Cara ran her finger over the slick satin. "The color certainly brightens my mood."

"It has a breakaway zipper front that I'm hoping doesn't break away before you want it to. Hook some stockings onto the attached garters, slip on the G-string, and you're in business. Figuratively speaking, of course."

Cara had never worn stylish lingerie that made her feel sexy; she could never afford it. Robbie had once bought her a pair of crotchless panties and pasties, but she hardly considered that tasteful lingerie.

Leah helped her into the corset. "Take a deep breath." She breathed in while Leah pulled the back laces tight. She stood back to admire her. "You look incredible. Put on the stockings and pumps."

After Cara put on the G-string, Leah helped her clip the sheer, black stockings to the garters—a task she would never have been able to do on her own. Cara paraded around the living room like a prized show dog.

"Ryan thinks I want a commitment," she told Leah. "That's why he won't sleep with me."

"That's what the hubs said, too."

Cara put her hand on her hip and struck a pose. "Not every woman wants a serious relationship."

"Men seem to think we do. Bend over and touch your toes."

She did as she was told and surprisingly, her breasts remained intact. "Men need to get over themselves."

Leah gave her an appreciative whistle. "Too bad Ryan can't see you like this. I'm sure he'd change his mind real fast."

And then it hit her. She knew how she'd seduce Ryan without him realizing it. "Oh, I plan on making Mr. Garridy very aware of the fact I have on extremely sexy lingerie underneath my clothing.

It'll be tough to tell when I'm wearing my work clothes though. Maybe you can drop a hint here and there."

Leah arched an eyebrow. "Drive his imagination wild?"

Cara smiled wickedly. "Make him want me so much that he doesn't realize he wants me until I make him want me so much."

"Um, yeah, what you said."

She strutted around in her heels, feeling empowered by the satin and lace. "I'm tired of feeling like a victim. It's time for me to be in charge."

"I hear ya, sister."

"Take control of my destiny and stop being treated like a doormat."

"Are you going to roar right now?"

"I just might," Cara said. "I feel like unleashing the woman within." She made an expansive gesture with her arms, causing the break-away zipper to burst open.

Leah snickered. "A little too much woman. I'll have to fix that so you don't unleash the girls down in the restaurant."

Cara's seduction plan began to take shape. "Why don't you wait on fixing it so I can use it to my advantage?"

CHAPTER 13

Ryan breathed a sigh of relief. A busload of tourists on their way to Atlantic City had come into Bella for dinner and every table was filled. It would certainly make up for the lousy week in sales.

If only it could be this busy every day.

Even though he was running around taking orders and bussing tables, he was still very aware of Cara's presence. Even more so after Leah had mentioned Cara had on a defective corset that could burst open at any moment.

"Let's hope she doesn't make any sudden movements or large gestures," Leah said.

He was able to see the outline of bright pink under Cara's white shirt, a shirt that strained across her bust. He noticed the black laces as well. What was holding up those sheer black stockings—the ones with the thin line running up the back of her calves and thighs? He could only guess at what she had on underneath the short skirt she wore and the idea of it was making him nuts.

What he did know for sure was that she was flirting with Oz and he didn't like it, so he had to create reasons to get her away from the bar area.

"Can you fill this bottle with olive oil, Cara?"

"Tell Brady table six wants to meet him."

"Go to my office and get … "

Before fulfilling his last request, she said, "I feel like there's a tiny pebble in my shoe. Let me just shake it out." She sat on one of the tall bar stools and crossed her legs. Then she removed one of her heels and began shaking it.

Ryan was treated to a full view of Cara's shapely leg encased in stocking. His eyes traveled further up to the smooth, bare skin between the hem of her skirt and the top of the stocking. He sucked in his breath. There was the garter holding the stocking in place.

He looked up, meeting her eyes, which held a challenging expression. She slipped her pump back on and stood up. "Much better," she purred.

Ryan ordered a Scotch from Oz, even though he had told himself he needed to cut down on his drinking. He sipped it slowly as he followed Cara's every move.

"'Night, Ryan," she said at the end of her shift.

"Thanks for your help. It was a busy night."

She gave him a bright smile. "There was a lot to clean up, but look at the place now." She opened her arms wide and thrust her chest out. Her corset exploded open.

"Whoops," she giggled. "I've had a bit of a wardrobe malfunction. Good thing it's only you here to see my nipples through the shirt. I'd better go upstairs and take everything off."

He watched her swaying behind as she walked away. "Sweet dreams," she called over her shoulder.

Ryan went behind the bar and poured himself a double.

...

"What's the matter, Dino?" Cara asked.

Dino squinted up at her. "Your perceptiveness astounds me. How can you tell I am out of sorts today?"

"You're not your usual cheery self."

Not to mention, it's a bright, sunny day without a cloud in the sky and your painting looks like a gory crime scene.

Dino leaned back and studied his masterpiece. The sea was a tumultuous blood-red color, the sand consisted of black and gray brushstrokes, and the gulls resembled evil gargoyles. He put his brush down and sighed. "I have increased in girth."

Cara sat down on the sand, cross-legged. "What does that mean?"

"It means I got fatter." He dug into his jacket pocket and pulled out the usual baggie he carried filled with celery sticks and baby carrots. He offered her one and she chose a piece of celery. Dino bit angrily into a baby carrot. "The wife knows I've been cheating on my diet."

She shrugged. "So get back on your diet."

He looked at her like she had just suggested he go parachuting naked. "Listen, girlie, if it were that simple, I'd look like Dean Martin. Trouble is I hate all this rabbit food." He gnawed on a piece of celery.

"Yeah, but you don't want to drop dead on your wife, do you?"

Dino picked at his teeth with his pinkie, which looked like a Vienna sausage with hair.

"When I was younger, I could really pack it away. An overflowing plate of *spaghetti alle vongole*. That's *clams*, by the way."

"I know what *vongole* means."

"Fried calamari, zucchini, and baked clams topped with golden-brown bread crumbs drizzled with olive oil. Crunchy, yet soft." Dino wore a pained expression. Cara wasn't sure whether he might cry or have an orgasm.

"Speaking of food, I have a problem." Maybe she could distract him by focusing on her dilemma instead.

His ears perked up and he leaned forward in his chair. "*Dimmi.*"

"All right, I'll tell you. The restaurant I'm working for is about to go down the tubes. If it goes under, I'm out of a job. If I'm out of a job, I'll have to go crawling home to my brother with my tail between my legs."

"He's family. Family always helps out when it's necessary."

"My brother would always help me out, but that's not the point. It's time for me to be independent. I'm turning thirty and

I need to be able to stand on my own feet." *Preferably in a nice set of Dolce & Gabbana heels.*

"You need to find a husband to take care of you."

"I'm in this mess *because* of a guy."

Dino regarded her thoughtfully. He looked like a wise Buddha—if Buddha happened to be Italian with a dyed black pompadour.

"Which restaurant is it?" he asked.

He stroked his chin for a few moments after hearing the name. "There's your problem, girlie. It tries to be too fancy-schmancy. The regulars in Crabclaw are mostly blue-collar, working families. When they go out to eat, they want authentic and simple. And big portions for their hard-earned money."

"That's exactly what I told my boss, but no one listens to me. Everyone thinks the chef is like the Second Coming."

"I'll see what I can do." His words had an almost ominous tone to them.

"You're not gonna whack the chef or anything, are you?" she asked, only half-kidding.

"Don't worry 'bout it." He picked up the paintbrush again and dabbed at his possessed seagulls.

Cara waved goodbye and headed down the beach. She had come to learn when Dino started painting again, the conversation was over.

•••

He was in the middle of crunching numbers in his office that afternoon when Cara called down the stairs. "Ryan, I have a small problem."

An open spreadsheet on the computer screen showed him numbers he wasn't happy with. The acid in his stomach began to churn. He leaned back in his chair and shut his eyes. Bella was sinking fast. He needed to make a decision about the fate of the restaurant, and soon.

"I think the toilet is clogged."

His eyes snapped open. "Try a plunger. There's one under the sink," he shouted up to her.

"I did. It's still not working."

With my luck, it'll be an expensive problem with the piping and I'll have to replace the entire system.

Ryan popped two antacids, rolled up his shirtsleeves, and trudged upstairs. The door was ajar, so he pushed it open without knocking. "I'm here. Show me—" The rest of the words froze in his throat.

Cara was looking out the window with her back to him, wearing nothing but silk chiffon and lace. Ivory lace on top held by delicate ribbon ties at the shoulders, with a sheer skirt that fell just below her hips. Underneath were ivory lace panties that did nothing to cover her tan line. His gaze traveled from her smooth back down to her small waist, and lower to the full round cheeks of her ass. Ryan's chest, groin, and fists tightened all at the same time.

"Damn," he muttered under his breath. There was only so much a man could take.

She turned. "Oh, you're here."

She looked like a goddess in ivory with the sunlight streaming in behind her. Her face was bare of any makeup and her hair fell in curls, which almost reached the lace cups holding her breasts. *Her breasts.* Breasts he wanted to bury himself in for three days. He forced himself to look away.

"Come, I'll show you the problem," she said.

He held up his hand to stop her. "No, you stay here. I know where the bathroom is." Once inside the bathroom, he adjusted himself and took a deep breath. He was aching to explore every part of her with his hands, his fingers, his tongue. Maybe just one time. Maybe right now, here, it'd feel so good, and be so easy—

He stopped himself. No, this was Cara he was talking about. There'd be nothing easy about her. She almost got married, which meant she wasn't a no-strings-attached kind of girl, despite what she told him. In a short amount of time she'd want what every woman wanted: a ring on her finger, and he just wasn't the man for the job. Even if his penis begged to differ.

Ryan grabbed the plunger underneath the sink and two thrusts later, the toilet was flushing fine. *At least that went smoothly.* Unfortunately, he was going to be tortured by a mental image of Cara in that lingerie for the rest of the day.

"All fixed," he told her, heading straight for the door.

"That was fast. You're so amazing."

Was she kidding? He kept his head down. "It's probably one of my only talents."

"Oh, I'm sure you have many more talents, Ryan."

Her suggestive tone made him look up to finally meet her gaze. He saw hunger in her eyes, like she wanted to have him for lunch.

He shook his head, pointing his finger at her. "I know what you're doing and it's not going to work. I'm not going to be your Band-Aid."

She laughed softly. "I don't know what you're talking about."

"You're playing this cat-and-mouse game, but you're not going to win."

Cara raised an eyebrow at him. "What's wrong? Are you starting to feel like prey?"

"Don't be ridiculous. I'm never the mouse in the game."

"Then you don't have anything to worry about, do you?"

• • •

She had underestimated Ryan. He was a lot harder to crack than she'd thought. Short of purposely tripping and falling on top of him naked, she wasn't sure what to do at this point. She had been convinced the sheer ivory babydoll she wore the other day would seal the deal. Cara had to put a lot of paper down that toilet to clog it. Yet when he came up to plunge it, he had hardly glanced at her.

"How are things going with Ryan?" Leah asked.

Cara was in the midst of lighting candles on the tables for the dinner crowd. "Well, the slutty corset thing didn't work so I tried being a goddess with the babydoll, and he completely ignored me."

"That's not physically possible, unless he's made of stone, or heavily medicated, or a eunuch." Leah collected all the salt and pepper shakers and began to refill them. "How did the babydoll fit, by the way?"

"Like a dream. Don't change a thing."

"What about the panties?"

"Surprisingly, they didn't ride up my butt."

Leah looked pleased. "What do you have on tonight?"

"The plum-colored mesh teddy with the lace-up sides, although at this point, I could have on a trash bag for all Ryan cares."

Leah pulled out Cara's shirt from the waistband of her skirt, unbuttoned the last three buttons and tied the shirttails in a knot. "Is the underwire digging into you?"

Cara shook her head no. "Why did you tie my shirt?"

"I want to see for myself what's up with *Signore* Garridy."

When Cara approached the bar, Oz whistled. "Your outfit looks good on you, but it would look better on my bedroom floor."

And to think she didn't even need to try with Oz. He was a done deal.

"The village called, Oz. They want their idiot back. One screwdriver for table three."

He grinned. "I can tell I'm wearing down your resolve."

"Have you ever had a woman throw herself at you?"

"Oz has women throw themselves at him all the time."

Cara could believe it. He was gorgeous enough.

"So what do you do?"

Oz handed her the mixed drink. "I tell them to take a number. Oz will get to them all in due time."

Too bad that talking thing he did kept getting in the way.

"Hey," Johnny-boy said to them in passing.

"Why doesn't he ever talk?" she asked Oz.

"He may be a man of few words, but he's a wealth of information. No one knows women better than Casanova Johnny-boy."

Casanova? Before she could ask Oz to explain himself, Leah pulled her away.

"I have never seen Ryan wound so tight. He looks like he's about to blow and I know why."

Cara stared at her blankly.

"He's snapping at the kitchen staff. I have never seen him do that before." Leah looked like she might burst from excitement. "It means my lingerie is a bona fide success in making men hot and bothered."

She was still doubtful. "Maybe he's just having a bad day."

"What the hell is wrong with Ryan tonight?" Ginny asked, joining them. She had her dark hair pulled back into her usual tight bun, which accentuated the hollows of her cheeks.

Leah threw Cara a knowing glance. "Seems a bit tight at the seams, does he?"

"I think he needs to get … well, you know."

"Victory will soon be yours," Leah whispered in Cara's ear.

Brady teetered over to the bar and pounded on it with his fist. "Another Jack, my good man."

"That's his third one already," Ginny said.

Cara tentatively approached Brady and asked how his little girl was doing. His face instantly brightened. "I did this all for her." Brady yanked up his chef's jacket and turned around. Everyone gasped. There was a full-color scene from *The Wizard of Oz* tattooed across his entire back.

"Jesus, Mary, and Joseph!" Leah exclaimed. "There's the Emerald City in the distance, and the field of poppies with Dorothy running across it."

"And the Scarecrow, Tin Man, and Lion," Ginny added.

"You even have Toto," Cara said, amazed.

"It's my daughter's favorite movie."

"It's a good thing her favorite movie didn't involve Barney the Dinosaur," Oz said.

Ryan stalked over, his eyeballs looking like they might explode. "Do I pay you all to stand around and look pretty?" His mouth dropped open when he saw Brady's tattoo. "Brady, am I going to have to pay you to keep your jacket *down*?"

"Sorry, Boss. *Jinkies.*"

"Hey, that's Velma from Scooby Doo," Oz said. "Scooby and the gang with the Mystery Machine would have been a cool tattoo."

Ginny and Oz scurried back to work. In a louder voice than was necessary, Leah asked, "Can you hand me one of those glasses above the bar, Cara?"

When she reached up to get the glass, her shirt rode up, revealing the provocative laced-up side of the teddy she wore. Ryan cursed softly under his breath. Leah chuckled.

"Do you think you two can squeeze some work into your busy night?" Ryan said in a clipped tone.

Leah grinned. "And then some."

Cara glanced up at Ryan and attempted a smile. His eyes were a tumultuous green—the color of a dense pine forest. He did not look happy. "Untie your shirt and tuck it in or I'll write you up in violation of dress code. Understood?"

She swallowed, nodding once. Cara had never seen this side of Ryan before—bitchy and unyielding—and she didn't particularly like it. She was done playing their game, even though it had been one-sided all along. It was time for her to find a man who wanted her. Someone like … Oz.

•••

The cool water sprayed down Ryan's back and legs. This was a defining moment for him: spending a Saturday night alone, taking a cold shower to ease his sexual frustration. If this was what getting older was going to be like, he wanted no part of it.

Scroll through your phone, choose a woman, and call her, he kept telling himself, but each time he thought about a woman, it was always the same one, in various pieces of lingerie. *Damn her for making me unable to concentrate on anything except untying the satin laces of that teddy, or lifting up the nightie she wore with those lace panties the other day.*

He grew hard despite the chilling water. He wanted her so much and he wished he didn't. Cara was a good person, even if she was a little rough around the edges. She'd had enough heartache already. She didn't need his indecisive, gun-shy attitude messing with her head.

Still, her acting like a sexual temptress was enough to make any sane man lose it. Ryan was only human. He had needs, physical ones. He made the water warmer and grabbed the bar of soap. How could any man resist a woman standing in front of a sunlit window in sheer lingerie?

Ryan soaped himself up, letting his hand move down past his belly. Every curve of Cara's body, each angle—even the dimple on her ass—had all been visible through that gown. He'd barely been able to look at her, that's how afraid he was of losing control.

Control. He stroked himself harder. It was becoming almost impossible to stay in control around her. She wanted him. He wanted her. But then what? Either he'd grow bored or she'd blow up at him eventually, because he couldn't give her more.

More. God, he wanted more of her. Wanted to know if she would moan softly while he sucked on her breasts. If she would gasp when he bent her over, grabbed her hips, and thrust inside her. Ryan stared down at the swollen head of his penis, imagining Cara being in control of it, stroking it, guiding it toward her lips, between her thighs.

His legs shook as he envisioned himself coming inside her. Squeezing every last drop out of himself, he prayed he would finally find some relief.

He didn't.

CHAPTER 14

Cara stretched the second sheer, black thigh-high stocking over her knee and yanked it up over her thigh. She walked around the living room to see whether the elastic bands underneath the lace trim would hold up. So far, so good. The bands were a little tight, which caused the upper part of her thighs to spill over the lace, but she supposed that was better than droopy stocking knees.

She reached for the magenta lace bra and thong and put them on. Too bad Ryan wouldn't be seeing her in any of this, because she had to admit she looked fuctastic, as Leah would say. She was even turned on looking at herself. Cara had never felt truly sexy before, but wearing Leah's lingerie made her feel sensual, with a little bit of naughty thrown in.

Her self-confidence needed to be built back up after Robbie. And Oz was just the man to help her. He was fun, handsome, and appreciative of her assets—granted in a bordering on sleazy kind of way—but still … she could have a good time with him, without it turning into something serious.

So what if Ryan had created more heat between them than she had ever felt with anyone simply by feeding her? He probably fed all his women salami. No more pining for men who didn't want her. She didn't need to put a gun to any man's head to be with her.

It was probably best she and Ryan remain friends. She valued him as a friend and didn't want to do anything to screw that up. Still, it had pissed her off that he had lumped her into a category with all the other women who wanted a relationship. She needed a relationship like she needed twenty extra pounds and upper lip hair.

After Cara dressed she went down to the dining room. Everyone was already assembled around a table, waiting to see what Brady had in store for them to taste. Ryan gave her a formal nod of acknowledgment. She couldn't help but notice how handsome he looked in a pale yellow, linen shirt that brought out the flecks of gold in his eyes.

Oz glided over to her. "Hey, beautiful, should I call you in the morning or nudge you?"

She attempted her most seductive smile. "I think you should nudge me."

He began to choke on what she guessed could only be his own saliva. Brady cleared his throat, thrusting a wine-filled glass in Oz's face. "'94 Moshin Pinot Noir, well-balanced and earthy. Don't choke on it."

Oz took a big gulp and avoided Cara's eyes.

Brady turned his attention to her. "Are you going to indulge me tonight by tasting the lobster broth, Miss Bensonhurst?"

"I suppose," she mumbled, even though lobster was her least favorite shellfish.

"For the main course, we have a *porcini pappardelle* with braised shredded duck and mushroom," Brady announced.

Ginny picked around the pasta and ate only the duck and the mushrooms. Leah scarfed it down while Oz tried a bite but seemed more intent on polishing off the glass of wine. And Ryan looked as if he wanted to snap off all their heads.

When it was time to set up tables for dinner, Leah asked her what she had on. Cara unbuttoned the first three buttons of her shirt and showed Leah the bra.

"Nice. Breasts are a bit high. I could set my drink on them, but that's not necessarily a bad thing."

Ryan stepped out of the kitchen, caught a glimpse of her in the bra and immediately headed back into the kitchen.

"The lingerie isn't having the effect on Ryan I'd hoped for," Cara said, buttoning up her blouse.

"What's your next plan of attack?"

"I've decided to give up on Ryan and set my sights on Oz instead."

Leah cocked her head. "Did you go to bed last night and wake up stupid?"

"At least I won't have to beg."

"True, and you might even catch an STD to boot."

"Come on, Oz isn't that bad."

"In three weeks if it burns when you pee, don't come crying to me."

Two statuesque model-types walked in, each as thin as a candlestick. Before Cara could approach to seat them, Ryan swooped in and hugged them both. As he led them to a table outside, he told Cara, "Bring a bottle of that Pinot Noir on the house, with three glasses."

And let me guess: Hold the bread and bring a steamed artichoke for them to split?

Oz handed her the wine on ice. She didn't want to ask. Really, she didn't. "Friends of Ryan?"

Oz smirked. "Depends how you define 'friends.'"

She made a gurgle of disgust in the back of her throat and headed outside to serve the happy threesome their *vino*.

Ryan was sandwiched between both women. "Cara, this is Bri," Ryan said, motioning to the grinning strawberry blonde on the right.

"Brie, like the moldy cheese?" she asked.

The girl's smile faded. "No, like Brianna."

"And this is Pita."

"Oh, People for the Ethical Treatment of Animals. Was your mother an animal lover?"

"It's Pita, like the bread, not PETA," she said, indignantly.

Cara tried to hide her smile as she poured them each their wine. "I'll send over your server," she said before stomping over to the bar. "Bimbo alert at table three, Leah."

"Raspberry vodka, coconut rum, Blue Curacao liqueur, Sprite … what else is in a Blue Balls?" Oz asked.

"Peach schnapps, sweet and sour mix," Cara told him. "You call yourself a bartender?"

"The best in South Jersey."

"Uh huh." She snorted. "I'd bet I know more drinks and what goes in them than you do."

"I'd put my money on Cara," Ginny said. "Table eight needs a Manhattan."

"Whiskey and sweet vermouth!" Cara and Oz said at the same time.

Leah rubbed both hands together with glee. "How about a little competition after we close for the night? I've got twenty bucks that says Cara will kick your ass, Oz."

"Who's going to vote for me, then?"

"Ryan can," Ginny said. "It'll be girls against guys."

This will work out perfectly. "Winner gets to choose whatever he or she wants. Since I'll be the winner, I choose to spend the night with Oz."

Every mouth dropped open, including Oz's. Finally, Ginny said, "I think that would make you the loser."

Oz's cheeks reddened. "But … but … " he stuttered.

"Oz, you wouldn't be able to handle Cara," Leah said.

"Oz can handle any woman—" he started to say before Ryan descended upon them.

"This is like high school all over again. I'm very close to issuing detention."

"Sorry, boss," Ginny said. "Cara just bet Oz she would spend the night with him if she won their drink competition."

"What the hell?" Ryan looked outraged.

"Don't worry. It'll be after hours," Cara said.

"Oz needs a man in his corner so we put you in for twenty," Leah informed Ryan. "Nothing like a little healthy competition between the sexes."

• • •

The score was six to five in her favor, but it was Oz's turn so he had a chance to tie. Growing up with a brother had made Cara very competitive. She didn't like to lose, and the fact Oz was keeping up with her caused her blood to race.

"Ready, Oz?" Leah asked. He nodded slowly, seeming uncharacteristically nervous.

"Tell us what goes into a Stiletto," Ginny said.

Cara rolled her eyes. "That's too easy."

"No, it's not!" Oz said. "Amaretto, bourbon … " He hesitated. "Orange—" Cara gasped, and he quickly said, "No, wait, lemon juice."

"Very good, Oz," Leah said, consulting the thick bartender's guide open on her lap. "You almost fudged that one. It's now a tie."

"All right, Cara," Leah said. "What's in a Bosom Caresser?"

Cara flipped through her memory data bank. She remembered a distant cousin of hers ordering it at a wedding reception where she had been playing bartender. The pig had been staring at her bosom when he ordered it.

"Brandy, Madeira, and triple sec." She smiled proudly, knowing she had nailed it.

"No! That's wrong," Oz said. "It's cognac, Orange Curacao, grenadine, and egg yolks."

Ginny made a gagging noise. "That's disgusting."

Leah held up the guide. "Well, the book lists what Cara said."

"Actually, they're both correct," Ryan said.

They looked over at him. Ryan had been so quiet, they'd almost forgotten his presence. *Almost.* Cara had been well aware of him sitting there slouched in a chair, arms crossed, shirtsleeves folded to his forearms, looking dangerously sexy.

"Last one, Oz. You miss this and you'll actually be the winner, instead of the loser. Right, Cara?" Leah winked at her. "Long Island Iced Tea—"

"That's way too easy!" Cara interrupted.

Leah held up her hand. "You didn't let me finish. What do you substitute for cola to make it a Jersey Tea?"

"No fair. Oz is from Jersey. I'm not," Cara said.

"From the look on Oz's face, I don't think it matters," Ginny said.

There were beads of sweat all over the man's forehead. He closed his eyes, rocking back and forth on his heels. "Wild Turkey?" he guessed.

Leah made the sound of an angry buzzer. She lifted Cara's arm. "And the winner is Cara from Bensonhurst."

Ginny clapped. "Poor Ozzie."

"So what's the answer?" Oz grumbled.

They looked to Cara. "Hell if I know. Jägermeister?"

"It is indeed Jägermeister," Leah exclaimed. "Tequila is substituted with Wild Turkey in a Pittsburgh Tea, Oz."

Cara danced around the bar area savoring her victory. Ryan still hadn't moved from his chair. She caught his eye and smiled at him. He didn't smile back.

He had his chance.

Cara went in search of Oz, who had mysteriously disappeared. Now that she had him, she wasn't sure what she was going to do with him. Oz in theory was one thing; Oz in reality was another thing altogether. Did she really want to be with him when the only one she wanted was Ryan?

Oz was in the kitchen, pacing and visibly distressed. She hurried over to him. "Are you having a panic attack?"

"There's something I have to tell you." He held her by the shoulders. "I live with my parents."

Laughing, she told him, "That's okay, Oz. Today's economy sucks. Lots of people still live with their parents. I'll sneak in through a window." She went to put her arms around his neck, but he dodged her. Then it hit her. He didn't want to be with her, either. Cara's hand flew up to her mouth. "Here I am, throwing myself at you and you don't want me." She stifled a sob. How could she have been so blind and desperate? "I'm sorry."

He went to her. "No, I'm the one who's sorry."

"You've been giving me signals all night, and I've been too stupid to pick up on them."

"You're not stupid. I'm the idiot. It has nothing to do with you. You're a beautiful and sexy woman."

"If I had a friggin' dollar for every time a guy has told me that lately." She covered her face with her hands. He pulled her hands away.

"Cara, listen to me. I'm a virgin." He spit it out so quickly, the words tumbled together. "There, I said it."

She took a step back. "Huh?"

"I've never had sex with a woman."

Her immediate reaction was that Oz was trying to soften the rejection. His age, his good looks, not to mention his nasty mouth made his excuse seem implausible. The bashful, ashamed expression on his face told her otherwise.

"Why not?"

He shrugged. "I've never found the right woman, I guess. I've waited so long that now I want it to be something special."

"You're kidding, right? Is this a trick to make you seem more vulnerable and sensitive?"

"Of course not! And it'd be great if you stopped staring at me like I'm some freak of nature."

"An endangered species is more like it." She shook her head in amazement. "I can't help it. I've never seen a male virgin your age before, up close and personal."

"Your reaction is the reason I don't broadcast it."

"All those cheesy come-ons and sexual comments you dish out? Here I thought you were just overcompensating for having a very small penis."

He managed a smile. "I'd appreciate it if you didn't go and tell the whole staff about this. Oz has a reputation to uphold."

No one would believe her even if she did say something. "Do you have any prospects in sight to relieve you of this, um, condition?"

He blushed. "I've always had a tiny crush on Ginny." They strolled out of the kitchen and through the dining room arm in arm. "She has a boyfriend though."

Ryan was behind the bar printing out register tapes.

Cara hugged Oz like she would her brother. "'Night, Oz."

"Goodnight all." He gave a wave and headed out.

"What happened? Your big date fall through?" Ryan asked without looking up.

"Easy come, easy go." She flinched as he slammed the register drawer closed. "Right now I have a date with my bed."

He came around the bar and strode toward her so purposefully she took a few steps back. "Correction. Right now you have a date with me in your bed."

CHAPTER 15

Ryan was done playing games and making excuses. Done watching Cara flirt with Oz. Done lying about an early meeting with a fish vendor—which was what he had told Bri and Pita when they wanted to take their party back to his place. They couldn't believe it, either. But all he could focus on was that damn "competition" and whether Cara would wind up in bed with Oz.

He was tired of trying to fight his attraction to Cara. He wanted her, and he planned on having her. All night. He didn't wait for any reaction to what he had just said. He picked her up and threw her over his shoulder, flipping the lights off and the alarm on as he went.

She screeched and struggled in his arms while he was given a nice view of her legs in thigh-high stockings. He carried her up the stairs and into the apartment. When he put her down, she glared at him, hands on hips.

"This is your seduction technique?" she said.

Ryan sat down in one of the straight-backed chairs. "I'm very direct once I decide I want something. Now take off your clothes."

"Are you kidding me?"

"I'm done talking, Cara. Take them off." His voice came out sounding harsher than he had intended. "Please," he said more gently. "I want to look at you."

She held his stare. A moment passed, and then another, before a small, triumphant smile played across her face. She began to slowly unbutton her shirt. His groin tightened in anticipation of seeing those magnificent breasts. She took off the shirt and threw it at his head. He managed to catch it before it smacked him in the face. With her shoulders back, she was practically bursting out of her bra.

"Now, the skirt."

She reached behind her. The sound of the zipper going down filled the room. Cara shimmied out of the tight material and again aimed for Ryan's head. It landed on top of the plant next to him.

His breathing grew shallow as his eyes took in the vision of her standing in front of him in lacy thigh-high stockings, and heels. She was all curves and soft flesh and wild curls. So different from what he was used to in a woman, and yet she surpassed anything he could have ever imagined.

He stood and walked slowly over to Cara, taking her hand and leading her to the wall. "Turn around."

She did as she was told. Ryan brought her arms up over her head and held them against the wall. He came up behind her. With his warm mouth against her ear, he whispered, "Do you know what all this teasing of yours has done to me?" She let out a soft moan as his erection pressed into the small of her back. "And that's only the half of it."

He moved her hair aside and lightly kissed her neck. She shivered. His lips moved down to her shoulder and across to the other one. He brushed his rough, stubble-filled cheek against her soft skin. Skin that smelled like … mint? He licked her. "Why do you taste like peppermint schnapps?"

"I read somewhere it was an aphrodisiac."

"Maybe for a recovering alcoholic."

"Should I go and wash it off?"

She tried to turn around, but he held her firmly in place. "I finally have you where I want you. You're not going anywhere."

She took a deep breath when he unhooked her bra and let it out once his hands came around to cup her breasts.

"Better than I dreamed," he murmured, trailing kisses down her back. He kneeled behind her so he could ease her panties off. It was then he turned her around to face him. "Tell me what you want," he said, looking up at her.

She responded by lifting her leg and resting it on his shoulder. Ryan wanted to take her hard and fast against the wall, but he forced himself to slow down. He inhaled her scent, touched her, licked her, and when he felt her leg begin to shake, he brought her over to the bed.

Cara tore at his shirt, followed by his slacks and briefs. She made a move to take her shoes off. "Leave them on," he said.

"Do you want me to walk on you with them?"

He nudged her down onto the bed. "You'd probably like that, wouldn't you?" He bit into the flesh of her calf and licked his way up to her inner thigh.

"Now why would you say that?"

She arched her back when his tongue entered her. Ryan waited until she was wet and hot and breathing heavily before answering. "Because you've been torturing me these last two weeks, and I think you've enjoyed it."

She gave a wicked laugh. When he slipped a finger deep inside her, a desperate moan escaped her lips. A moan that let him know she was very close to the edge. He grabbed a condom from his pants and rolled it on. *Slow down*, he had to tell himself once again.

She crooked her finger at him. "Come here, big boy." Wrapping her hand around him, she guided him inside her. When he sank his entire length into her, she gasped. Ryan knew he needed to pace himself, at least until she came. Considering how long he had anticipated this moment, it was going to be a difficult task for him.

He matched the thrust of her hips, her tongue, and when he heard her begin to pant, he thrust harder. She grabbed his ass and forced him deeper into her. Ryan felt her tighten around him and it was all he could do not to come while he moved with her through her spasms. "Oh, oh God," she groaned.

He couldn't wait any longer. Lifting her knees up to his chest, he drove himself deep inside her. Three thrusts and he was a goner.

"Oh God," she said again.

"God wasn't responsible for that orgasm," he said. "I was."

She sighed. "You're both one and the same right now. Take it as a compliment."

He kissed her lips, reluctantly hauled himself off her, and went to the bathroom to dispose of the condom. When he came out, Cara had her shoes and stockings off. Just as well. He was planning on another round, a much longer one, and he didn't want to rip the stockings.

"I'm going to jump in the shower," she said. "Is it okay if I don't see you out?" She kissed his cheek on the way to the bathroom. "That was great, by the way. Thanks."

Had he just been given the bum's rush? Ryan was stunned. What happened to spending the night together so they could pretend to cuddle? Where were the awkward morning goodbyes? More importantly, where was the middle-of-the-night sex and wake-up blowjob?

He would have never thought there was a woman out there who wanted less intimacy than he did. Until now.

•••

Thinking about Ryan the next morning made Cara feel tingly. In all areas. She had hit the sexual jackpot. It made her realize how terrible Robbie had been in bed. His idea of pleasing her meant letting her have the last piece of pizza and control of the remote for the night.

Robbie's betrayal still stung, but the swelling had gone down. It was now more an issue of her bruised ego. Ryan had showed her what she had been missing, namely the ability to achieve orgasm with an actual person other than herself.

Things were looking up. She had taken Ryan's advice and registered for school a few weeks ago so she could finish up and get her degree. Once she had her degree, she'd get a better paying job and be able to afford a place of her own. She certainly couldn't stay in Ryan's apartment forever. Cara was taking definitive steps toward her future, and this time she wouldn't let anything, or anyone stand in the way of her goals. Especially not a man. Ryan was ideal, since he didn't want anything more than she was willing to give. It was a win-win situation for the both of them.

If only the restaurant wasn't about to tank. She didn't want to have to look for another job while in school. She liked the people she worked with—especially her boss. *Her boss.* It should have felt taboo to be sleeping with her boss, but it didn't. And while it was a little weird to be living in his apartment rent-free, that situation would change soon.

Cara made her way downstairs before the lunch shift. Ryan was in his office, staring off into space. He gave her that irresistible smile of his when he saw her and pulled her onto his lap. He kissed her deeply, so deeply it left her breathless and a little dazed.

"Hello to you, too," she said.

"How did you sleep?"

"Like a fat man after a huge plate of spaghetti."

His eyes were a light gray, matching his charcoal gray shirt. A lock of hair fell into his eyes and she smoothed it away.

"I have good news," he said. "I got a call this morning from a man who wants to rent out the entire restaurant tomorrow night."

"That's great!"

"He's offering a ridiculous amount of money just to ensure privacy for an important meeting. Maybe it's the Secret Service or FBI, although he had a pretty thick Italian accent."

"Did he say what his name was?"

Ryan read from a notepad on his desk. "Dino Pelagatti."

Dino. The literal translation of his last name was "to skin cats." It gave Cara the chills. "Did he happen to mention what kind of meeting it was?"

He shifted her on his lap. "No, he said it would be men only, and we needed to get rid of the 'frou-frou' menu and serve some 'real Italian food.'"

One big problem came to mind.

"Any suggestions as to what I should tell Brady?" he asked, reading her thoughts.

"He's fired?"

"I was thinking more along the lines of giving him the night off. Sort of like a 'Chef Appreciation Day.'"

"Who's going to decide the menu?"

He nuzzled her neck. "You and I can brainstorm later on tonight, among other things."

•••

A half-hour before the dinner shift that Friday evening, Leah showed up at Cara's door, cat carrier in hand. "I have a huge favor to ask you."

Cara let her in, eyeing the container warily. "As long as it doesn't involve a cat."

"This sweet kitty won't be any trouble," she said, setting the carrier down on the floor. Ouch mewed frantically. "He hates this thing." The second Leah popped open the door, the kitten tore out of it like he was being chased by an angry dog.

After watching the feline make his rounds of the apartment, Cara said, "I don't do cats."

"Please, I'm begging you. It's my anniversary, and the hubs surprised me with a weekend at a bed-and-breakfast. We're supposed to leave as soon as my shift is over."

She stared into Leah's pleading face. "I thought the great thing about cats was that you could leave enough food and water for a month and they'd be fine by themselves."

"Usually, except there's one teensy tiny issue."

Ouch jumped onto the sofa and began to scale down the back of it with his claws. "What's that?"

"He's had a sinus infection, so he needs antibiotics." Cara scrunched up her face and Leah began speaking faster. "If you interrupt the cycle, he could get it again. I've already given him his dose for today and since we'll be back on Sunday, all you'd need to do is give him his pill tomorrow. Easy peasy."

"All right, I guess."

Leah threw her arms around Cara's neck and hugged her. "Thank you!"

"Where's his food?"

"I left all his things outside the door. I didn't want to freak you out until you agreed." Leah brought in a litter box and sack of litter, a large bag filled with cat toys, a cat post, a cat bed, a cat blanket, and lastly cat food, a cat placemat, and cat dishes.

She watched Leah set up all the stuff, feeling a slight sense of panic. She'd never had to take care of an animal before. What if Ouch fell into the toilet and drowned? Or tumbled down the stairs and broke a paw?

Leah handed her a pill bottle. "Give him one of these sometime tomorrow. All you have to do is stick the pill in his wet food. You have to make sure he eats it though. He's a tricky little fucker. If he doesn't eat it, you'll need to hold him and shove the pill down his throat."

"You're kidding, right?"

"No, why?"

"Your kitten is going to bite the hell out of my hand."

"The secret is to not let him know you're about to give him a pill," Leah said, heading out the door. "Bye, sweet boy. Be good for Auntie Cara."

Ouch was sitting on top of the table by the window, batting the leaves of a plant. Cara shut the door, hoping Ryan knew something about cats, because if he didn't, she had a feeling she was in for a few surprises.

• • •

For the first time in months Ryan felt hopeful about the future. It was a big change from wanting to tie an anvil around his neck before jumping into the bay. Renting out Bella tomorrow night would give him some immediate cash flow to get a few vendors off his ass before they took him to collections. Maybe they'd even be willing to supply him again.

He needed to come up with a menu to make this guy, Dino, happy. He was willing to let Cara help him in that department. Actually, he was willing to let Cara help him with a lot more than just food, which was a first for him. He wasn't used to the feeling of wanting to see a woman two nights in a row. He chalked it up to pure novelty. As soon as they got their fill of one other sexually, they'd both move on. Ryan was secure in knowing she wouldn't demand more from him. This gave him freedom to be himself, to indulge passionately without having to worry about her wanting a marriage proposal from him.

He still wasn't sure what his inner voice was trying to tell him that night he turned Cara down in the kitchen. Maybe the timing hadn't been right or the stars hadn't been aligned properly. All he knew was that it now felt right. And he was going to enjoy *it* for however long *it* lasted.

Ginny came to him, shaking her head sadly. "The man's an emotional train wreck. How does his wife put up with him?"

She was referring to Brady, but whatever meltdown his chef was having couldn't dampen his good spirits. "Don't worry, I'll handle it," Ryan said cheerfully. He went to find Brady. "Brady, my man, what's up?"

"My princess has the chicken pox."

"That's awful. You don't … I mean, you've had them, right?"

"Everyone gets them as a kid," Brady said, sniffing hard. "The point is my little girl is miserable. Miserable!"

A bottle of Jack Daniel's sat on the counter. "Did you bring that from home?"

"Yeah, it's going to be a long night."

The bottle was almost halfway gone. "That wasn't full to start, was it?"

Brady studied the bottle of JD, his eyes red and swollen. "I don't think so."

The rare optimist in Ryan wanted to believe his chef hadn't already consumed that much liquor. In fact, his mood was so good, he was willing to give Brady the benefit of the doubt. Until Brady said, "My knife. Who stole my goddamn knife?" It was when they both realized he was holding it in his left hand that Ryan became worried.

He asked Cara if she could keep an eye on Brady. She groaned. "That guy got on the crazy bus and forgot to get off at his stop."

"He's gone through half a fifth of Jack and I'm pretty sure he's not done. Do this for me and I'll make it up to you later."

Cara gave him a reassuring smile. "Since you put it that way …"

Two hours later, Brady stumbled out of the kitchen, practically falling into the table of diners in front of him. "Hello, good evening, thank you for coming out tonight to eat. 'Course you had to eat anyway, but thanks for choosing … where are we again?"

Ginny and Cara scurried over to Ryan. "You need to get him out of the dining room *now*," Ginny said.

"I thought I told you to watch him, Cara."

"The last time I went into the kitchen, he told me if he saw my face in there again, he'd bite me."

Ryan ran up to Brady, who was in the process of asking a couple who hadn't yet ordered how they had enjoyed his food.

"You're needed in the kitchen, Brady. *Immediately*." His drunken chef wobbled away as he attempted damage control. "I'm so sorry. Please accept a complimentary dessert on our behalf."

The man laughed and pointed. "I think you have a way bigger problem than us right now."

Ryan's eye followed the man's finger. Brady was lying on the edge of the fireplace, passed out. All the filled tables snickered as Brady began to snore.

"I'll get the guys to help carry him away," Cara said, sprinting to the kitchen.

CHAPTER 16

Cara was curled up beside him on the couch, which was a small consolation considering the night he'd had with Brady. He leaned his head back, sighing. "It's a good thing we're renting out the restaurant tomorrow, because chances are there wouldn't be any customers anyway."

"Yeah, that was a bad scene."

Ryan shot up from the couch like he'd just spilled scalding hot coffee in his lap. "Jesus, what was that?"

Something orange and fluffy had jumped up onto the back of the couch, next to his face.

"That's a cat," he said. "How did a cat get in here?"

"I'm kitten-sitting for Leah. I hope that's all right."

"Last time I was around a cat, my eyes swelled up to the size of basketballs and I started to sneeze."

"You're probably allergic."

"I guess we'll see." Ryan scratched the kitten behind the ears. "You're a cute little—Ouch!"

The kitten sank his teeth into Ryan's finger and Cara tried not to laugh. "You guessed his name."

"Ouch, huh? Clever." He examined the teeth marks on his index finger.

She picked up the wannabe Jaws by the scruff of the neck and dropped him on his cat bed. "Stay," she told him. Which, of course, he didn't.

"Okay, let's get to work."

"My thoughts exactly," he said, knowing a surefire way to relieve the stress he was feeling.

She wagged a finger at him. "Work first, play later, Mr. Garridy."

"Come over here and kiss me once, and then we'll work." She sat on the far end of the couch. Ryan patted the couch next to him. "Come closer, little girl." She slid closer to him. He took her face in both hands and kissed her deeply, with a passion that practically overpowered both of them.

She lay back on the couch, taking him with her. His hands roamed her body, his mouth never leaving hers.

"Ryan, we need to … "

He dragged his lips off her. "We need to make love," he said. "Now."

"You said one kiss."

"I lied." He started to unbutton her shirt.

"Think of the meeting tomorrow. We don't have much time to prepare."

His hands stilled. She was right, of course. He took a deep breath and pulled himself off her.

She ran her finger along the stubble on his jaw. "The sooner you listen and agree with my ideas, the faster you can be inside me."

Ryan's eyes narrowed. "Something tells me you have a lot of ideas."

• • •

Cara was feisty and opinionated, and she was driving him mad. They had been going 'round and 'round with ideas, but couldn't seem to agree on anything. It was after one in the morning. He was exhausted, his eyes itched, and his nose was starting to run.

Cara stood in front of him. "Look at me and tell me what you see."

He dropped his head into his hands. He needed to choose his words carefully. What he wanted to say was *I see a loud-mouthed Italian who always demands her way.*

"I see a strong-willed woman with a lot of hair?"

"I'm a middle-class Italian-American who equates food with family."

"That's what I meant."

"Italian men are coming here with big appetites. They eat fish on Friday and pasta on Sunday."

"That doesn't mean they don't want their food fancy."

She put her hands on her hips, reminding Ryan of a bossy, strict schoolteacher he'd like to take over his knee. "Dino does not want his food fancy."

"I don't see why we have to change the menu—wait, how do you know what Dino wants?" She remained quiet. "Cara?"

"I may know him." She looked down and started brushing imaginary crumbs off her skirt.

"Cara?"

Her head snapped up. "Okay, fine. I do know him."

He stood and began to pace. "Why didn't you tell me this earlier?"

"All I did was ask Dino for advice. He agreed with me about the residents of Crabclaw wanting authentic and simple food."

"Bella caters to the tourists who come from the city and want fine dining."

"The tourist season is only three months long. It's not enough to sustain you for the rest of the year. You need to make a change or you're sunk. That is, if you aren't already."

The previous owner of Bella had raved about the booming tourist season and how Ryan would make more than enough during that time to get through any slow periods he may have during the winter. What a tool Ryan had been.

"We're not getting anywhere, and my throat feels like I've swallowed a ball of cat fur," he said, rubbing his eyes. "Tell me what you think we should do."

"Burn the place down and start over?" When she saw he wasn't amused, she led him back toward the couch. "Sit down and listen to my plan.

• • •

Poor baby. Ryan looked miserable slumped on the couch, his eyes swollen and red. Cara's natural inclination would have been to assume the role of nurturing caretaker. Run out and buy him an antihistamine and massage his shoulders. But where had selfless caregiving gotten her with Robbie? She would help Ryan with business, but that was it. She believed in him, but she wasn't his mother and she certainly wasn't his girlfriend.

"The men can choose between two antipasti, like stuffed mushrooms and fried calamari," she said, thinking of Dino's preferences. "Three *primi*, three *secondi*, three vegetables."

Ryan looked horrified. "Only three choices?"

"You wanna do this the easy way or the hard way?" He slumped down lower into the couch and she continued. "They can choose spaghetti for the first course. Bolognese, marinara, and with clams."

"No risotto or gnocchi?

She shook her head. "Takes too long to make. We need to keep it simple. Main course will be the fish of the day, stuffed veal chop, or a steak."

"No chicken?"

"Absolutely not." Ryan grunted, but said nothing. "Spinach, fried zucchini, or a mixed salad as a vegetable, cheesecake or *gelati* for dessert, and of course, enough wine, espresso, and after dinner drinks to keep everyone happy."

Cara dropped down in the chair opposite Ryan, exhausted. She shot up at the sound of a blood-curdling scream. "I'm sorry, kitty. I didn't see you there."

Ouch ran to the center of the room and began to furiously lick his fur. Ryan smirked. "Great cat-sitter," he said, and then he sneezed.

"We have to get you out of here." She helped pull him up from the couch. "Let's finish talking downstairs."

She didn't want to go downstairs to talk. She wanted to undress him and feast on his gorgeous naked body, but she guessed from his bloodshot, puffy eyes it would have to wait. They made their way to the kitchen. As soon as Ryan reached the side door, he yanked it open and stuck his head out for some fresh air. He sucked in a few deep breaths.

This was all her fault. She shouldn't have agreed to cat-sit without running it by Ryan first. It was his apartment, after all. Cara mumbled yet another apology. He regarded her thoughtfully for a moment, his eyes soft and appealing. Then in a matter of seconds, they changed to dark and intense. She held his gaze, too drawn in by it to look away.

She was overcome with longing. How could she want him so much when just a few weeks ago the entire male race had made her sick to her stomach? If a man had never touched her again that would have been all right, and now here she was, craving Ryan, needing him like butter on toast. She tore her eyes away from him and glanced up at the clock on the wall. It was going on three in the morning.

"It's late," she said.

Neither of them moved. He reached out and stroked her hair, but his fingers became tangled in her curls. He yanked his hand, taking her head with him.

"Ow, I'd like to keep my hair, thank you."

"Sorry," he said.

She untangled her hair from his grasp. "Damn curls."

"I love your curls. They make you look like a wild animal."

"Or an escaped mental patient," she said, starting to laugh.

Ryan started to laugh, too. "There is nothing smoother than trying to seduce a woman and getting your fingers stuck in her hair."

"Or seducing a man while he's having a severe allergy attack."

Soon they were both laughing hysterically. Deep belly laughs that made Cara's sides hurt. He sneezed, which caused her to laugh even harder.

"And then … and then you sat on the cat," he said, wheezing.

"You almost jumped out of your skin when you first saw Ouch next to your head."

"Cats freak me out. They don't blink."

She was finally able to catch her breath. "Thank you, Ryan."

"For what?"

"For making me laugh like that. It's been a while."

"You deserve to laugh like that all the time. You're beautiful when you do." He kissed her lightly on the lips. "Get some sleep."

•••

Cara woke with a start. Ouch was chewing on her finger like it was a piece of corn on the cob. She squinted at the clock. Six-thirty. "Way too early, cat." She shoved her finger under the pillow and fell back asleep. Fifteen minutes later, she felt a paw in her curls, so she grabbed the pillow next to her and whacked Ouch with it.

What woke her next was the vigorous scraping sound in the bathroom. It went on for what seemed like hours. What the hell was that cat doing in there?

Then it hit her. A stench so powerful, it made her gag. She had never smelled anything like it. It was a lot of stink for a little cat. Moments later, Ouch jetted out of the bathroom and ran full speed around the apartment. He began to howl. Was this a ritual of cats after they pooped, like a victory dance?

She hauled her tired body out of bed to make sure the kitten didn't slam into any table legs.

What the—?

There was a brown ball hanging from his butt.

"You've got to be friggin' kidding me."

Cara grabbed a tissue and managed to catch Ouch on his third pass around the room. She quickly removed the offending ball and ran to the bathroom to flush it down the toilet, along with the load that had been dropped inside his cat box. She hoped this wasn't a premonition that she was going to have a shitty day.

When she came out of the bathroom, Ouch was circling around his food bowl. He rubbed up against her calves.

"Let me guess. You're hungry?"

His food reeked of tuna, making her gag once again. She dumped the entire can into the bowl and hid one of the pills in it. When she put down the food, Ouch raced to his dish. He sniffed the contents and walked away. She picked him up and placed him in front of his bowl. He licked where she had touched him and again walked away.

She began to panic. "How am I supposed to get you to take this pill? If you don't take this pill, you'll get sick again. Do you want to get sick again? Do you?"

He flicked his tail at her, jumped up on the back of the couch, and gazed out the window.

Cara retrieved the pill from the slimy, stinky tuna that was now lodged under her fingernails. After tiptoeing over to the unsuspecting kitten, she grabbed him from behind, pried open his mouth and crammed the pill inside. Ouch contorted his pint-sized body as he emitted a low growl.

Uh-oh. That doesn't sound good.

He bit down hard on Cara's hand, and left scratch marks over the entire length of her arm while he struggled to get away. She shrieked and dropped him to the floor. Blood oozed from the gashes. The pill fell from his mouth before he ran and hid under the bed. She dialed Ryan's number.

"I need you to search 'how to give your cat a pill.'"

He chuckled. "Not having any luck?" She heard him clicking away on the keyboard. "Have you tried the burrito method yet? It says here it *pawsitively* works. Get it?"

"Yeah, I got it. What's the burrito method?"

"You wrap a towel around the cat like a burrito so he can't scratch you."

She examined the wounds on her arms and wished she had heard of this method sooner. "Please help me. I can't get him to take his pill and if he doesn't, he'll get sick again. Leah trusted me to—"

"Calm down. I'll be right up."

Cara breathed a sigh of relief as soon as she saw Ryan. Strong, capable Ryan. He'd get the job done. He already held a white towel in his hands. "Where is he?" She pointed to the bed with her bloody arm. His eyes grew wide as he started to laugh. "Did that tiny creature do that?"

"That 'tiny creature' is the devil in disguise. Trust me."

Ryan kneeled down next to the bed to coax Ouch out. Once Ouch registered it was Ryan instead of the evil, pill-pushing Cara, he calmly wandered out. Ryan scratched him behind the ears, threw the towel over him, and while wrapping the kitten up in it, yelled, "The pill! Where's the pill?"

Before she could reach them in time, Ouch had twisted out of the towel, sunk his dagger teeth into the web part of Ryan's hand, and then proceeded to claw his way down Ryan's torso. He scampered back under the bed.

"Oh boy," Cara said.

Ryan yanked up his shirt. "Look at these welt marks on my chest! Jesus, my hand is bleeding!"

"Don't cry to me about it. I warned you."

He went over to his desk and pulled out a phone book. He dialed. "Hello. Can you give me some suggestions for how to give my cat a pill?" He hung up a moment later.

"Well, what did they say?"

"Either sneak it into his food or try the burrito method."

"So, what are we going to do now?"

He shrugged. "I've only ever had dogs. With a dog you stick the pill in a spoonful of peanut butter and they lick the whole thing off without ever knowing what hit them. Cats are a different species altogether."

They crouched down next to the bed. This time when the little devil ventured out again, Ryan swiftly wedged him between his knees and held his front and rear paws. "Grab his head and shove the pill in!" Cara did just that, and held Ouch's mouth closed while the kitten twisted from side to side like a freshly caught bass on a fishhook. When she was sure the pill had been swallowed, they both let go at the same time. Ouch hissed and ran off. Ryan sneezed.

"I am never cat-sitting again," Cara said.

• • •

"Did we go out of business?" Ginny and Johnny-boy wanted to know when they saw the *Closed* sign on the door.

"Change of plans, guys," Ryan explained. "We have a private party coming in. They rented out the restaurant for the night."

"For what?" Johnny-boy asked. "A bachelor party?"

Ryan didn't want to know. He probably should have asked, but he was so flabbergasted when he had heard the amount of money he was going to receive in cash, all reason and sensibility fled.

"A business meeting," he said.

"Must be some business," Ginny said.

He checked on Cara, who was in the process of explaining the change of menu to the sous chef. "Forget fine dining. We're doing 'casual authentic' this evening."

"Can you keep an eye on things in the kitchen while I handle the dining room?" Ryan asked, surprisingly calm over the fact he was allowing a woman, any woman, to have this much control over a situation that could make or break him. He was smart enough to know he wasn't able to handle this all on his own. It was bad enough he was surviving on only four hours of sleep.

"Sure thing, cookie," Cara said, giving him a playful look that kicked his pulse up a notch.

No time to think about why my pulse is kicking up a notch.

"Listen," he told Oz, "you know how you like to kid around with Cara by making sexually inappropriate comments that I've chosen to ignore, but could theoretically interpret as sexual harassment?"

"Um, I guess?" Oz said slowly.

"Well, don't do it anymore."

Where the hell did that come from?

An enormous man sauntered into the restaurant, trailed by two other men. His heavily sprayed black pompadour reminded Ryan of Elvis, and the retro look was completed by a gray and white bowling shirt buttoned at the neck with a black T-shirt underneath.

"The name's Dino," he said. Ryan shook his hand. "This here's Frankie on my right and Joe on the left."

Frankie's shock of red hair contrasted with his pale pallor, and his deep-set, blue eyes darted around the room like a Ping-Pong ball. Joe was an olive-skinned, heavy-lidded man, so tall and thin he reminded Ryan of a drainpipe.

"How many more people are you expecting?" he asked.

"About twenty," Dino said.

Ryan led them to the dining room. "How about an aperitif while you wait?"

Without bothering to ask the other two men what they wanted to drink, Dino ordered three Negroni.

When Ryan returned to the bar, Oz's eyebrows looked like they were pinned to the top of his scalp. "What's the problem?" he asked.

"What kind of meeting did you say they were going to have in there?"

"Business—as in 'none of our business.' Do you know how to make a Negroni?"

"Sure. It's gin, Campari, sweet vermouth … " Oz's voice trailed off.

Five more men, all in dark suits walked in. Ryan brought them to the dining room and stopped short. All the tables had been pushed together to form one long banquet-style table. A lone table had been moved to the center of the room.

"We did some rearranging," Dino told him. "You don't mind, do you?" Ryan absently shook his head as Dino slapped him twice on the cheek. "That's good."

He wandered back to Oz in a daze. "Ginny, take these cocktails to the men and tell Cara to come see me, please. ASAP."

Ginny nodded. "You look lovely tonight," Oz said.

Her brows knitted together. "Where's the rest of the comment? You know, ' … but you'd look lovelier sitting on my face.'"

Oz grimaced. "The compliment stands alone."

Ginny stared at him stone-faced for a moment before walking away.

"Are you turning over a new leaf?" Ryan asked Oz.

"I think I need to plant a whole new tree."

Another handful of men trickled in, followed by a man who wore a dark, bulky trench coat. His face looked like it had been rearranged by Picasso. He approached the bar and asked for a whiskey, neat.

"Is that a machine gun under your coat or are you just happy to see me?" Oz joked.

"It's a machine gun," the man said, opening his coat to reveal a 9mm submachine weapon.

Oz poured his whiskey with a shaking hand while the man pulled out a twenty and dropped it on the bar. Ryan directed him to the dining room. There were a bunch of .22-caliber handguns with silencers on the tables.

"What the hell is going on here?" he asked Cara when she joined him.

"Can you be more specific?"

"Who are these men?"

She shrugged. "I only know Dino."

"Don't they look a little suspicious to you?"

"They look like the uncles I used to see only at weddings and funerals."

"They all have guns, Cara," he said, his voice changing to a harsh whisper.

She didn't appear fazed. "And?"

The last two men arrived, sporting pinky rings and too much cologne. Ginny led them to the back, but when she returned she had a pinched expression on her face.

"I started reciting the menu choices," she said, "and the *fat* one told me he wasn't taking meal suggestions from a 'skinny molink' like me. He said he only wants 'the meatball mistress.'"

Everyone looked at Cara.

"I'm guessing that would be me."

CHAPTER 17

Dino wanted Cara's meatballs. When she informed him they weren't on the menu and perhaps he'd prefer a nice meat sauce, he said, "It would be a quintessential disaster if there weren't any meatballs. I promised the men your Sicilian meatballs. They would be very disappointed and quite possibly not want to return here ever again."

She quickly counted heads and dashed over to Ryan. "They need meatballs," she told him. "No negotiation." She scribbled out a list and thrust it in front of Johnny-boy's face. "Please go to the store and buy these extra ingredients." Ryan handed him cash and he took off. "In the meantime, serve the antipasti and bring them wine. Lots and lots of wine."

Cara bolted to the kitchen. "Slight change of menu, boys. We're making meatballs." She thanked God Brady wasn't around to make her life even more of a living hell. This night needed to come together for Ryan's sake. For all their sakes. She had to do whatever was needed to make sure they succeeded.

After what felt like two hundred meatballs later, if she never saw another meatball for a year, that'd be fine with her. She had flecks of ground meat stuck in her hair, her feet were killing her, and she felt on edge from all the yelling around her in the kitchen. "Behind! Hot! Sharp!" She had no idea how the staff did it night after night. It was hectic and sweaty, and only a matter of time before you chopped off a piece of your finger.

"Dino had me send Oz, Leah, and Johnny-boy home," Ryan informed her. "He wants the kitchen staff gone in ten minutes. You and I are to handle the desserts and after-dinner drinks before they get down to the 'business' part of their meeting."

How long the 'business' part would take was anyone's guess, so once the men had been served, Cara and Ryan sat at the bar and waited. Ryan nursed an amaretto. He had surprised Cara with coffee and a splash of amaretto, topped with whipped cream dusted with cinnamon. The almond-flavored liqueur brought memories of past family holidays rushing through her.

"My dad used to make this for me and my brother on Christmas Eve. We'd dunk almond biscotti in it."

"I always had an amaretto after dinner in Italy, or anisette."

She scrunched up her nose. "Anisette tastes like black licorice to me."

"It helps with digestion."

"Maybe so, but it still tastes yucky." She paused. "How come you never talk about your family?"

"What's there to say?"

"You could try telling me a little about them. I know your parents are still married and you have a younger brother. That's it." Ryan massaged the side of his jaw, his eyes looking everywhere except at her. "Do you have some deep, dark family secret you don't want anyone to know?"

He smiled. A smile that didn't quite reach his eyes. "No secrets. Except for the time I snuck out my window at midnight to meet my girlfriend."

"What happened?"

"I didn't get caught, but she did. She was grounded for a month."

"Her father didn't rat you out?"

"He was my baseball coach and I was his star player. He didn't want anything to ruin my concentration."

"Oh brother," she said, rolling her eyes. "Good to know he had his priorities straight."

"Hey, I took our high school to the championships. I was a star. Had my picture in the town paper and everything."

"Your dad must have been proud."

"Everyone was. Overnight, I transformed from a complete goober to a god. I had girls lining up for me."

Cara punched him lightly in the shoulder. "Does that mean you're still a god?"

Ryan stood and stretched his legs. "Nah. I'm back to being a goober." He walked over to the dining room and peeked in.

She let out a big yawn. "Do you think they're almost done?"

He put his finger to his lips and motioned her over. She looked inside. One man sat at the front table with a glass of red wine, and a gun and a knife in front of him. Everyone stood. Words were said in Italian.

"What are they saying?" Ryan whispered.

"I think that man is about to get baptized."

Dino went over to the man and took his hand. He pricked the man's trigger finger with a needle, squeezing it until a sufficient amount of blood oozed from it. With his other hand, Dino held up a picture of a saint and squeezed a few drops of blood onto it. He reached into his pocket for a lighter and set the picture on fire. The card was quickly passed around from hand to hand while more words were said in Italian.

Ryan looked to her for translation. "The blood symbolizes that man's birth into the family," she explained. "He's to live and die by the gun and the knife, and if he disobeys any of the rules, he'll burn just like the picture of the saint."

"Please tell me this is a joke." One by one the men lined up to kiss both cheeks of the now "baptized" man. "I feel like I'm watching a movie."

"A movie I don't think we should be watching." She pulled him away. "Let's sit down and act like we didn't just witness some kind of bizarre initiation ceremony."

"Is there a chance I could get arrested for hosting this? I mean, they're maf—"

She clamped a hand over his mouth. "I wouldn't say that word out loud if I were you."

Ryan gave her a knowing look and nodded. Cara slowly took her hand away. He dropped his forehead to the bar and began to thump.

"What are you, autistic? I have a nephew who does the same thing." It was Frankie, one of the guys who had first arrived with Dino. Ryan lifted his head.

"He does it to relax," Cara said.

"Dino says you're having some problems with the restaurant. Whatsamatta? You a deadbeat? You don't pay your debts?"

"No, I—" Ryan started to say.

Frankie slapped him on the back. "Ay oh, you don't gotta explain. Hard times come upon us all. Let me know if you ever need my help. Frankie the Firebomb. I do good work and nobody will ever know nuthin'."

Before Ryan could respond, the men started to file out, murmuring to each other about getting home before the wife cut them off at the knees. Dino and Joe were last.

"How was everything?" Cara asked.

"You got a talent with them meatballs," Dino said. "Maybe you can cater my granddaughter's wedding. Two hundred and fifty guests."

Cara imagined making meatballs for all those people and felt a little queasy. She smiled and nodded anyway.

"You're good people," Dino said as he pinched Ryan's cheek. "Joe, give him a dollar."

Ryan held up his hands. "You don't have to give me a dollar."

Joe pulled out a roll of hundred dollar bills. He peeled off ten and left them on the bar.

"We got another meeting in three weeks," Dino said.

Ryan stared at the money. "You and your business associates are welcome anytime."

"I assume you'll want my meatballs again?" Cara asked.

"Why else would I come, girlie?" Dino grinned, his gold canine tooth shining in the light. "*Buona notte*."

As soon as the men exited, Ryan pulled a roll of antacids from his pocket and popped four of them. "I can't do this without you," he said, chomping down on them.

"I know." She loved the feeling of his needing her even though she'd never admit it out loud. "Look, we're both helping each other get back on our feet, right?"

Ryan was silent for a moment. "I suppose that's one way of putting it," he finally said. He took her hand and led her outside.

Cara groaned as she sat down and removed her shoes. Ryan brought her legs up onto his lap and began massaging her tired, achy feet. She leaned her head back and admired the star-filled sky, enjoying what would probably be one of the last warm nights of the summer.

"You don't see stars like this in Brooklyn," she said.

"I saw them every night growing up in Connecticut."

"Connecticut, huh? You must have been born with a silver pacifier in your mouth."

"More like gold or platinum, depending on the market."

She always suspected Ryan came from money. After all, he brought her back to a place he simply called a smart "investment." His condo was furnished with Murano glass and white linen furniture. She had been petrified to drink a glass of Merlot for fear she'd spill a drop on his sofa.

"You're struggling to save a failing restaurant. You've obviously depleted your own resources. Is there a reason you don't ask your father for help?"

"That's a dumb question," he snapped.

"Why?"

"When you ask someone for help, there are always strings attached. Besides, my father thinks this whole restaurant idea is ridiculous. He'd much prefer I work for him, but I can't do it. It would be torture for me."

"A regular salary, normal hours, and much less stress. Yeah, that sounds like it would be a real bitch," she said with a hint of a smile.

He pulled her chair closer to his. "I'd have to work side by side with my brother, and yes, that would be a real bitch."

"Sibling rivalry?"

"Something like that. Now shut up and come sit on my lap."

As she rose, she gave a quick glance around to make sure the street was empty. Then she hiked up her skirt and sat facing him, straddling his hips. Ryan's hands came around to cup what little lace covered the cheeks of her ass. She brushed a bit of hair off his forehead, swept her finger over his brow and down to his lips.

He grabbed her wrist and kissed the inside of her pulse, then moved her hand down to his crotch.

"You're already hard."

"I was hard the second you lifted your skirt."

She rubbed the length of him through his pants. He pressed her hand harder into him as he nestled his face in her chest.

"Couple at twelve o'clock," Cara whispered. He lifted his head. The couple nodded to them as they passed by. When they were out of view, Ryan kissed her long, slow, deep, and hard, all at once. His hand moved up her thigh and rested on top of her panties. When his fingers found her, she was already damp for him. He moved one, two fingers inside of her, matching his movements to her breathing.

"Should we take this inside?" he asked, his eyes a deep, rich brown—much darker than they had been only moments before.

She shook her head no.

Ryan let out a low chuckle. "Whatever the lady wants." He squirmed underneath her, reaching into his pocket and pulling out a condom package.

"You carry one everywhere you go?"

"Boy Scout motto. Be prepared."

Cara kneeled in front of him, reaching to unzip his pants. She took the package from him, ripped it open, and rolled the condom down onto him with her mouth.

"Wow."

"Girl Scout motto. Have many talents," she said, straddling him once again.

"Pull your panties to the side for me."

As soon as she did, he thrust hard into her. Cara buried her face in his neck, holding onto him tightly. His movements were full of need and hunger and rawness. She was building up to an intense orgasm when the memory of Annemarie sitting on Robbie flashed in her mind.

This was the very same position I found them in.

She felt herself starting to drift to an ugly place, a place she no longer wanted to visit. She clenched her eyes shut, trying to annihilate the bitter memory.

"Open your eyes, baby. Look at me." When she did, he told her, "Stay with me." She swallowed, nodding. "I'm not going to move. You're in complete control, okay?"

Their eyes locked on each other. Ryan's hands stayed on her hips, squeezing, holding onto her like she was his last chance. Cara became lost in the pleasure of the moment. He was so in tune with her, he knew the exact moment she came. He pumped into her deeply, causing her to gasp and moan his name.

"You're so fucking beautiful when you come." His mouth went to her neck, licking and sucking until his breathing became too heavy. "So tight, so sweet," she heard him whisper before he shuddered and let out a hissing breath.

His head fell forward onto her shoulder. Cara pressed her lips to his sweaty temple. A wave of panic hit her when she realized the tenderness of the emotion coursing through her. What was the matter with her? Great sex did not equal love. These feelings for Ryan were simply lust. *Don't ruin it by getting sensitive and attached.* She should be thanking him for ridding Robbie from her psyche.

"Spend the night with me," he said, bursting her neurotic bubble.

She couldn't do it. Cara needed to get away from him, get her head on straight. "I still have to take care of Ouch."

"Right, I forgot about him. Tomorrow night, then."

Of all the men in the world, Ryan was the worst one to have delusional domestic fantasies about. He was still the same man she had met months ago—a womanizing commitment-phobe. Nothing had changed. And yet, now that she was sleeping with him, everything had changed.

• • •

The animal gods were smiling down on her that morning. Ouch had let her sleep in later than eight, which she desperately needed, what with the meatball madness coupled with her insane orgasm. She smiled and stretched. Ryan sure knew how to please a woman.

Of course he did. He had lots of practice.

And just like that, Cara's mood soured.

If she didn't care about Ryan, why should it even matter? He was supposed to be her sexual salve, her rebound, not The One. As long as she kept that in perspective, there wouldn't be a problem. Ryan was an attentive lover and they had incredible chemistry. He had the unique talent of making her feel like she was the only woman he wanted. But for all she knew, he could be sleeping with five other girls—spreading his seed, pollinating, or whatever it was that males claimed they had the biological urge to do.

She jumped out of bed and on the way to the bathroom stepped on a toy mouse. It let out a sick squeak. She kept forgetting there was a cat in the apartment. Where was the pint-sized puma, anyway?

She slowly made her way into the living room in case Ouch was lurking behind something, ready to pounce. He wasn't. He was curled up in a ball, nestled in the corner of the couch, one tiny paw covering his eye.

How adorable is that? He wasn't so bad. If she didn't count the permanent scarring she'd probably have up and down her forearms and around her ankles, he was pretty cute. Ouch woke up and noticed Cara staring at him. He stretched his sinewy torso and began to lick himself.

Maybe she would get a kitten once she was in a place of her own.

Ryan was allergic to cats.

So what? Ryan won't be in my future.

Ouch flew off the couch. A sad, low mournful cry escaped from his mouth. It sounded like a didgeridoo, that spooky wind instrument Cara's Anthropology instructor had brought in to show the class. "Wow-Wow-Wow-Wow."

"What's wrong?"

The cat crouched close to the ground, making a gagging noise.

"Are you choking?"

"Urka-Urka-Urka-Urka." His abdominal muscles contracted and Cara realized he was about to throw up.

"No, not on the rug!"

Her yelling caused him to run and spread droplets of who-knows-what on the carpet. He stopped and gave one last hack. Whatever he threw up was the size of a small mountain goat.

"Holy crap."

Ouch shook his head, flicked his tail at her, and strutted away. Cara stood there for a moment in shock, unsure of what she had just witnessed. Had he hacked up a piece of his intestine? A mouse? She went over to inspect it. It looked like a cigar, covered with pieces of plant leaves and bile.

Forget the whole cat idea.

When Leah arrived later on to pick up her *Exorcist* kitty, Cara decided not to ruin her friend's mood with all the vomit, blood, and poop-filled details.

"How was my little munchkin? Any problems?" she asked, scooping the kitten up and cradling him in her arms.

"He was an absolute *angel*," Cara said.

Leah almost choked on her gum. "Angel, huh? He must have been on his best behavior. Any problems giving him the pill?" Cara shook her head. "I guess I know where I can leave him if we ever go away again. Auntie Cara's."

She managed a smile, even though the only way she would take care of Ouch again was if Leah had his claws, teeth, and stomach removed.

"How was your trip?"

"Fuctastic," Leah said, "and I mean that in all senses of the word. I love being married. I have the best husband in the world."

Cara felt the slightest twinge of jealousy over Leah's marital bliss, but quickly brushed it off. Maybe one day she'd have it, too.

"How are things with you and Ryan?"

"What can I say? The lingerie finally worked."

Leah bent down to open the cat carrier, shoved Ouch in head first and quickly slammed the door, latching it in place. Ouch started howling. "You'll be careful, right?"

"You mean safe sex? Of course."

"That's not what I'm talking about. I meant with your heart."

"My heart's not getting involved."

Leah threw her a skeptical look. "Just remember who you're dealing with, okay? Ryan's not the settling-down type, and I don't—"

Cara held up her hand to stop her. "Want to see me get hurt. I know, and I won't."

After she helped Leah with all of Ouch's stuff, she flopped down on the sofa. Leah's words of warning played over and over in her mind. *Ryan's not the settling-down type.* Well, neither was she. At least, not anymore. She'd enjoy the time they spent together, and once she was done with school and had her degree in hand, she'd thank Ryan for all his help and move on. She was different from all the other women who thought they could change him. Cara knew you couldn't change a man who didn't want to change. As long as she remembered that, her heart would be just fine.

CHAPTER 18

Ryan leaned back in his chair after signing the last of the checks he had written. Dino's money had helped. A lot. And while it hadn't fixed everything, he had been able to take care of paying the vendors who threatened to break his legs.

Sure, he could have taken the coward's way out. Burn down the restaurant to collect the insurance money. He might have considered it three weeks ago when he felt all was hopeless, especially when Frankie the Firebomb said: "Let me know if you ever need my help. I do good work, and nobody will ever know nuthin'." But he'd never be able to live with himself. He wanted Bella to succeed, and for the first time in a long time he actually believed it had a chance. Ryan wanted to be successful on his own, without his father's aid. That was the difference between him and his brother. Well, that and the small matter of integrity.

He heard faint footsteps upstairs and smiled. Ryan didn't necessarily believe in fate, preferring to believe a person created their own destiny. But how else would he describe his meeting Cara?

He likened a woman to a puzzle. A challenge at first, but as the picture became clearer, the mystery gradually faded. When he fit the last piece into place, it was time to move on. There were many facets to Cara, and yet he couldn't seem to put them together. It drove him nuts. He hadn't felt unsure around a woman since the ninth grade. Not since his ex-wife had a female gotten under his skin, and he had sworn it would never happen again. So far, he had kept that promise.

It was because of Cara that the restaurant was still afloat. Surprisingly, he didn't feel threatened. Or powerless. He regarded her as his partner. He felt comfortable with her and *wanted* to be around her. This was new to him. What had previously made him extremely anxious now gave him a sense of … hope.

There was that word again. Maybe he had finally healed from his divorce or maybe he was simply growing up. Whatever it was, Ryan wanted this relationship with Cara to work. He didn't want it to be only about sex, despite what she said.

There, he had said it. Without breaking out in a cold sweat.

…

Ginny stood at the open door to the apartment biting her thumbnail, a shell-shocked expression on her face. To say Cara was surprised would be an understatement. Ginny had never visited her before. Ginny hardly talked to her, period.

"Can I come in?"

Cara swallowed her mouthful of powdered doughnut and opened the door wider. "Sure."

Ginny sat ramrod-straight in the easy chair, with her purse clutched tightly in her lap. "I hope I didn't catch you in the middle of anything," she said, her voice quivering.

"You're actually saving me from exceeding my calorie count for the week."

Ginny eyed the box on the coffee table. "Are those powered doughnuts?"

Cara wiped at her mouth and cheeks. "Did my white mustache give it away?"

"Do you mind if I have one?"

"Am I supposed to call your sponsor to talk you out of this? A doughnut is wheat, dairy, and sugar."

"I know, and I haven't had one in at least ten years."

Major dilemma. If she gave Ginny a doughnut, was she going to throw it up after? It was one thing to cheat with a piece of bread; a doughnut was an entirely different level of sin. In terms of sin, it was up there with cheating in poker and coveting thy neighbor's husband. Then again, Ginny was an adult. If she wanted to take the express elevator to Hell, that was her choice.

"Help yourself."

She took one and sniffed it. The tip of her tongue lightly touched the powder. Smiling, she took a huge bite. Cara watched in awe as Ginny practically made love to the doughnut. When she was finished, Ginny leaned back, licked her fingers, and asked for another one.

"Hold on a minute, Olive Oyl, why don't you tell me what's going on with you to make you fall off the wagon."

She covered her face with her hands. "My boyfriend of two years just broke up with me. He said I was too uptight and rigid, and he couldn't see himself marrying someone who reminded him of his strict American history teacher in high school."

"What a jackass."

"But it's true!" she wailed. "I am uptight and rigid."

Cara couldn't dispute that. She handed Ginny another doughnut. "You're Brazilian. You're supposed to be loud and passionate, and have a big ass."

"See, I'm a failure even to my culture."

She studied the other woman for a moment who was in the process of chowing down her second doughnut. "I have to admit I'm a little surprised you came to *me* about this."

"I needed advice and it's pretty obvious you're way more ... " She looked down at Cara's cleavage. " ... uninhibited than I am."

Cara wasn't sure that counted as a compliment.

"Plus, after all the women we've seen Ryan with, the fact that he chose you says a lot."

Her cheeks grew warm. "You know about me and Ryan?"

"Everyone knows about you two. He stares at you like he wants to rip your clothes off every time he sees you. That's how I want men to look at me."

Everyone at Bella knew they were sleeping together? And more importantly, did Ryan really look at her like that?

"Ginny, you don't want all men to look at you like that. Only the one you're interested in."

"Tell me how I can be more sexy." She reached for another doughnut.

Cara slapped her hand away. "You can start by laying off the doughnuts. And you might try taking your hair out of that bun. Men like to run their fingers through hair. They don't want to get stabbed with a bobby pin."

"Let me write this down." She dug inside her purse for a pad and pen.

Cara had to look away so she wouldn't laugh. "It also wouldn't hurt to gain a few pounds. Men don't want to feel like they're going to bed with a broomstick."

Ginny chewed on her bottom lip. "For the last few years I've been terrified of losing control of myself, especially when it comes to eating. I used to be much heavier, you know."

"You don't have to lose complete control. But don't deny yourself the great pleasures of life, either. Namely food and uninhibited sex."

She nodded. "I need to loosen up a bit."

"Also, there's a fine line between dressing provocatively and dressing slutty. Your shirts buttoned all the way up to the neck make you look like you're being strangled, but you don't have to have your boobs hanging out, either. You can straddle the line, but don't cross it." Again, Ginny's eyes dropped to Cara's cleavage. "I can't help it," she mumbled, crossing her arms over her chest.

Ginny rose. "You've given me some great suggestions. I don't know how to thank you."

"No problem." Cara walked her to the door. "By the way, have you ever thought about Oz? I mean, in a romantic way?"

"Are you kidding?" she said. "I've dated two men in my lifetime. He's been with probably three hundred girls. Oz has way too much experience for me. He'd think I was frigid."

Virgin. Frigid. Cara was sure there had to be some similarities between the two.

"Sometimes people aren't always as they seem, Ginny."

She shook her head. "I can't think of other men right now. It's way too soon."

Famous last words.

• • •

Ginny came to work that night with her dark hair flowing down past her shoulders, fire-red lips, and the first three buttons unbuttoned on her work shirt. She strode confidently past Oz on the way in, and Cara worried the poor guy might have a stroke.

"Sweet mother of God," he said under his breath.

They gathered in the kitchen to taste Brady's specials of the day. Brady was back to work and strangely subdued. Ginny was the first one to try everything. Cream of eggplant soup, roasted butternut squash ravioli, and smoked mozzarella chicken over whipped potatoes with Marsala sauce.

"Are you feeling all right, Ginny?" Ryan asked.

A drop of Marsala slid down her chin. "Of course I am. Why do you ask?"

"You don't usually ... er, I mean, you seem ... " Ryan threw Cara a pleading look to help him out.

"Ginny is exploring her newfound appetites," she explained.

"About duckin' time," Brady grumbled.

Johnny-boy nodded his approval, eyeing her up and down. Cara put her arm around Ginny and steered her away from the men.

"I like what you've done with the hair, but I'd go up a button."

"Too slutty?" Ginny asked.

"Unless you want your customers to think you're on the menu."

"Right," she said, buttoning up.

When the two of them approached the bar, Oz practically fell over himself to get to Ginny. "Can I make you something to drink, Ginny? Anything your heart desires."

"What am I, day-old milk left out in the sun?" Cara said.

Ginny smiled. "That's sweet, Oz, but I've got to get to work now."

"You have to score me a date with her, Cara. Please," Oz begged, the moment Ginny was out of earshot.

"I tried to put in a good word for you, but she thinks you're the equivalent of a male prostitute."

"Nothing could be further from the truth."

He appeared so visibly distressed, she felt sorry for the guy. "I know that, and you know that, but no one else does. How about asking her on a date yourself?"

He ran his hand nervously back and forth over his bald head. "I don't know how to do that. How would I do that? I can't do that."

She was starting to think she should become a love and sex therapist.

Ryan came up behind her. "Should I be jealous of my bartender?" he whispered into her ear.

"Definitely not." She smiled without turning around, remembering what Ginny had said earlier about Ryan wanting to rip off her clothes.

"Then get to work or I'll have to reprimand you later. In my office." And with that, he pinched her waist and took off toward the dining room.

• • •

Ryan looked up when he heard a single knock on his already open office door. It was twenty minutes until closing. Johnny-boy was standing there with his hands clasped behind his back.

"What's up?"

"I hate to do this to you, but I've got to give my notice."

"Are you moving to another restaurant?" *A busier one?*

Johnny-boy cleared his throat. "Actually, I'll be moving to the city where there'll be a lot more acting opportunities for me."

He had no idea the guy was an actor, but now the whole James Dean look made more sense. "Are you moving to New York alone?"

"No, with Kathleen, the woman you've seen waiting for me at the bar a number of times."

"Ah, yes," he said, remembering the older woman with a body as tight as her skin. "Good luck to you."

Ryan didn't want to train a new waiter, but given the changes he was planning to make with the menu—changes he was betting on to draw a much larger crowd—it was inevitable. He knew a complete overhaul of the restaurant was needed and he finally had the incentive to do it, not to mention the funds, especially after Dino's next "meeting."

The problem was Brady. He dreaded having to tell his chef about the new concept. He wasn't sure what Brady's reaction to the change in menu was going to be. He might break out in tears or break out his knife. He'd have to ask Cara what she thought the best approach would be when dealing with his unpredictable chef. Maybe he'd have Cara do it for him.

Wait, what?

Since when did he ever ask anyone for advice? What had this woman done to him?

She kept him on his toes. It was unnerving. And exciting. He sure hadn't seen her coming. But now that she was here, he wasn't planning to let her go.

Later that night, when it was just the two of them left in the restaurant, Cara came up to the bar where he was studying the night's receipts and said, "That old guy is at the door. He won't take a bag of food from me. He said it's got to be from you."

He looked up. "Who, Edward? How do you know about that?"

"I saw you one night."

He followed her to the kitchen. Ryan checked the bag and added another loaf of bread. "This is Cara," he told Edward. "It's all right with me if she feeds you."

He nodded. "Don't want nobody to lose their job is all. I've said it before and I'll say it again. You're a good man, Mr. Garridy."

"Stay warm, Edward. It's chilly out there," Ryan said, slipping him a twenty. He shut the door and locked it. He caught Cara staring at him. "What?"

She put her arms around his neck. "You're a good man, Mr. Garridy."

"I'm a horny man, Miss Manzoni."

"Don't try and change the subject."

Which was what he always did whenever someone pointed out any of his positive qualities. "Okay, I'm a good man." He ran his lips over the side of her neck. "Let me show you how good I am."

She sighed with pleasure. "I know how good you are."

His hands reached around to cup her behind. "Yes, but I keep getting better. Come spend the night with me and I'll show you."

Ryan took the opportunity on the way to his condo to drop both bombs on her. "By the way, Johnny-boy gave his notice, so you'll be taking his place. And you and I will be revamping Bella's entire menu immediately."

• • •

Ryan bolted upright in bed when he heard his phone ringing. He usually checked to see who was calling first, but this morning he didn't. Big mistake. It was his father.

"How's the restaurant business treating you?" his father's voice boomed through the phone lines. "Do you have people waiting to get in the door? A write-up in the *Times* yet?"

Ryan was about to do what had by now become habit whenever he spoke to his dad. Give brief answers that didn't encourage any more conversation, and then tell him he had another call to take, but this morning he figured he'd have a little fun.

"The restaurant is doing better than I imagined. I changed the menu, which brought in a new clientele and now the place is packed every night. I'm raking in the dough."

"Is that so?" His father's surprise was obvious. "It's good to hear you finally got it on track. I didn't think you would. I'm proud of you."

It would have mattered more to Ryan if his dad were proud of him even when he wasn't succeeding.

"Don't you think it's time you patched things up with your brother so you can join us for the holidays? Bury the hatchet, as they say."

Only if he could bury it in his brother's back.

"I don't think so," he said.

"I don't know what went on between you and James, but it has gone on long enough. Your mother hasn't seen you in ages. Why don't you plan a visit?"

Ryan shifted uncomfortably, aware that Cara was awake and watching him. "Bella's so busy at the moment. I can't get the time away."

"Your mother misses you."

"Tell her I miss her, too. I need to answer my other line, Dad. We'll talk again soon." He disconnected and tossed his phone on the bedside table.

"Any particular reason you lied to your father?" Cara asked.

"Just wanted to make his day. He's only proud of me when I'm doing well at something."

"Of course. No one says they're proud of someone when they majorly screw up."

He gave her an exasperated look. "You wouldn't understand."

"True. I don't have any parents to make proud anymore, so what would I know?"

"That's not what I meant," he said, reaching for her. She dodged his hand and rolled out of bed. "It's complicated," he continued. "The problems with my family go way back."

"I guess it's all in how you look at things, Ryan. Me? I'd give anything to be able to have problems with my family again." She disappeared into the bathroom.

"Come back to bed," he called.

"I have to get ready for class. By the way, you owe me a few espressos for keeping me up half the night."

"How did I keep you up half the night?"

She popped her head out. "I thought you said you always moved to the other side of the bed when you spent the night with a woman. You were practically on top of me the entire night."

Ryan looked over at the far side of the king bed, which didn't look slept in at all. He shook his head in dismay.

He was turning into a woman.

CHAPTER 19

"Authentic and simple, with large portions to feed working-class families." This is what Cara kept repeating to him every time he began to doubt he was doing the right thing by changing Bella's menu. "Everything will work out. Trust me," she said. Ryan wasn't entirely convinced, but she said it so confidently, he was willing to take a chance.

"Tell me again why you're studying psychology instead of something more practical like restaurant management?"

"Oh please." She snorted. "I'd hardly call myself an expert in the restaurant field. I've been coming to this town for years, so I know the type of people who live here."

He stretched his arms over his head, attempting to work out the kinks in his back. They had worked well into the night trying to come up with a new menu and he was both tired and sore. "You know a heck of a lot more than I did when I bought Bella."

"That's not saying much." She laughed as he threw a couch pillow at her. "You could have just signed up for a dating service if you wanted to meet women. It would have been much cheaper."

"But then I never would have been ripped off by you."

She threw the pillow back at him, aiming for his head. "I'm never going to live that down, am I?"

"No, but it'll be a great story … " He was about to say, " … to tell our children."

Ryan swallowed hard. He was in love with her. How in the world had he fallen in love with Cara Manzoni from Bensonhurst?

• • •

Why was Ryan looking at her like she was a piece of modern art worth a million dollars and he couldn't figure out why.

"What's the matter?" she asked. His cheeks were flushed, yet the rest of his skin was pale. "Are you having another allergic reaction?"

"No, I—" He stopped short and bolted up.

"Ryan, you're starting to worry me. What's wrong?"

"Nothing, baby. I just got a little dizzy all of a sudden. Not a big deal." He leaned down and kissed her on the cheek. "I feel fine now, but I've got to go."

"You're leaving *now*? It's two in the morning."

"I'm on this round of antibiotics for a sinus infection and if I miss a dose, well, you know what can happen. Remember Ouch?"

Cara waited for an invitation to sleep over, but when it didn't come, she knew he was lying about the antibiotics. Ryan grabbed his jacket, phone, and keys before heading for the door. "Besides, we should both get a good night's sleep."

He was choosing sleep over her. She pressed her lips tightly together and said nothing. "See you tomorrow," he said, and then was gone.

Which was probably a good thing or else she might have seriously hurt him.

Don't be obtuse. It's obvious he's tiring of you. He's creating distance, like all men do when they're getting ready to dump someone.

She tore off her clothes, decided against wearing Ryan's T-shirt to bed, and went to brush her teeth. *Here I am, being a fool again, thinking Ryan could be satisfied with only me. How naïve.*

She'd beat Ryan to the punch by creating some distance of her own. She would have "the talk" with him next time she saw him. They had been spending too much time together, she'd say. Cara needed to focus on school. They could still see each other, but she needed space.

As long as she didn't succumb to his easy smile, deep kisses, or sexual magnetism, she'd be fine.

But when she walked into the apartment the next day after shopping for some warmer clothes, Ryan was running half-naked on the treadmill. Again, he hadn't heard her when she came in because of his headphones. She was careful not to startle him. Cara leaned against the wall, trying not to drool over his breathtaking physique. His lean, muscular thighs, tight buttocks, flat stomach, and chiseled forearms, all covered with a layer of glistening sweat.

A sweaty Robbie had never turned her on. But seeing Ryan drenched with perspiration made her feel like she was an aggressive, hungry lioness and Ryan was a weak, unsuspecting zebra, drinking water at the river's edge.

He decreased the pace on the machine so that it slowed, and eventually stopped. Ryan bent over to stretch his hamstrings, giving Cara a nice view. She inwardly groaned. Creating distance would be so much easier if the man weren't so damn hot.

He pulled the earphones from his ear and grabbed a towel.

"Behind!" she said, mimicking the kitchen staff who yelled that every time they stepped behind someone with something hot.

He spun around. "Thanks for the warning."

"You look very, very good right now," she said, stalking him.

His eyebrows shot up at her suggestive tone. "How about I take a quick shower and then—"

"How about you stay the way you are and let me have my way with you." Cara ran her hands up and down his sweat-soaked chest.

The look of surprise on his face was worth the price of admission. "I'm covered in sweat and I stink, and … something tells me you don't mind at all, do you?"

She stripped off every single article of clothing she had on. When she was naked, she commanded him to lie down on the treadmill. Cara lay on top of him. She kissed his forehead, his temples, licked his neck, tasting him, breathing in his distinct scent.

Then she slid Ryan's shorts down. Her mouth went around him. She savored his saltiness, taking pleasure in hearing his moans and gasps, until he stopped her. "There's a condom in the drawer over there. Get it quickly."

When she sank down on him he grabbed her hips, forcing himself deeper inside her. "You have no idea how you feel." His voice was low, almost unrecognizable.

She teased him by going excruciatingly slow until he begged her to go faster and when she did, when she knew he was almost to the point of release, she'd slow down again.

Ryan nipped at her bottom lip. "You're playing with me."

"Mmm-hmm," she said, finding that rhythm she knew would bring her to the edge.

"Tell me you're close."

"So close," she breathed.

When he brought her face down for a kiss, it was hard, urgent, letting Cara know it was his turn to take charge. He wrapped his arms around her, nudged her to the floor, and rolled on top of her, slowing the pace.

She groaned in frustration while he chuckled. "Now you know how it feels to not be in control."

"I'm never in control when it comes to you, Ryan."

His eyes never left hers as he began to move steadily. She ran her fingers through his hair and along his back, urging him to go faster. It wasn't until she arched her hips that he drove into her, their bodies slapping together in a rhythmic frenzy.

"Now," she moaned.

Ryan's body tightened as he thrust deeply a few more times, drawing out her waves of pleasure before he let himself go. He whispered her name, clutching her tighter until she almost couldn't breathe. They lay together for some time, listening to each other's breathing return to normal.

She didn't know where her body ended and his began. It was awe-inspiring. And unnerving. It complicated things and she didn't need any more complication in her life. It was a sad day when phenomenal sex was viewed as a complication, but there it was. And Cara knew she needed to do something about it before it was too late.

"I love the way you feel on me, but I can't breathe," she said.

He gave her a quick kiss and pried himself off her. "I don't think I can walk, much less work."

"Are you complaining?"

"Hell no." Ryan made his way to the bathroom. The water in the shower turned on. "Come here, you wildcat," he called.

A naked Ryan was a dangerous Ryan. Even worse was a naked Cara with a naked Ryan. Mentally, she listed all the reasons why she shouldn't join him in the shower, but as usual, her body won out.

• • •

Karma sure had a way of coming around and kicking him in the ass. How many times had Ryan given the very same speech to women that Cara was giving him now? "I need more space." "It's not you, it's me." "I'm not ready for a more serious commitment." For all the times these women had called him a jerk, he now officially knew where they were coming from. It was humbling to hear these excuses.

"You've been so great to me, Ryan," she told him. "In fact, it was you who encouraged me to go back to school, which is why I'm saying I need more time to focus on my school work. We can still see each other, of course. I mean, we work together after all, but maybe limit the nights we spend together to … " She ticked the days off her fingers. "Tuesday, Thursday, and Saturday."

He sat there calmly listening to her ramble on. They had just had two rounds of unbelievable sex, and now she was telling him she needed "more time for herself"? He didn't buy it. She would have given him the speech before pouncing on him, not after.

Cara began to pace. "Obviously I'll have to find my own place to live. And I intend on paying you back the money you lent me for the clothes."

Ryan knew this had something to do with running out on her so abruptly the other night, but the precise moment a man realized he was in love with a woman was a scary thing—exhilarating, yes, wonderful, absolutely—but scary, nonetheless. He had his head on straight about it now. He was in love with Cara. They were amazing together; he wanted more time with her, not less.

So how was he going to help *her* get her head on straight? He wouldn't pressure her right away. He'd give her the space she claimed she needed for her studies. During the days. With her added responsibilities at the restaurant, she'd be around him more, anyway. But the *designated* nights would be his to claim. Those nights would be when he would prove himself by making passionate love to her, when he would make her cry out his name, and realize how right they were for each other.

"So you're okay with what I've just told you?" She stood in front of him, hands on hips, waiting for a response.

No, he wasn't okay with it, but the last thing she needed was for him to become an overbearing, insensitive boyfriend.

"Uh, sure."

Her eyes flashed with what looked like anger. Why should she be angry? Ryan was giving her what she said she wanted. He reached for her, but she evaded his grasp.

"My space has to start now. Sorry, but I need to get some homework done."

His jaw went rigid, but he chose to portray a casualness he didn't feel. "No problem. I'll see you later."

...

That was easy. Cara's fears had been confirmed. The fact that Ryan hadn't objected to her needing more space proved he didn't much care which way their relationship went. He was only supposed to be a sexual Band-Aid. Isn't that what she said? His sole purpose had been to get her mind off Robbie, and he had served that purpose. A little too well. She should have known she wasn't the type of woman who could remain emotionally detached after making love with a man.

Why couldn't she be more like the women in this day and age? The ones who treated men like boy-toys for their own pleasure and satisfaction, who were okay with not having a serious relationship with every man they slept with. Instead, Cara had become the type of woman Ryan had complained about. Attached and wanting more.

Damn my sensitivity.

She desperately missed her mom and dad. They had always been there for her when she needed to talk, especially about boys. "Follow your heart," her mom would have said. But Cara had followed her heart with Robbie and her heart had been broken. How could she ever fully trust another man when she was so scared of getting hurt again?

Her grandfather would have told her to make meatballs. There was no problem that couldn't be solved by getting back to basics. "Food never betrays you, Cara; it comforts." He used to say the feel of the raw meat through his fingers and the aroma of the spices calmed him. Preparing meatballs had a meditative effect on him; it allowed him to clear his mind and focus on the task in front of him.

Since Cara wasn't able to make meatballs, she did the next best thing. She went to the beach. The sun was shining, but the air was brisk, so she wore her new jacket. She could have used a scarf. And gloves. Probably a hat, too.

Surprisingly, Dino sat in his same spot, painting. She jogged over to him. He acknowledged her with a nod while she hopped back and forth on one leg trying to stay warm.

"I can't believe you're here," she said. "I figured you'd pack it up once summer was over."

"It's my excuse for getting out of the house." He leaned back in his chair and studied his picture.

Cara tilted her head in confusion, trying to figure out what the heck he had painted.

"Rocks and sand," Dino said, answering her unspoken question. "What does it look like to you?"

She gave it some serious thought. "The rocks make me think of overstuffed cream puffs covered in rich, dark chocolate, and the sand resembles whipped cream filling, spilling out all around them."

Dino stared off into sea. "I know this restaurant," he said, and started packing up his things.

They had two cream puffs each, along with cappuccinos at a café called Fratelli, which means "brothers" in Italian. They were good. Not as good as her mother used to make whenever she or Anthony brought home an A, but still good. Cara noted the owner of the restaurant didn't charge them.

She gave Dino a hug when saying goodbye, which made him blush.

"What was that for?" he asked gruffly.

"I was feeling homesick, but I feel better now. Thank you."

Cara was determined not to let the situation with Ryan affect her mood or her work. They could still have fun together for the time being. She simply had to keep her feelings for him in check, so she didn't get hurt.

Her spirits quickly did a nosedive when she came down for work and heard Ryan informing Brady about his decision to change the menu. She braced herself for the inevitable storm.

"So, you're going to transform Bella into a restaurant for commoners?" Brady bellowed.

Ryan's posture grew straighter. "I don't look at it like that, Brady. Either we change things or Bella becomes a restaurant for ghosts."

Brady spotted her. "So you think pouring tomato sauce over everything is the answer, do you?"

"It's a better bet than trying to get people to eat duck livers covered in candied Brussels sprouts, and pickled pig's feet stuffed with truffles," she shot back.

"You listen here, Brooklyn—"

"At least I know real food when I taste it."

"You wouldn't know real food if it bit you in the—"

Ryan quickly intervened. "Knock it off." He turned to Cara. "Brady is a master at what he does. Please don't insult him." Brady stuck his tongue out at her. Ryan pivoted to Brady and said, "I think Cara may be right about the more simple tastes of this neighborhood. We're going to try the new menu and see what happens." She stuck her tongue out at Brady.

Brady removed his apron and tossed it on the counter. "Like I always say, 'There's no place like home.' This Pop-Pop is going home."

"You're walking out twenty minutes before the dinner rush?" There was panic in Ryan's voice.

"*Rush* being the operative word. Yes, as a matter of fact, I am. Let Brooklyn take over; she's done it with everything else."

"You don't care about getting a favorable reference from me?"

"Nah. Being away from my kid was killing me. You're giving me an excuse to become a stay-at-home dad and write a cookbook for kids."

"A cookbook for kids?" Cara and Ryan said together.

"For kids with a more discerning palate. Mac n' cheese with creamy béchamel and sharp cheddar, crab fish sticks with a sour cream and mustard sauce, lamb-feta burgers." Brady waved to everyone in the kitchen. "*Sayonara*, my peeps."

In a deathly calm voice that betrayed the frantic look in his eyes, Ryan said, "What am I supposed to do now?"

"Start looking for another chef?" she suggested.

Ryan's hand went to his stomach. "You wouldn't happen to have any antacids, would you? I'm all out."

Leah wandered into the kitchen, a bewildered expression on her face. "What the hell happened to Ginny? Did she go to bed last night and wake up a hussy?"

Ginny wobbled in wearing stilettos identical to Cara's, her long hair flowing around her shoulders. "Brady just told me he quit to become a house-husband and write a cookbook. Is he joking?"

"I'm afraid not," Ryan said. "He didn't see eye to eye with me on Bella needing a menu change." He pointed to Ginny's head. "You need to do something about your hair."

She shook her mane like she was in a shampoo commercial. "You mean like highlights or layers?"

"Put it in a bun like you used to. There are health codes."

Ginny teetered away, mumbling something about how men were always trying to squash her individuality.

"And to think she was the sensible one of all of us," Leah said.

"I need a minute alone in my office," Ryan said. He went inside and shut the door.

Leah looked concerned. "Is he all right?"

"I think he's a bit overwhelmed with all the changes."

"Speaking of changes, did you have something to do with Ginny's transformation?"

"I might have suggested some things she could do to let out her inner ... " Cara searched for the right word.

"Beast?" Leah suggested. "She grabbed my bag of pretzels and scarfed them down like she hadn't eaten in a year."

Cara laughed. "She's making up for lost time."

"She keeps eating like that and she'll have to make up all her time in the gym."

• • •

Ryan ransacked his desk drawers, searching for a loose antacid that might have escaped the package. His ulcer was acting up and he knew having a drink would only make the pain worse.

Where was he supposed to find a chef as good as Brady, and on such short notice? Maybe this whole menu change wasn't such a good idea. But what choice did he have? Bella was skiing downhill fast and he was desperate. Actually, Bella had already reached the bottom of the hill, but thanks to Dino's money, not to mention future money, he had a shot at resurrecting it.

He wanted the restaurant to succeed and he wanted Cara to be proud of him. He had wasted enough time wallowing over his failed baseball career and his failed marriage. Back in the game now, he was up to bat and intended to hit a home run.

Ryan stepped out of his office with a newfound confidence. Whatever obstacles were thrown his way, he'd deal with them. That was life. One curveball after another. He could handle anything.

Anything except his brother, James, who was heading his way.

James looked the same as he had almost three years before, right down to his smug smile.

"Long time, no see, brother," James said, extending his hand.

Ryan looked down at the hand and then back up to his eyes. "What are you doing here?"

"Dad sent me to check out your place. He said you told him it was a raging success." He smirked. "I can tell I'll have to wait hours for a table."

"You came, you saw, now leave."

James sat at the bar. He eyed the two younger women one stool down. "Not just yet. It was a long drive and I need a drink."

Ryan clenched his jaw so tightly he was surprised his teeth didn't shatter. "One drink. And then you need to get the hell out of my restaurant."

"Bartender." James snapped his fingers at Oz. "Hennessey. Neat."

Ryan's cell rang, and as he stepped outside to answer it there was only one question going through his mind.

Would I take greater pleasure from throwing my brother's pompous ass out on the sidewalk myself, or should I have someone from the kitchen do it so I can watch?

CHAPTER 20

Cara almost didn't recognize Johnny-boy sitting at the end of the bar. It was the first time she had ever seen him in street clothes. He had on dark blue jeans cuffed at the ends; a pressed, white T-shirt; and black work boots.

"I like your glasses," she told him, pointing to his tortoise-color frames.

"Thanks."

"I hear you're off to the big city."

He nodded. "Yep."

"Going to pursue an acting career, huh?"

"Gonna try."

She waited for something, anything from him. "Okay then. Take care of yourself."

"Same to you," he said, tipping his head to her.

She was about to leave when she stopped herself. "Do you mind if I ask you a question?"

"Ask away."

"Why do you think men cheat?"

"Fear of a woman's power," he said with conviction. "Love for one woman can feel overpowering and all-encompassing to a weak man. So if he cheats on his woman, he deludes himself into thinking he'll lose some of that love for her." He leaned into Cara. "He's then able to handle love by falsely assuming he has the upper hand."

That was more than Johnny-boy had uttered to her their entire working relationship. "Is this personal experience speaking?"

He shook his head. "I worship women. I love women and respect them." He smiled. "I was raised by a single mother and two older sisters. I'm perfectly happy letting you ladies have the upper hand. In case you haven't noticed, I don't say much."

"No kidding."

"Women just want someone who listens to them. It's very simple. Men make it so much harder than it needs to be."

Cara patted him on the shoulder. "Your mom and sisters did a great job."

An older woman returned from the restroom and joined Johnny-boy.

"Oh, is this your mother?" Cara asked.

"This is Kathleen. We're moving to New York together," Johnny-boy said.

Yeesh. It was like asking an overweight woman when she was due. Cara took note of the jewels on Kathleen's fingers and the diamond tennis bracelet, along with her Balenciaga purse. It finally dawned on her what Oz and Ryan had been hinting at the whole time. This was Johnny-boy's sugar mama, or cougar, or whatever you called an older woman who was into much younger guys.

Oz rushed up to her. "I need to talk to you."

"Excuse me," she said to Johnny-boy and Kathleen. She followed Oz to the opposite end of the bar. "That was awkward. What's up?"

"A man claiming to be Ryan's brother just walked in, and judging by the look on Ryan's face, I don't think he's too happy to see him."

• • •

Cara studied Ryan's brother. They were both tall with a slim build, same golden-brown hair. The eyes were different though. Ryan's were expressive, changeable, while his brother's were dark and judgmental. There was something about him she didn't trust, which struck her as weird considering she hadn't said two words to the guy. Ryan must have his reasons for being estranged from him. She only wished she knew what they were.

Ryan's brother caught her staring at him and his eyes immediately dropped down to her chest. Subtlety was not one of his virtues, but since he was related to Ryan she'd give him a little slack.

He crooked his finger at her, motioning her over. "I couldn't help but notice you checking me out," he said.

Very little slack.

"It's more like morbid curiosity. Sort of like watching a car wreck on the side of the road."

"James," he said, introducing himself. "And I don't bite. Unless you want me to."

"I'm not up to date with all my shots, James," she said. "I'm Cara. I work with Ryan."

He let out a low whistle. "Ryan's always had excellent taste in women, whether they were for work or for pleasure. Or both."

Her lip curled in disgust. So much for trying to get to know the family. "Well James, charmed, I'm sure."

She turned to leave, only to have him grab her arm and pull her closer. "I was thinking of getting a motel room tonight. Maybe you and I can—"

All Cara saw next was James being pulled backward and Ryan's fist crashing into his upper cheek. James fell to the floor.

"That's what I should have done three years ago, you son-of-a-bitch!" Ryan said, kicking his brother in the ribs.

Oz ran out from behind the bar and grabbed Ryan. "Chill out, man. That's enough."

Cara had never seen this side of Ryan before. She knew what it was like to fight with a brother, but there was more to this troubled relationship than the typical sibling issues.

James sat up, holding his nose. There was blood trickling down his face. "How does it feel to not be the golden boy anymore,

Ryan? Feels like shit, doesn't it?" He stood up slowly and reached for a wad of napkins to dab his nose.

"What are you talking about?"

"I'm the oldest son, and yet I was always following in your footsteps. I was supposed to be the better one, the more successful one."

"It's my fault you couldn't make the cut in baseball? Or top me in commissions in the family business?"

James lunged for Ryan, but Johnny-boy jumped between them. "I couldn't make the cut at anything with you in the picture. Dad couldn't get a hard-on for anyone else!"

"That's why you screwed my wife? Because you were jealous of me?"

"No, I screwed your wife because she was a hot piece of ass."

And there it was. The clue that had been missing this whole time. Cara couldn't believe after all they shared, Ryan hadn't told her it was his brother who had betrayed him.

He grabbed James by the front of his shirt and slammed him against the bar. "You ruined my life for a quick roll in the hay?"

James pushed back with all his strength. "Trust me. It wasn't quick. And it wasn't one time."

Ryan went for his brother again, but this time James nailed him with an upper cut to the eye.

"Stop them before they kill each other!" Cara shouted.

It took both Oz and Johnny-boy to pull the brothers off one another.

"Go report home to Daddy, big brother. Tell him what a fuck up I am."

"I don't need to. You've already proven it these last few years." James twisted free and grabbed his leather jacket off the stool. He spit once on the floor before staggering out.

She ran over to Ryan. "Are you all right?" She tried to touch the cut underneath his eye, but he knocked her hand away. "Why didn't you tell me it was your brother who slept with your wife?"

He stared at her, his eyes unfocused. "Does it really matter, Cara?"

Shouts came from the kitchen. "Fire!"

The remaining customers fled the dining room. Ryan snapped to attention and bolted toward the kitchen. Cara followed. Smoke billowed out through the double doors as Chris and Manny came running out.

"Where the hell are the fire extinguishers? Get a goddamn extinguisher!" Ryan yelled to his sous chef.

"I tried all the extinguishers, Ryan," she heard Chris say. "There's nothing coming out of them."

"Oz, grab the fire extinguisher by the bar!" Cara said, remembering where she had seen another one.

By the time Oz made it back, flames had engulfed the entire kitchen.

"We have to get out of here!" She pulled Ryan away. "Somebody call 911!"

Sirens sounded in the distance. They all made a run for the front door.

"Is everyone out?" Ryan asked, his eyes darting around frantically.

"Yes, go!" Oz said, shoving him outside.

Cara stood with Ryan in the middle of the street, along with Chris and Manny, Ginny, Oz, Leah, Johnny-boy and Kathleen, and a few remaining customers. They were all in wide-eyed disbelief.

"What happened in the kitchen?" Ryan demanded to no one in particular.

"There was a grease fire, but it was a small one," Chris said. "I don't understand why it spread like it did. I used the extinguisher next to the stove, but nothing came out."

"When did you get the extinguishers last serviced, Ryan?" Oz asked.

"Serviced?"

Two fire engines pulled up, along with a wailing ambulance. Three police cars followed.

"Clear the way!" One firefighter worked on connecting the supply hose to a hydrant, while another two with hoses barreled through the front door of the restaurant. Two more firefighters, one wielding a chainsaw, used the ladder truck to get on the roof and create a hole for the smoke to vent.

Dazed, Cara watched the thick, black smoke pour out of Bella. She gave Ryan's arm a slight squeeze for comfort, but he remained rigid and impassive. Oz had his arm around Ginny in an attempt to keep her warm. Leah muttered curses under her breath while Johnny-boy wisely kept silent.

A black luxury sedan pulled up at the curb half a block down. Dino and Frankie the Firebomb stepped out.

"I'll be right back," she told Ryan. Cara met both men halfway. "How did you know about the fire?" she asked Dino.

"I always know what's happening with my properties."

"You own this building?"

Dino nodded. "How did the fire start?"

"I guess there was a small grease fire that got out of control. And a problem with the fire extinguishers."

Dino and Frankie exchanged looks. "That's most unfortunate for Mr. Garridy," Dino finally said. "Insurance doesn't pay out on negligence."

Still in shock, she mumbled, "Everything I own in Crabclaw is in that building."

"Let me know if you need anything," Dino said.

She didn't know what she needed at this point, or would need in the future. All her things were probably ruined, either from fire, smoke, water damage, or all three.

When Cara made her way back to Ryan, he took her by the arm, pulling her out of everyone's earshot. In a harsh whisper, he said, "Did you do this?"

"Did I do *what?*"

"You caused this?"

"The fire? You think I set fire to your restaurant?"

Ryan's features twisted into a furious rage. "Did you tell them to do it?" He motioned toward Dino and Frankie.

"Are you out of your friggin' mind?"

"Why are they here? How did they know about the fire if they had nothing to do with it?"

She stared at him, open-mouthed, trying to wrap her mind around the fact that he had just accused her of torching his place. "This is Dino's building."

"It makes perfect sense now."

"What makes perfect sense?"

Leah ran over to them. "The fireman needs to interview you both about what happened." Her eyes jumped from Cara to Ryan, and back again to Cara. "What's going on?"

Cara was barely able to get the words out. "Ryan seems to think I started the fire."

"Are you insane?" Leah cried.

"I didn't say she started it, but I think she had something to do with it."

"What reason would she have for trying to burn your restaurant down?"

"For the insurance money," he said, as if it were perfectly obvious. "It'd be a perfect way for us to start from scratch, wouldn't it? And with your connections to a trained professional—"

"You mean Frankie?"

His silence said it all. Her head spun. The man who had given her a place to stay, along with a job, who had made love to her like she mattered—the man she realized she had fallen in love with—was accusing her of being an arsonist. The betrayal she felt was worse than when she found Robbie cheating on her.

"I can't believe you'd think I had anything to do with this."

Leah jabbed her finger at Ryan's chest. "You need to stop talking crazy and get it together. Go find out what the hell happened with your restaurant. And you," she said to Cara, "need to talk to the fireman, and then you're coming home with me."

• • •

A couple hours later, only a few people remained at the scene. Some police, the restoration crew who was in the process of boarding up the windows and hanging yellow caution tape, and the arson investigator. Ryan stared at Bella, his baby, in disbelief. All his hopes and dreams had been extinguished. Literally in less than a night.

The arson investigator, a balding man in his fifties, approached with a pen and pad. "We won't know for sure what caused the fire to spread for another day or so," he said. "I'll need all your insurance information, and anything else you may think is pertinent to this case."

Frankie the Firebomb's face flashed before Ryan, but he decided to stay quiet on his suspicions until he read the official fire report. How could a small grease fire get so out of hand? And why hadn't the fire extinguishers done their job?

His mind was reeling from many unanswered questions—the most important one being Cara's involvement. He would have never suspected her until Dino and Frankie showed up out of nowhere. It was obvious Dino was willing to help Cara out, but how far would he go?

"Burn the place down and start over," she had joked a while back.

Emotionally and physically drained from the evening, he was no longer able to make sense of anything. His brother had brought back so many feelings he wasn't prepared to deal with—feelings Ryan thought he had long had under control. His head hurt, acrid smoke filled his nostrils, and the realization that he had fallen in love with another woman who couldn't be trusted made his chest ache.

The sense of defeat he was experiencing again didn't anger him like it had in the past. Defeat was an all too familiar emotion, almost comforting in the way that becoming numb was disturbingly comforting. Ryan took one last look at Bella before turning his back on her.

CHAPTER 21

Two days later, Cara returned to the restaurant to see whether anything of hers in the apartment was salvageable. The front door was wide open. Ryan stood behind the bar, lost in thought.

"I came by to see if I could grab some of my stuff," she said. He appeared tired, worn out, with dark circles under his eyes, but she refused to feel sorry for him.

"Hey, Cara," was all he said.

After an awkward silence, she asked, "Can I go upstairs?"

"I just got a call from the arson investigator. Turns out the grease fire grew out of control due to a faulty hood and duct system. A hood and duct system I should have had serviced months ago but didn't, along with the out-of-date fire extinguishers."

"Great, now I can sleep better knowing you don't think I'm an arsonist anymore. You can collect your insurance money and start over."

"That's just it," he said with a short, bitter laugh. "My insurance company won't pay out due to negligence on my part."

Her heart was breaking for him and his sad situation, but she still couldn't forgive his accusations and blind mistrust. "That's too bad."

"I'm sorry for the things I said to you, Cara. I … there was no excuse—"

"Don't worry about it," she said, stopping him. "You have bigger problems on your hands."

"It's just that you had joked about burning the place down, and then Frankie showed up and told me he did good work. You kept saying everything would work out, to trust you."

Her temper flared. "I told you everything would work out because I believed in you, Ryan. That's what people do when they're in a relationship. They trust each other. They open up to each other."

"Is that what you would call what we were in? I thought it was 'physical therapy.'"

"How could it have been anything else? God forbid you have an emotional investment in anything. You're so afraid of failing that you take the *why bother* approach with everything you do."

He looked as if she had just slapped him. "Where is this coming from?"

"You couldn't trust me enough to tell me it was your brother who had betrayed you, especially after I poured my heart out to you over my own betrayal?"

"That's the difference between men and women. Women talk. A lot."

"Don't give me that. It's because you don't trust anyone. You're waiting for an excuse—any excuse—for someone or something to let you down. At the first sign of trouble, what did you do? You accused me of burning down your restaurant."

"I said I was sorry."

"They're just words, Ryan. They mean nothing."

"What do you want from me?"

She wanted his trust, his willingness to be open and honest with her. Most of all, Cara wanted his love. But she also knew she couldn't force these things from him if he wasn't ready.

"Right now, I just want my stuff."

• • •

He waited three days before going to see Cara. Leah answered the door but didn't seem surprised to see him. When she invited Ryan in, he shook his head.

"I'm allergic to Ouch and I'd rather have a clear head when I talk to Cara."

"Do you have any idea what you're going to do now?"

He smiled. "Not a damn clue."

Cara came to the door. She, unlike Leah, appeared surprised and not very pleased to see him.

"Before you slam the door in my face, I want you to hear me out."

She stepped outside the door, closing it behind her. He had to resist the urge to pull her into his arms and kiss away her anger over the many stupid things he had said.

"Would it help if I apologized again?" he said.

"I'm not angry at you anymore. In fact, I'm completely … "

Uh-oh. If a woman wasn't angry anymore, it meant she was—

" … apathetic."

Worse than angry. He sighed. "I was wrong. I made a mistake. Can we move on from here?"

"Where do you want to move to? Having sex on the kitchen counters? Or the bar?"

"Absolutely. But only if you want to, of course," he said, grinning.

She turned away. "I should have known better. I don't do casual, Ryan. I never have. Sleeping with you was a huge mistake."

His face dropped. "How can you say that? We're amazing together."

"No, we have amazing sex together. There's a big difference."

"Isn't that all you said you wanted?" He was fishing, urging her to admit she had feelings for him.

"Yes."

"So that's all it was for you? Just sex. Nothing more?"

Cara pushed the curls back from her eyes. "It was just sex. Nothing more."

He let out a whoosh of air from his lungs. "I see."

"I've decided to go back to Bensonhurst to stay with my brother until I graduate. I'm leaving here once the semester ends."

He touched her arm. "What would you say if I asked you to stay in Crabclaw with me?"

If she was surprised by his invitation, she didn't show it.

"I'd tell you that for once I'm doing what I need to do for myself." She opened the apartment door and stepped inside. "Goodbye, Ryan," she said, before quietly shutting the door.

• • •

Cara and Leah stood next to the Pimpmobile. Leah hugged her tightly. "I'm going to miss you, but I'm glad you'll be home with your family for the holidays."

"I'll miss you, too. Thanks for putting up with me this last month so I could finish the semester. I have only one more to go before I get my degree."

"Then what are you planning to do?"

"Get a job as a cocktail waitress." They both laughed.

"I almost forgot to tell you Ginny called this morning. She's working at a restaurant called Alberto's two towns over. Guess what else she told me?"

Cara stupidly hoped it was a snippet of news about Ryan. It had been an excruciatingly long month being in the same town as him, without seeing him. The further away she was from Crabclaw, the sooner she could begin to forget him.

"She's going out on a date with Oz. Can you believe it? Slut-boy."

"Oz isn't that bad. I think they make a cute couple."

"Whatever," Leah said, rolling her eyes. "How about you? You ever plan on speaking to Ryan again?"

She shrugged. "Who knows? Maybe one day." She opened the driver's side door and slid in.

"Is there a reason you didn't tell him you were in love with him?"

"What makes you think—? Oh, never mind." There wasn't any point in trying to pretend with Leah. "Because he never told me he was in love with me, that's why."

Leah gave her a look that said she was as thick as a six-dollar milkshake. "The fact that he came here to talk to you means he loves you. That he asked you to stay in Crabclaw with him means he loves you. Geez, Cara. What more do you want from the guy? His left testicle?"

"You don't get it. Ryan might be happy with me for a little while, but he's never said anything to lead me to believe there is any kind of future between us. You even said so yourself. He's not the settling down type."

"People change when they meet the right one. When I met my husband, suddenly I didn't want anyone else."

"If you recall, our agenda was different," she said. "Ryan and I were supposed to be casual fun only."

"When did that change for you?"

Cara was quiet for a moment. "When I decided to sleep with him the first time."

"It was never casual for you, was it?"

"No, but I did a good job making him think it was."

"I guess that makes you the winner for the best actress award," Leah said drily. "You know, in all the time I've known Ryan, I've never seen him do as much for a woman as he did for you. The man put a roof over your head and gave you a job, even after you screwed him over. He shared your bed, not to mention he trusted you enough to make decisions for the well-being of his restaurant."

"He never said he loved me, Leah."

"He didn't have to, you dope. Actions speak louder than words, especially when it comes to men. You think Jeff tells me he loves me? Only when he's had too much to drink and then it's just sloppy talk. But he shows me he loves me by putting the toilet seat down or surprising me with a weekend away to a B&B."

Cara slammed the car door and squinted up at Leah, shielding her eyes from the sun. "Suddenly you're a cheerleader for Team Ryan?"

"What I'm trying to say is, instead of accusing him of having trust issues, maybe you should examine your own."

"You couldn't have this therapy session with me a few weeks ago? You had to wait until the day I was heading home?"

Leah grinned. "I've had way too much coffee this morning. The excess caffeine suddenly made everything painfully obvious to me. You're welcome."

"Send me your bill." She started the car and the Pimp roared to life. Leah blew her kisses as she pulled away.

Once again, Cara was leaving behind heartache and heading toward the unknown.

CHAPTER 22

"Eddie, another Scotch, please." Ryan drained the last of his drink and pushed the glass toward the bartender. He glanced up at the TV screen above the bar, but couldn't make out the score of the basketball game. Not that he cared about the score. He didn't care about much these days.

Bella was history and so was the woman he loved. And for good reason. He'd accused her of burning down his restaurant, for God's sake. Talk about having some trust issues. Ryan's biggest regret was never telling Cara he loved her. He'd wanted to so many times, but could never get the words out. What was he so scared of? Trusting another woman fully and getting hurt again? Didn't everyone say that was the risk you took for love? Except he had taken a lot of risks already in his life, and they hadn't paid off.

His defeatist attitude made him sick and yet he couldn't seem to change it. Boy, had his past royally screwed his future.

Staring down at his fresh drink, he knew it should be the last one for the night before driving home. Although he hadn't yet reached the comfortably numb state he needed in order to go home to his empty condo. It was ironic that what was perfectly acceptable before was now intolerable. He used to welcome being alone, especially after a wild dating frenzy or whenever a relationship turned sour.

But that was BC—Before Cara. Now whenever he was alone, his thoughts went to her. The more he drank, the blurrier the thoughts became until he eventually passed out in bed. What a life.

"Ryan?"

He turned slightly. It was Ginny. "How are you doing?"

"I'm good," she said. "How are you?"

"How do I look?"

"Like crap."

He nodded. He had always appreciated her bluntness. "What are you doing here?"

"I'm … meeting someone for dinner."

"Good for you." He toasted her with his glass. "Make sure he treats you like a queen. You deserve no less."

"How's Cara?" she asked.

An innocent question that took him a moment to answer. "I wouldn't know. She went back to Brooklyn."

Her surprise was obvious. "But I thought … I mean, you two were perfect together. I'm sorry. It's none of my business."

"No, it's fine. I was the one who messed things up. I take full responsibility."

Ginny cocked her head to one side. "So, what are you going to do to get her back?"

He smiled wryly into his Scotch. "Cara deserves better than me."

"Oh, Ryan." She sighed. "The entire time I worked for you, I saw women come and go. None of them brought out the best in you. Until Cara. And let me say right now, you were a mess when she met you. All those other women were with you when you were at the top of your game, but not Cara. She lifted you up. You both lifted each other up. That's what makes a truly great relationship. Someone who sticks by you through the bad times."

He finished off his drink. "Relationships are too complicated for some of us."

"You're many things, Ryan Garridy, but I never thought quitter was one of them." She pointed. "Look, there's Oz." Ginny went over to him and motioned in Ryan's direction. They came over, and Oz shook his hand.

"This is a coincidence," Ryan said.

Ginny blushed. "Imagine that."

"Just stopped in to grab a burger. Anyone want a burger?" Oz asked.

"I could go for a burger," Ginny said.

"How about you, Ryan?" Oz said.

"Nah, I think I'll go home. You guys have fun." He stood, steadying himself.

"You okay to drive, bro?"

He sure hoped so. "Yeah, no problem. Oh, and by the way, Ginny, you should wear red more often."

"Thank you."

Before Ryan stepped out into the night, he turned just in time to see Oz place his hand on Ginny's lower back. She looked up at Oz and gave him a smile. The same appreciative, intimate smile Cara used to give Ryan.

•••

Fate. Ryan had never considered the word more than since he'd met Cara. How else could he explain the series of events leading her to him? Or the fact she was the last woman he ever thought he'd fall for and yet … he fell. Hard.

And how else could he explain meeting a man named Mike less than a month later, who happened to sit next to him one evening at that very same bar. His daughter was running late for dinner, he told Ryan, so he had some time to kill. They got to talking. Just so happened Mike was a therapist.

"There comes a point in everyone's lives when it helps to have an objective ear," he explained. "I don't tell people what to do. I help them get rid of what's blocking them so they can figure out for themselves what they need to do."

It'd probably be easier for Ryan to figure out what he needed to do if he were sober more often.

"You married, Mike?"

"Twenty-eight years this June."

"What's the secret?"

He was thoughtful for a moment. "Love is a decision. You make the decision to love a person and you stick with that decision through good times and bad. You never give up." He took out his wallet and offered Ryan a business card. "If you ever just want to talk."

CHAPTER 23

Five months later

"I'm heading out," Cara said to the bar manager as she zipped up her jacket and wrapped a scarf around her neck. It was the end of May and still chilly, especially at two in the morning. "See you tomorrow night." She waved to one of the bus boys.

Margo, one of the other cocktail waitresses, caught up with her. "How'd you make out tonight?"

"I had to do a tequila shot, since I was the one who got Mr. 'I think there's a hole in my glass because all my beer is gone, so I get a free one, right?'"

Margo laughed. "At least he tips well. Some asshat left me a religious pamphlet instead of a tip. *The Power of God*. Is God gonna pay my rent this month?"

Cara stopped in her tracks. Standing in the doorway was Ryan. Her heart surged at the sight of him. She hadn't allowed herself to think about him these last months, but seeing him now made her realize just how much she had missed him.

Still, she was cautious. Why was he here, and why did he have a piano keyboard under one arm? "How did you find me?" she asked.

"Leah."

"Next question. Why?"

He took a step toward her. She took a step back. "Remember when you said I was so afraid of failing, and that's why I wasn't able to make an emotional investment in anything? You were right."

"Is this guy your boyfriend?" Margo asked.

"No," Cara answered as Ryan said, "Yes."

Ryan said to Margo, "You see … I'm sorry, I didn't get your name."

"Margo."

"You see, Margo, I met Cara when I was a different man. A man who was down on his luck, had one too many disappointments in life, was unable to commit to anything." Ryan went over to one of the tables and set his keyboard down. "I'm a changed man now, and it's all because of this woman right here."

"Awww, how sweet," Margo said.

Cara started to say he was full of it, but Ryan wasn't done with his speech. "I did some therapy during these last few months, although I have to say, Cara, you're much more therapeutic for me. What the counselor did teach me, however, was that failing miserably is an inevitable part of life, even if my father doesn't happen to think so."

"You poor thing," she heard Margo mutter.

"It's all right, I don't need pity, Margo. I just need love. Love from this woman." He held out his hand to Cara, who was beginning to wonder whether there were hidden cameras filming this whole thing. "And to show you just how much progress I've made, I'm going to sing my own version of a well-known song. Do you know 'Mandy' by Barry Manilow?"

"Barry Manilow?"

"My mom loves Barry Manilow," Margo said.

"I can't sing very well and I haven't played piano since junior high."

"You don't have to do this. You really *don't*," she emphasized.

"Of course he does," Margo said.

He tapped a few keys on the piano. "I plan on failing miserably at this song, but the huge emotional investment I've made in the words are worth the humiliation." He winked at Cara.

"Oh no," she groaned.

Ryan cleared his throat and started playing a few chords on the keyboard.

> First time that I saw you there,
> Sick as a dog with all that hair …

He had an audience. The manager, bus boys, and remaining bartenders and servers had all gathered 'round to see what was going on.

"Please tell me this isn't happening," Cara said as Margo shushed her.

> A shell of a woman,
> Bitter attitude,
> Crying all the time,
> All day and night.
>
> Made me want to dry your eyes,
> Make you laugh, at least a smile.
> I didn't want love twice.
> You became my whole life.
> Didn't realize
> Until you left me, oh Cara.

His voice cracked as he hit the wrong note, but he quickly got back on track.

> You came and you made me your meatballs,
> But I kept you away, oh Cara.
> You grilled me and drilled me with questions,
> And you forced me to change, oh Cara.

Mouths were agape. The men laughed at the meatball line. The women gazed at him with longing and adoration. With the next lines, he looked up from the keyboard and stared straight into Cara's eyes.

> I'm standing here a broken man,
> Have no idea who I am.
> Life's been a fight,
> Elusive love,
> Emotions wrapped up so tight,
> Now nothing makes sense, oh Cara.
>
> You came and you healed me, I thank you.
> But you sent me away, oh Cara.
> You showed me that love isn't scary,
> So I ask you today, oh Cara.

She bit down on her lip to keep from crying. She no longer cared about anyone else in the room, except for Ryan. He had put himself out there *for her*. It didn't matter if people thought he was a fool; he was *her* fool.

> Can't rewind the past
> Need your forgiveness,
> Want you in my life,
> I'm begging you please, oh Cara.

Ryan's voice cracked again. He stopped playing for a moment. "And now for my grand finale. Listen closely." His voice quivered a little as he started to sing again.

> You came and you made me more manly,
> But you sent me away, oh Cara.

> You trusted and loved me completely.
> Will you marry me please, oh Cara?

There were collective gasps all around. Margo sighed. "If you don't marry him, I will."

Everybody clapped. They quickly disbanded to give the couple some privacy. Cara went to the man who had just asked for her hand in marriage—the last man on Earth she ever dreamed would utter those words.

"I can't believe you did this. You were awful," she said, laughing and sobbing at the same time. "But I loved it."

"I *was* awful," he agreed. He took her hands in his. In a more serious tone, he said, "I told myself I'd never get married again, Cara. I closed myself off from that possibility, because I didn't want to risk going through the hell I went through a second time."

"What changed your mind?"

"You surpassed whatever dream girl I had conjured up in my mind when you passed out at my feet that day at the farmer's market."

She smiled through her tears. "I'll admit that was the exact moment I fell for you."

Ryan reached out and wiped the corners of her eyes. "To say I'm the luckiest man in this world would be an understatement. You've brought purpose to my life. I'm a better person because of you."

And then he finally said the words that sealed the deal.

"I love you. I adore you. I cherish you. You're the most beautiful, spirited, passionate, opinionated woman I have ever laid eyes on. There is no one else for me. You're it."

"Well," she said breathlessly.

"Trust me," he said, reaching for her hands. "I promise I won't let you down."

She knew he had been deeply hurt by love before, just like she had. She also knew that if and when he ever allowed himself to love a woman again, he'd never betray her. This truth resonated within her soul.

He pressed his forehead against hers. "You haven't answered my question."

She wrapped her arms around his neck. "You bet your sweet ass I'll marry you."

CHAPTER 24

Two weeks later, Cara stretched lazily in Ryan's bed in Crabclaw. Sunlight was attempting to break through the marine cloud layer. It was the beginning of summer. Her favorite time of year. Figuring it had to be around nine, she was horrified to see it was actually past eleven.

After having a big celebration lunch with Anthony and the family after her graduation ceremony, she and Ryan had headed back to the shore. He stopped at a small, intimate restaurant that overlooked the bay, where they drank champagne and had a few appetizers. Then Ryan announced he was going to do things the "proper" way.

He got down on one knee and presented her with a single solitaire diamond ring.

"Isn't this much better than the sound of a hundred cats being run over by a cement mixer?" he said, slipping the ring on her finger.

She giggled. "Your singing wasn't *that* bad."

When they arrived at his place he carried her into the bedroom and undressed her. They made love passionately, with an intensity that took Cara's breath away. The level of trust and commitment they had finally reached had enhanced their lovemaking in ways she never believed possible.

Cara padded into the kitchen and poured herself a cup of coffee. Ryan was sitting at the dining room table, scouring the online classifieds. She kissed his cheek and sat down with him.

"See anything for me?" she asked.

"A position for a counselor or a server?"

"Both? Neither?"

"With a BA now, you can do whatever you want."

She snorted. "Yeah, the possibilities are endless."

"You have a lot to keep you busy. Planning our wedding, being a fit model for Leah's designs, planning our wedding, psychoanalyzing me, planning our wedding."

She gave him a purposefully blank look. "Yes, but don't you think I should plan our wedding?"

He gave her that slow, sexy smile of his—the one that could launch a thousand orgasms. "I think you should plan our wedding." His cell phone rang. "I don't recognize the number, but it's local." He answered, "Ryan Garridy."

After about five minutes of Ryan listening to whoever was on the other end, along with a few uh-huhs thrown in, he handed the phone to her.

"It's Dino. He has a business proposition for us."

• • •

A bit more salt, Cara decided after tasting the primavera sauce bubbling on the stove. She savored her last few minutes of peace and quiet in the commercial kitchen.

"How late am I?" Leah said, waddling in. "I had to stop along the way and take a fucking piss for the hundredth time."

"Relax. You're not late. And you know you can't use that language once the baby comes."

"I know. I'm going to pull a Brady and replace the f-word with 'duck.' Duck you! That's ducking great! And so on."

Cara looked down at Leah's enormous pregnant belly. "Are you sure you're up to helping me cater Dino's granddaughter's wedding today? I don't want your water breaking on his lawn."

"I would kill to have my water break today, so I can pop this girl out. Look at me! I can barely move. I'm thinking of designing a line of lingerie for pregnant women. Whales and Walruses."

Ryan burst in, immediately going to Cara's side. "Do you think you should be standing for this long?"

"I'm only three months pregnant. I think I can still operate at a normal functioning capacity."

"I'm fine, Ryan," Leah said. "Thanks for asking."

He smiled sheepishly. "You're looking radiant, Leah. Radiant and round." His cell rang. "*Mangiamo* Meatballs," he answered.

If someone had asked Cara when she had first arrived in Crabclaw where she thought she'd be in two years' time, she certainly wouldn't have said, "Married and pregnant, cooking five different kinds of meatballs and sauces for the catering company I co-own with my husband (financed by Dino)."

"I just booked us a party for eighty balls and sauce, plus sides," Ryan told her. "We're going to need help with this one."

"Okay, I'll ask Oz and Ginny when they get here."

Leah chuckled. "They agreed to help you? I'm surprised you were able to get them to leave the apartment."

"No kidding," Ryan said. "Every time I call Oz to ask whether they want to go out with us, he tells me they're staying in for the night."

"They're … a new couple," Cara said, smiling to herself. "Remember when we used to be like that?"

Ryan came up behind her, putting his arms around her belly. "How do you think we made this baby so fast?"

She twisted around and kissed her husband full on the lips.

"Ugh, newlyweds," Leah grunted. "I'm starving. How about a ball before we hit the road?"

"Great idea," Cara said, feeling content and fulfilled. She had good food, good friends, the love of her life, and a baby on the way. She couldn't ask for anything more. "*Mangiamo*. Let's eat!"

About the Author

Tiffany N. York lives in Southern CA with her spirited son, diva Chihuahua, three to five cats, and two tone-deaf parakeets. She writes romance to escape reality. You can visit her at *tiffanynyork-author.com*.

A Sneak Peek from Crimson Romance
(From *Colleen's Choice* by Holley Trent)

Colleen Sanders took a bracing breath before mashing the last few digits of the number she never expected to dial again. Slinking off her seat edge, she took sanctuary beneath her abused cherry desk, gripping the edge of her phone base as she went.

Her father had stripped the carpet from the big office two years past and had never gotten around to replacing it. The staff lingering in the hall could probably hear every blink—every whisper—even through her closed door.

She curled into the corner, drawing her knees up to her chin as her target picked up his extension.

"Greg Quinton."

"Greg. Hi." She swallowed the lump in her throat and lowered her voice to a whisper. "How are you?"

"Great. That you, Colleen? Sounds like your rasp."

"Yeah, it's me."

"Was just thinking about you—talking about you, actually—at the retreat last week. Miss you around here."

She pinched the bridge of her nose between her thumb and forefinger, and mentally berated herself for her lachrymose tendencies as of late. Ball-busting Colleen had never been a crier. She hadn't even cried during that one lacrosse match freshman year when a freak collision resulted in her dislocated shoulder and broken nose, although she had introduced the Emerald Springs residents in attendance to the less refined components of her vocabulary. The official had tossed her a yellow card for that outburst. She'd framed it.

"Miss all of you, too," she confessed.

"Hey, can you speak up? I can hardly hear you."

"No. Listen, do you … " She closed her eyes and willed her churning gut to calm. This was just *Greg*. Out of all the calls she'd had to make in recent weeks, this should have been an easy one. Another deep breath. "Listen, do you have any work for me?"

"Work?"

There was surprise in Greg's voice, and Colleen couldn't tell if it was pleasant or otherwise.

"Yes. Got any design work for me?"

A pause. Greg rustled some papers on his end of the call in Seattle, and there was a thump, followed by a loud, squealing whine.

Colleen yanked the phone back from her ear and held it away until the infernal racket ceased.

Greg came back on the line. "Sorry! Sorry."

Colleen put the phone back against her ear and whispered, "What happened?"

"Got so excited I dropped the phone. We're short some boot designs and have been in a frenzy trying to develop new motifs. I'm pretty sure the timing of your phone call is in direct response to the bargains I made with at least three pagan gods last night."

Her shoulders fell with her relief, and she blew out a breath. "Can you pay me up-front?"

Another pause. "How are things at the farm? Any better?"

"No." Why bother explaining? Greg already knew the dirt.

"Damn. Hey, I'll walk the invoice up to accounting right now. We'll try to get the check cut before FedEx gets here. I'll send you specs as soon as I'm back at my desk."

"Greg, thank you. Really. Thank you. You're getting me out of some serious hot water."

He laughed, and Colleen heard the sound of his heels clacking against the concrete floors at the Markson Outfitters corporate headquarters. Already on the move, Greg was. Colleen had learned a lot about efficiency working under that guy for all those years.

"Pays to have friends in high places, huh?" he asked. "Don't worry about it. You're doing me a massive favor. When you see the deadline, you'll understand."

Colleen laughed, too, and couldn't remember the last time she'd heard that sound coming out of her mouth. Things in her life hadn't been conducive to laughter in the past few months. "Thanks for the warning. I'll look for your email."

"Bye, love."

She put the phone in its base and crawled out from her hidey-hole. No sooner had she'd pulled up to her feet than the phone rang again, the display flashing an interoffice extension. She sighed and set the phone on the desktop before stabbing the speaker button. "Yes, Kate?"

"Colleen, you have some visitors here to see you," her secretary said.

Damn it. Kate had her on speakerphone on her end, too. That meant her dependable assistant had probably already told whoever it was that Colleen was unavailable, but they had insisted on having an audience. She couldn't bluff her way out of this visit as easily as she had with Sam Whitman earlier in the morning. Sam—marketing director at the neighboring Emerald Tea Farm—wasn't there to pay her any money, and she sure as shit didn't owe them any, so in her book, a meeting was unnecessary. Mercenary, true, but she couldn't turn Split Acres Farm around if she was on her ass engaging in idle chitchat all day. As it was, she was already digging the farm out of a grave that was filling in faster than she could shovel clear.

"And who are the visitors?" she asked, rubbing the bridge of her nose again.

"The septic tank contractor has finished his work and wants to talk to you … and Alan's here."

"Who's Alan?"

Kate had said "Alan" in manner indicating Colleen should already know that. She didn't.

"I … think you should talk to him."

That didn't sound good. Did she owe someone a paycheck and had forgotten?

No, that couldn't be it. She'd been staring over the foreman's shoulder for four weeks, approving every timecard to make sure he didn't let any overtime slip in. She'd issued pay for every single one of those hours.

"Fine. Let me just … " she opened and shut her desk drawer twice. " … finish up the filing I'm doing, and I'll be right out."

"Yes, ma'am." Kate clicked off.

"Damn it." The matronly assistant never called Colleen "ma'am" unless the situation required a certain performance. It was their unofficial code word.

Colleen shoved her socked feet into the powder blue floral-print rain boots awaiting her near the door and used the small mirror hung over the file cabinets to smooth the lumps from her hair. If someone suggested she had dressed in the dark that morning, the statement wouldn't have been so far from the truth. Being in a perpetual state of exhaustion, she rarely had her eyes open before arriving at Split Acres Farm's operations office, and Kate had poured that first pot of coffee down her gullet. Further, her lights were on the fritz at the old house. Sometimes they worked, sometimes they didn't, and sometimes she got a shock. Literally.

She looked haggard in that reflection. Until recently, she'd looked her age, maybe a little under it. She got good genes from her mother's side, but from her father's side, she got a major headache in the form of four hundred acres of unprofitable farmland. She was thirty-two but feeling pretty damn close to retirement age. No wonder her mother had always been so tired when Colleen and her brother, Jacob, were growing up. There was just so much to do, and she was doing it with far less staff than her parents ever had.

Oh well. She wasn't trying to win a sash and tiara. She just needed to deal with two visitors as efficiently and painlessly as possible.

She straightened her spine, smoothed her expression into the unreadable blank she always met the public with, and pulled open the door.

Showtime.

She was already talking before she'd cleared the end of the long corridor of mostly empty offices, and had her hand extended for the contractor to shake. "Thanks for coming out so fast, Bart." She caught a glimpse of a tall, dark-haired man lingering near the entryway, but she let him remain in her periphery for the time being. One thing at a time.

Bart switched his clipboard to his left hand and wrapped his big, rough, right hand around hers. "You should have called weeks ago when the plumbing started backing up. Would have been less of a problem."

She was perfectly aware of that. Less of a problem, but no less expensive to fix.

"Everything is in working order, then? Tanks are empty?"

He nodded and handed the clipboard over to her. He crooked his thumb toward the door. "Your custodian here looked it over and said it was fine. Signed off on the work. I just need a check."

All the words made sense. They were English, after all, but they didn't seem to apply to her particular situation. She squared her shoulders and cocked up her favored eyebrow. "I'm sorry?"

Bart took the clipboard back and pointed to something printed in the terms. "Payable upon completion. I guess you don't have a line of credit?"

Her teeth clenched, and she sucked a sobering breath through her nose. *Damn you, Daddy.* She'd waited as long as she did to call them in the first place because she expected to have money to pay the bill in the thirty days it took it to come due. Now she'd have to go rob Peter to pay Paul again.

She took the clipboard back and raised her chin, hoping to garner some sense of authority in the situation, but on the inside she was crumbling. Mess after mess, it never let up. How much more could she take?

"And my *custodian* signed off on it, you said?" She brought the paper up to her eyes and squinted at the scrawled signature. Alan … something-or-other.

Finally, she gave the man more than just her peripheral vision. She stared at him dead-on, expecting him to flinch and blanch like all the others did, but he lifted a hand in greeting and grinned.

Her jaw fell open, and she was stunned momentarily by the blue of his eyes, his chiseled jaw, his dark hair—deliciously unkempt and tickling the top of his collar—and the strong forearms her eyes skimmed down to as he twirled a ratchet wrench between long, tanned fingers.

A stranger, and if she had to guess, her father was to blame for him being there. Why did he agree to let her come home and do the job if he wasn't going to get out of the way to let her do it?

She closed her mouth and swallowed, turning her attention back to Bart. "Have a seat. I'll go cut you a check."

Bart shrugged, shuffled across the worn carpet, and plopped into one of the vinyl chairs near the door.

"Alan," she said, spinning on her boot heel and striding toward the hall. "Why don't you join me in my office and tell me about the work while I run this check through QuickBooks?"

"Yes, certainly, Colleen."

She stumbled a bit over her own feet, glad that no one, beyond the corporate sheltie lounging brazenly in the middle of the hall, could see it. She stepped over the dog and concentrated on her breathing as she approached her office.

Dear lord, he had an accent.

Get a grip, woman.

By the time she plopped her butt in her desk chair and punched her computer monitor button, her supposed custodian joined her in the office, and the blush inching up her neck had receded.

"Close the door, please."

He gave her a speculative look but put his hand on the doorknob and pushed.

She ducked her head behind her computer monitor, clicking her mouse blindly at nothing in particular. She couldn't see straight for some reason, and she didn't think it was low blood sugar.

Gorgeous man. Too bad she'd have to fire him.

In the mood for more Crimson Romance?
Check out *Maybe Baby* by Ashlinn Craven
at *CrimsonRomance.com*.